He raised an eyebrov planning to interview?

"No one."

"*¿Estas loca?*" The smile disappeared, and he pushed his chair back defensively, as if my brand of crazy might be contagious. "You intended to write an entire biography about a public figure without doing any research at all?"

"It wasn't a biography. It was a memoir." I tried to keep the testiness out of my voice. It didn't help that I agreed with him. Perfectly innocent trees would have perished for a hard-cover manifesto that portrayed Charles-Henri Banville as a non-toxic lifeform. "A memoir," I told him, "is not an objective account. It's simply Charles-Henri Banville talking about himself."

"A book that tells everything from his point of view? Everything he did? Everything he did to other people?" My host shook his head. "That's not what I need."

"That's all there was in the contract."

"Your contract, if I understand correctly, was about taking the lies that man told as the truth? If I knew another writer…" He paused. "But I don't, and unfortunately I have very little time. My lawyers will draw up the new contract and send it to you."

He didn't ask me if I wanted the job, but since I did, I saw no reason to make a fuss. He reached for the bill just as I slapped my voice recorder down on the table.

"You want research?" I asked. "Let's get started."

French Ghost

by

Corinne LaBalme

French Ghost

Cover Art by *Diana Carlile*

The Wild Rose Press, Inc.
PO Box 708
Adams Basin, NY 14410-0708
Visit us at www.thewildrosepress.com

Publishing History
First Edition, 2022
Trade Paperback ISBN 978-1-5092-3919-1
Digital ISBN 978-1-5092-3920-7

Published in the United States of America

Dedication

For my fabulous father, Guy Edouard Philippe, and the
Terrible Beagle Boys, wherever they are!

Acknowledgments

My thanks to Paris's ultra-genial DWG writing group for all their bright and brilliant comments on this story: Albert Alla, Peter-Adrien Altini, Peter Brown, Amanda Dennis, Nina-Marie Gardner (and Beanie & Bella), Rafael Herrero, Matt Jones, Rachel Kapelke-Dale, Samuel Leader, Ferdia Lennon, Marissa McCants, Reine Arcache Melvin, Chris Newens, Tasha Ong, Alberto Rigettini, Jonathan Schiffman, and Nafkote Tamirat...with special mention to Lady Helen O'Keeffe who always keeps the wit glowing and the rosé flowing at DWG meetings. And my heartfelt gratitude to Gary Lee Kraut, Sylvie Bardet, George Ellenbogen, and Audrey O'Reilly for their ever-pithy advice on the writerly life.

Chapter One

Charles-Henri Banville's funeral was a box-office smash. Sobbing movie fans from around the world gathered at Père Lachaise, Paris's A-List cemetery, to bid *adieu* to the man formerly known as France's greatest living actor. Police helicopters whirred above the ornate tombstones while tough young men in dark suits and mirrored glasses patrolled makeshift barriers that kept reporters, paparazzi, and TV crews at bay.

By contrast, the small but select group of VIPs inside the stone-cold crematorium chapel required no crowd control. In fact, this crowd controlled itself very well. None of these dry-eyed celebrities had racked up any florist bills either. Only one lonely wreath of carnations adorned the casket, and it bore the dutiful banner of the French Actors' Union.

I didn't connect the heavy-set brunette in the front row with Delphine Carroll, the once-waifish pop princess who won the 1979 Pan-Europe song contest, until she turned around and batted her eyes at the pallbearers, barely concealing her glee at outliving her ex-husband. The equally cheerful Yorkshire terrier peeking out of her handbag chewed happily on a squeaky rubber toy.

Swedish super-model Ingrid Svenson occupied the opposite pew, flanked by two towering Scandinavian teenagers who might, or might not, be Charles-Henri's twin sons. Charles-Henri always denied it, and his fancy legal team had blocked any meaningful child support ever since their birth. Nope, Ingrid didn't look especially bereft either.

By the time the priest got the show on the road, my own prayers were directed to the patron saint of antifreeze. My feet had frozen into icicles long before the altar boys started swinging the incense. When I'd packed my open-toe sandals for April in Paris, I sure hadn't planned on cooling my heels in a frigid French mausoleum.

I stared enviously at the fleece-lined boots worn by the redhead across the aisle who was tapping away at her cellphone. That was Jenna Bardet, the Franco-American VJ whose cable career nosedived after she slapped Charles-Henri with a sexual harassment suit. Unlike me, she hadn't bothered to dress up. Warm and comfortable in corduroy pants and a down jacket, she caught my inquiring eye and flashed her phone at me. A colorful video game. She winked and got back to her game.

I reached into my purse for my own phone when something sharp and hard smacked the back of my neck. I turned around. A rumpled, balding guy with a bland, forgettable face—Charles-Henri's former impresario, Marius Dubrovski—used the downtime to clip his nails. Charles-Henri made a neater job of it when he cut Marius out of the profits from his first major movie deal. I edged farther down the pew to escape the shrapnel.

I'd never met any of these people in person, but after eight weeks of non-stop research, I could update their Wikipedia entries in my sleep. I even knew the people who were conspicuous by their absence, like drug-challenged starlet Charlene Trent, the dead actor's last major lust interest, whose LAPD ankle-bracelet was keeping her anchored in Malibu.

There were people I didn't recognize, but not many. I'm a detail-driven Virgo, but there's no way I could have tracked down every dermatologist or dog-walker the actor ever met in his private life. Thankfully for researchers like me, stars as big as Charles-Henri don't have much private life. Messy details about his love affairs, arrests for public indecency, and on-set tantrums were all public record.

The pastor droned on about heavenly peace, a sermon that didn't seem too pertinent given that Banville, if true to form, was probably starting a bar fight in Hell. Since I didn't understand most of the long French words or care about learning them, I let my eyes wander aimlessly around the chapel. Then something— or rather someone—made me sit up straight and pay attention.

Tall, dark, and sexy standing in the back row. This guy was so gorgeous he could make a gargoyle drool. Longish black hair, piercing ebony eyes, and chiseled cheekbones that he must have borrowed from Christian Bale and forgotten to return. At his side, a veiled woman in a wheelchair clutched a single blood-red rose. Evidently, neither of them wanted to get up-close-and-personal with the corpse since there were plenty of empty seats in the orchestra section.

The tableau was bizarrely hot and gothic, but that's not what caught my attention. It was the *expression* on the man's face. In a room filled with people ready to dance a samba and uncork the Champagne, he was the only funeral guest who looked appropriately upset. Not in the "emotionally devastated" sense of the word. More like he was royally pissed off at something.

I could sympathize with that sentiment because I felt the same way. I had no idea why the incredible hunk was throwing a hissy fit, but I had a very valid reason for my own nasty mood.

That's because I'm Banville's ghost. When the undertakers shove his casket into the furnace, my career is going along for the ride.

Chapter Two

My name is Melody Layne, and I am a ghost writer.

If there was a support group called "Authors Anonymous," I'd be a regular at the coffee-and-doughnut table. There's real pain involved when you write books with other people's names on the cover. Ghost writers are the stunt doubles and understudies of the publishing world. It provides income, but not enough to compensate for the way it erodes the ego. I didn't set out to be a ghost writer. Nobody does. It's just the sort of thing that happens to starry-eyed journalism majors when they confront the reality of college loan payments.

Ghost writing anxiety runs deep, and it's more than missing out on the glory of a byline. It's the agonizing boredom. Most of my clients are egomaniacal business executives who are convinced that the public pants for every persnickety detail about their stock options. I try not to disillusion them because their corporate memoirs permit me to float a teensy, third-floor walk-up on Manhattan's trendy Lower East Side. That apartment—the envy of all of my friends—has hot running water almost every other day.

No writer ought to complain about steady work, and I don't...most of the time. However, my dream of writing a prize-winning biography that tops the bestseller list slips farther away each time I type "The End" on one of these yawn-inducing "as told to Melody Layne" volumes. If the alternative wasn't pushing sacks of fertilizer around in my dad's garden store in Saint Louis, I'd have headed back to Missouri.

Then, in the word-of-mouth way that most magic happens, everything changed. I'd just wrapped up an epic treatise on area rugs for the CEO of Discount Carpet City. He was so taken with the book that he recommended me to his brother-in-law, a drama coach who teaches foreign actors to speak like they were born and bred in Brooklyn.

And it was through that connection that, just two short months ago, I was eating melt-in-the mouth trout with heavenly hollandaise sauce at New York's elegant Pierre Hotel, while France's Greatest Living Actor asked me to ghost write his autobiography.

Long story short?

He was misunderstood.

The people who misunderstood him right now were puritanical studio executives in Hollywood. They wanted to cancel a seven-figure movie deal simply because Charles-Henri wagged his *beet* at them during a script conference!

Okay, I misunderstood him too. Three years of high school French wasn't much help, especially when Banville was slurring his words. My sister Abby, who majored in Frenchmen during her Junior Year Abroad, couldn't stop laughing as she informed me that *bite*— pronounced *beet*—means "dick" in French.

But I'd already signed the contract, and I'm not sure that understanding the full scope of Banville's vulgarity would have put me off the job. I was thrilled to sink my teeth into a Grade-A celebrity, even if he was far from the squeaky-clean role model he wanted me to portray in this memoir. For starters, when he wasn't trying to sneak his greasy fingers up my skirt, he was slipping them down the blouse of every female autograph hunter who leaned over our table.

Halfway through his third bottle of wine, he made it absolutely clear that the details of my contract would be finalized upstairs in his suite. That unappetizing idea nearly put me off the best food I'd eaten in weeks. I was gearing myself up to refuse when one of the autograph hunters dropped a black lace thong onto Charles-Henri's lap on her way back from the ladies' room.

I'll say this much for Charles-Henri: he asked the headwaiter to call me a taxi before racing to the elevator with his brand-new conquest. I figured the project was dead on the vine, so imagine my surprise when two days later Banville's London agent express mailed a $3,000 advance, a contract promising $2,000 on completion of the first draft, and a cool $10,000 on publication.

As soon as the check cleared, I posted my apartment on Craig's List. Despite my OCD issues that made living with someone else's stuff (or letting them touch my stuff) a source of existential agony, I signed on a six-month apartment trade with a Parisian doctoral student named Marie-Christine.

What could possibly go wrong?

Chapter Three

How about...*everything*?

It started out perfectly. Marie-Christine's fifth-floor apartment, a mix of Swedish modern and French antiques, was surprisingly comfortable. I didn't want to breathe too deeply next to the dining room tapestry which probably housed two hundred generations of dust mites but totally approved of another big antique, the Eiffel Tower, which was visible from the wrought-iron balcony. Back on Avenue C, Marie-Christine had a bird's-eye view of a methadone clinic, so I figured we were even on the sightseeing front.

The elevator in her nineteenth-century building was so small that I couldn't squeeze into it if I gained five pounds. That would help me control my newly discovered passion for *petits pains au chocolat* which totally outclass the glazed doughnuts back at the bodega. I was at the corner bistro on my second morning in Paris, indulging in one of these buttery-flakey pastries with a foamy *café au lait,* when *la merde* hit the fan.

My Spanish was slightly better than my French, so I'd already made friends with Alberto, the Cuban waiter. He slipped me a copy of *Le Parisien* newspaper that a customer left at the bar. Turning to the front page, I was pleased to see that Charles-Henri Banville was making headlines again.

But not this kind of headline. His name. His birthdate. Yesterday's date. There was an ominous black border around his latest publicity photo.

An obituary?

We had our first interview scheduled in *two days*. I'd run up my credit card on a state-of-the-art voice recorder that I hadn't even unwrapped yet. I'd given up my precious apartment, farmed out my cats to my sister, and moved halfway around the world for this job. How could this have happened?

I scanned the first few paragraphs, but the French just didn't make sense to me. Charles-Henri Banville had been declared dead sometime late last night, and his death had something to with a *lamproie*. What the hell is a *lamproie,* I wondered. Some kind of fancy sportscar?

I dropped the paper, switched on my tablet with shaky fingers, and typed Charles-Henri Banville into my search engine. I got the English-language obituary this time. The actor was in Bordeaux, on location for a French-Canadian miniseries about the life and times of King Henri I. Somehow, he'd slipped off the deck of the private barge he'd rented and drowned after a copious meal of stewed lamprey.

I looked up "lamprey" and nearly gagged. The definition was bad enough—*an eel-like marine or freshwater fish having a circular suction mouth with pointed teeth for boring into the flesh of other fish to feed on their blood*—but the picture was the stuff that nightmares are made of, a big-fanged mouth attached to a nasty, slimy snake. For some unfathomable reason, the French deemed these swimming vampires to be edible when stewed in sufficient quantities of red wine.

Lampreys were, as I read on, considered a great delicacy at the court of King Henri I…

Damn!

Now it made sense. Horrible sense. If there was one thing on which Charles-Henri Banville and I could have bonded, it was our dedication to research. Banville prepared for each of his roles meticulously. If serpent stew was the favorite food of the character he was playing, he'd want to chow down on it. And if I knew anything else about Banville, he'd been soaked in more red wine than the snake. Little wonder he'd flipped over the rails and gone overboard.

Unfortunately, this particular Frenchman didn't float.

How could he *do* this to me?

I know, I know…he didn't *decide* to drown in order to mess up my life. Nevertheless, that was the result. I'd already spent most of the advance on college loan payments, credit card bills, and my plane ticket. After writing a check to my sister to cover kibble and vet visits for my three rescue cats, the Bank of Melody Layne tottered on the brink of ruin. Banville's estate lawyers couldn't ask me to refund the advance?

Or could they?

I looked at my watch. It was barely four a.m. in New York. It would be cruel to wake Marie-Christine and tell her the house trade was off. No, I'd let her snooze in peace, if she could. By now she'd have figured out that the police sirens and car alarms were the *real* reasons that The City Never Sleeps.

In contrast, her apartment was blissfully quiet. I'd already gotten used to the pastoral chirp-chirping of the urban sparrows who nested on the balcony next to

Marie-Christine's geraniums. New York was built for business, but Paris basked in beauty. I was already free-falling into the soppy love affair that most expatriates had with City of Light. I just plain didn't want to leave. It was with real—and entirely selfish—regret that I emailed my condolences to the actor's London agent, Anthony Major, who forwarded me his personal invitation to the funeral in return. *"Couldn't stand the bastard when he was alive,"* he wrote. *"No interest in seeing him dead."*

My "American in Paris" idyll was over before it had begun. I stowed my tablet in my purse and set off for a day of sightseeing. If I had only a few precious days in France, I'd cram as much vacation into them as possible. I was going to hit the Left Bank, the Right Bank, the Champs-Elysées, the Eiffel Tower, Notre Dame, and everything in between. I wasn't leaving town without checking out the Louvre either.

Mona Lisa lived up to her reputation, as did the Monet paintings in the Musée d'Orsay. By the end of the day, I'd fallen completely in love with the quaint bookstalls on the Seine, the colorful cafés on every corner, the art galleries, and a pair of lime-green patent-leather stiletto pumps at a designer boutique.

The shoes, of course, were *way* beyond my budget, but I'd never have managed seven hours of tourism in those stiletto heels. Even in my trusty, rubber-soled sneakers, I was nursing a blister as big as Boise when I crammed myself into the tiny elevator with a bag of take-out *quiche Provençal* and shredded carrot salad.

After a restorative swig of supermarket Chardonnay, I dialed my own number.

Marie-Christine answered on the second ring.

"*Allô*, Melody! How wonderful it is, your apartment! You are enjoying Paris, yes?"

"Paris is beautiful, and so is your apartment. But I have some very sad news. Charles-Henri Banville…"

"*Mais oui*, this was reported on your CNN. It is an enormous tragedy *pour le cinéma.*"

"You see, I was working for him—"

"*Mais oui.* Then it is a great tragedy for you as well."

"So I can let you stay in the apartment through the end of the month, but after that—"

"*Mais non*," replied Marie-Christine. "Our deal, it was for six months."

Chapter Four

A half bottle of Chardonnay later, we'd come to an agreement of sorts. Marie-Christine was staying put, and I was up the Seine without a paddle. Somehow, it had slipped my mind that Marie-Christine was getting her doctorate in contract law. Turns out, she's pretty damn good at it.

In despair, I had a video chat with my sister Abby. As usual, I caught her in a fancy medical clinic, lounging under a plastic tree, with a briefcase full of narcotics.

"Hey, Mel, how's Paris?"

"It's fine, but there's been bad news for Charles-Henri Banville…"

"His loss," interrupted Abby. "He shouldn't have cheated on that Lithuanian underwear model." Abby works for a pharmaceutical company in Long Island and spends most of the day delivering gourmet lunches and swag bags to doctors. For that reason, she gets most of her news from six-month-old copies of glossy celebrity magazines.

"No, it's bad news in the sense that he's *dead!* He's dead and *gone!*" I spilled out the whole sorry saga. "I'm down and out in Paris with no possibility of sleeping in my own bed for months and months."

"Sleeping in your own bed wasn't all that great, Mel, not with that posse of pussycats holding raves on the quilt every night. They tried it with me, but let me tell you, I took care of those whiney little beasts once and for all."

Visions of burlap sacks flung over the Brooklyn Bridge turned my blood cold. "Abby, you didn't—"

"I bought three fuzzy cat beds and rubbed them down with catnip. Those critters can't say 'no' to drugs," she added with professional approval. "Honestly, Mel, no wonder your love life was flatlining. I can't believe Eric put up with that zoo for so long."

I didn't have a ready answer. I'd liked Eric. Who wouldn't like Eric? He was clever, clued-in, and an up-and-coming copywriter at a major ad agency. We both liked Szechuan dumplings, indie movies, and off-Broadway shows but, on the debit side, I hated his aftershave, the way he snored, and his irritating proclivity to analyze every situation in baseball terms. In truth, I'd been relieved when we split. When you came down to it, I enjoyed sleeping with Purrboy, Coolio, and Gigi, the crochety Persian rescue kitty, more than I did with him.

"You see what I mean?" said Abby said, misinterpreting my silence. "Let me tell you something about those European guys with the designer clothes and super haircuts. They're not gay! At least not all of them. When it comes to good-looking, fashionable straight guys, Paris is an all-you-can-eat buffet!"

"I'll settle for the gourmet food." I carried my tablet out to the balcony and flashed her a panorama of Paris rooftops and the Eiffel Tower, which exploded into its hourly show of sparkles. "I had chocolate rolls for breakfast, *salade niçoise* for lunch, and quiche and carrot salad for dinner."

"You can get that stuff at any gourmet store," said Abby. "What you can't get on Seventh Avenue are those luscious French beets I was telling you about. Promise me you'll try at least one of them before you come home. Honestly, Mel, if sexy Frenchmen in designer suits don't turn you on, you're a lost cause."

Chapter Five

Was Abby right? Had I morphed into the dreaded Spinster-With-Cats at the tender age of thirty-four? I was still pondering that idea as I headed back from the cemetery after the Banville funeral. Could this Paris problem be a wake-up call in disguise? Eric was only the latest in the long line of lemons I'd dated since leaving Missouri State. The last Frenchman I'd met, Charles-Henri Banville, was no advertisement for my sister's sales pitch for Latin lovers, but there were exceptions to every rule.

However, as I examined my fellow subway riders, I couldn't spot a single man who sparked my interest. Perhaps those dazzlingly dressed and beautifully-coiffed men of Abby's college days didn't patronize this particular subway line. They all looked too young, too old, too fat, too thin, too married, too single...heavens, was I *that* picky? I couldn't manage a flicker of interest in anyone at all? When, I asked myself, was the last time I'd seen a man who attracted me in the slightest way?

Oh yeah. I almost laughed as I checked my watch. Approximately forty-five minutes ago. The dark-haired guy with the bad attitude at the funeral. Something about Mr. Suave and Sulky utterly rang my chimes. On the other hand—and not that I get spooked about omens and portents—spotting the love of your life in a crematorium was too creepy for comfort.

So much for my love-life…what kind of positive spin could I put on my unemployment situation? Could I turn this exile from Manhattan into a career turnaround? American authors and Paris went together like macaroni and *fromage*. Ernest Hemingway, F. Scott Fitzgerald, and James Baldwin wrote brilliant novels here. Why couldn't I turn out an actual *factual* biography instead of another mindless memoir?

Unfortunately, my debut as a "real" biographer wouldn't star Banville. I'd barely met the guy; he'd been obnoxiously drunk for most of our abbreviated meal, and unfortunately, I lacked the cinema savvy that would interest an editor in a serious proposal about his professional life. If the contract had specified an "authorized biography" instead of an "as told to" memoir, it would be a different story.

On the plus side, Paris was a big cosmopolitan city with lots of egocentric people in the market for an English language book about themselves. Maybe some of them would be the kind of good-looking, well-groomed Frenchmen that my sister ran on about.

In this newly positive mindset, I switched my ringtone to "*I Will Survive*" and treated myself to a post-mortuary glass of Chardonnay in my neighborhood café. For the first time, I noticed the bulletin board papered with handwritten classified ads next to the cash register. There were notices for cleaning, childcare, ironing, and language tutoring.

Well, why not? I'd done some tutoring while I was in college. Schooling a few French people on gerunds and phrasal verbs could keep my head above the financial water until I nailed another ghost project. I ripped a page from my notebook and wrote, Private English Lessons from a Professional Author.

Alberto looked over my shoulder and said that thirty euros per hour was the going rate. "That's what I charge for salsa lessons," he said, pointing to his own note. I added the price and tacked it up on the board.

That night, I slept well for the first time since I'd got the news about Charles-Henri's death. In fact, I *overslept*. It was nearly ten in the morning, with bright sunshine streaming through the windows, when my cellphone blasted vintage disco at me. I checked the screen. It was an unfamiliar French number, which was not surprising since I'm not familiar with anyone in France. Could it be a potential English student? Already? If so, this was my lucky day.

"*Bonjour*," I purred into the mouthpiece.

"*This is Charles-Henri Banville and—*"

I hung up.

The phone rang again.

Same number.

"Drop dead! *Again!*"

I switched off the ringtone and got dressed. Charles-Henri Banville was *dead*. I'd seen him in his casket. If he was contacting me from beyond the grave, this ghost writer stuff was getting way out of hand.

By the time I'd brewed my coffee, I'd come up with less creepy explanations. Unfortunately, they were even scarier. What *living* person hated me enough to mess with my head like that? Only my family and closest friends knew about the Banville project. Where did this phone troll come from?

When I opened my email, I found a message entitled "*My Phone Call this Morning*" from an unfamiliar email address.

I apologize if I startled you. As my father's only legitimate son, I share his unfortunate name and mistakenly believed that using it would serve as introduction. His law firm gave me your contact details. We must speak with some urgency about the book that you are writing.

Charles-Henri had a "legitimate son" that the tabloids had missed? That was impossible. For the past thirty years, Charles-Henri couldn't sneeze without sending the tabloids into a flu alert frenzy. I rifled through my suitcase for the thick file-folders I'd accumulated on Charles-Henri Banville. As I carried them to the kitchen table, my email pinged again. This message came from Anthony Major, Banville's London-based theatrical agent:

In response to a request from the Banville family, I transferred your coordinates to the legal team handling his estate.

With an estate as large as this one in play, I'd expect the lawyers to be more suspicious when surprise relatives start popping up. I mean, *I* was suspicious of this guy, and I sure didn't have any claims on the actor's equity. Something didn't add up. I unfolded the Banville timeline that I'd painstakingly constructed from internet sources, press releases, and news clips. When, where, and with whom could Charles-Henri have played baby-daddy?

Okay, he married French pop star Delphine Carroll in 1977. Divorced barely three years later after a very highly publicized miscarriage. Australian starlet Lucy Paige was next on Banville's merry-go-round, but she didn't grab a gold ring. His affair with fashion model

Ingrid Svenson didn't wind up in marriage either. Those Swedish kids that she brought to the funeral might be his sons, but they sure didn't share his name.

Charlene Trent? Engaged with cameras flashing in 2015, followed by an equally public breakup about ten minutes later. There was a Colombian fiancée who perished in a hang-gliding accident two months before they were scheduled to tie the knot, and a Bulgarian pageant winner who'd stood him up at the altar after he slept with her sister.

Not for the first time, I reflected that Charles-Henri's bedroom had been a lot like the United Nations parking garage…but without all the security measures. When had this so-called "legitimate son" been conceived, where had he been hiding all his life, and what did he want with me?

Forget about how Perez Hilton and the celebrity trolls missed this kid.

How had *I* missed him?

Chapter Six

After poring over my notebooks for two hours, the possibility of a second Charles-Henri Banville made less and less sense to me. The use of the word "legitimate" in the email implied that Banville had been married to his mother when he was born. How could that be unless Delphine Carroll's child had survived and been switched with a stillborn at the hospital?

While that sort of thing happened all the time on daytime television, it didn't play in real life. For one thing, Delphine Carroll still obsessed about her miscarriage in interviews. If she'd discovered a long-lost child, the story would be plastered all over the papers by now. It was more logical to assume there was nothing remotely legit about this guy and that he was simply making a play for the Banville millions.

If this con artist thought I could help his case, he was in for a surprise. In the short time we'd spent together, Banville hadn't confided anything to me except a sincere desire to rip off my underwear. I looked back at my email. Anthony Major, Charles-Henri's agent, had passed my name to the lawyers. Perhaps he could shed light on the situation. I dialed his number in London, and after getting past a pit bull of a PA, a clipped voice told me I had five minutes.

"Mr. Major, it's about—"

"—that ridiculous book? You can keep the

advance, but all further payments are canceled."

"I'm actually calling about…"

"The idiot really believed that a cheesy memoir would be enough to whitewash his reputation." Major laughed. "Nobody wanted to work with him anymore. The insurance costs alone made him unemployable. Did you know he started a fistfight on the set of *Adieu, Marseille?* Broke his costar's nose and caused a two-week production delay. And after that, he had the goddam nerve—"

"His son is trying to contact me," I cut in, conscious that my five minutes were running down fast.

"Chuckie had a kid?" asked Major. "Someone better put the poor little bugger down before he hits puberty."

"If he has an adult son, do you have any idea who the mother might be?"

"The man piled up sexual harassment charges, but I don't recall any paternity suits." A long pause. "If he had kids, only his best friend would know."

"He had a best friend?"

"He had no friends at all." Wishing me good luck, Major rang off.

The second hand on the wall clock kept ticking, mocking me for not being able to come up with a reply to a simple email. Of course, it wasn't a simple email, was it? *Legitimate son? Unfortunate name?* And why was this pop-up relative interested in a memoir that would never be written about someone he didn't appear to like? If he was winding me up for a nondisclosure agreement, he was wasting his time. I had nothing to disclose.

And that was the dilemma: I had absolutely

nothing up my sleeve. After ten minutes of fruitless mental meandering around that fact, I wrote a first draft that expressed the truth, the whole truth, and nothing but the truth:

The memoir was to be based on a series of interviews that never took place. I regret that I can be of no assistance…

Damn, I didn't want to send that. After weeks of research and moving halfway across the world, I'd already made a serious investment in this project. Plus, on a purely personal level my curiosity was piqued by this mystery man. I brewed another cup of coffee and brainstormed with myself. With no other jobs on the horizon, this was my only tenuous chance at a paycheck. What could I offer this man now that a traditional "as told to" memoir was off the table?

Table?

Yes, that was it. A coffee-table book. Something I could pull off easily with my own research to date and a few gushing quotes from his acting colleagues. A subtle hint about "a fitting tribute to a theatrical legend" might appeal to some vestige of family pride. My fingers hovered over the keyboard as I searched for the right words.

Unfortunately, I sneezed and hit send.

The reply came in seconds.

With modifications, I see no reason why the original contract cannot be honored. Is it possible to meet tomorrow at the Café de la Paix? 10 a.m.

What? I sat back and took a deep breath. Was something finally going right for a change? If this guy really was the son of Charles-Henri Banville, he'd be able to greenlight an "authorized" biography of his father. That could be the biggest break of my career. I reread the message. "*Modifications*" didn't surprise me. After all, the original contract was for a piece of self-serving PG propaganda "as told to Melody Layne." Without a Ouija board, Charles-Henri wouldn't be telling me much at all.

The Café de la Paix was the cherry on the sundae. I'd peeked in the windows of this landmark restaurant located next to the Paris Opera house yesterday. It had been one of Ernest Hemingway's many Parisian watering holes, but the menu prices posted in the window were frightening. On my own, I couldn't afford water, much less water mixed with coffee beans, in that historic bistro. I emailed back and accepted.

The next obstacle was dressing to impress. The low-end knits that wowed the guys at Discount Carpet City wouldn't make the grade in Paris. Luckily, I'd packed the slinky, charcoal gray designer wrap-dress that Abby gave me last Christmas. I'd already worn it to the funeral, but this guy hadn't seen it. There sure weren't any sobbing relatives on view at the gravesite. With the possibility of a paycheck in the future, I dove back into my stacks of Banville research. If I ever have the nerve to get inked, my tattoo will read "*Be Prepared.*"

Chapter Seven

The interior of the Café de la Paix was all gold paint, starched linen, and potted palms. Almost every table was occupied by a single man. As the hostess was busy on the phone, I took a spin around the room on my own, figuring that Charles-Henri Junior would bear a passing resemblance to Charles-Henri Senior.

Therefore, I was on the prowl for someone with sandy-blond hair, aquamarine eyes, and high-cheekbones...hold on. I glanced at myself in one of the mirrors. I fit that description pretty well myself. If it was open season on claiming Banville genes, I had a better shot than anyone else I saw in this room. I was heading back to the reception desk to see if there was a reservation for "Banville" when the man at the corner table folded his newspaper and stood up to case the room.

OMG. It was the hunk from the funeral!

Here he was—all six-foot wonderful of him—in Ernest Hemingway's hallowed Café de la Paix. What could be a more perfect place for an American writer to meet the love of her life?

Except...I was here for business, not pleasure. Where was this Banville guy? I scanned the room again, and as I did, Mister Heart Throb took two steps forward and stared right back at me. I swear I *felt* his gaze taking in my strappy sandals, wandering up my legs, lingering over the V-neck of my dress, before meeting my own eyes. This was more than electricity. I felt like my insides were being flash-fried. If there had been any warmth in that gaze, I might have dissolved into a puddle on the glossy parquet floor.

"Miss Layne, I presume?"

He gestured to the empty chair across from him without a flicker of enthusiasm. This was Banville's son? If he was pleased to meet me, he hid it very well. Had I already managed to offend him in some way? I sat down and tried to get a mood reading from him. Silky black hair, chiseled cheekbones, and chocolate-brown eyes that were just as dry as they'd been at the funeral. To judge from his frown, he was still royally pissed off about something.

"I apologize for startling you yesterday, Miss Layne." His English was perfect, but there was a rolling trill going on with the "*r*" that didn't ring entirely French. "I mistakenly presumed that using that...*name*...would serve as a reassuring introduction. I realize that it must have been a shock to receive a telephone call from a person you thought was dead."

"It was, but I'm equally sorry I hung up on you."

A waiter in black tie materialized at our side.

"We'll have..." My host stopped. "I'm sorry, what would you like?"

"Café au lait."

"*Un crème et un express, s'il vous plaît.*" That seemed to kill the conversation again. He stared at the floor gloomily until the waiter showed up with our order.

"You don't look much like your father," I ventured when the silence began to get on my nerves.

"*Por suerte*," he muttered. After ten years in New York, I speak fairly fluent Spanglish. Why would he think it was a blessing not to look like his father? And why would his go-to language be Spanish instead of French? I unwrapped a sugar cube, more for something to do than from a desire to sweeten my coffee.

"The lawyers showed me Mr. Major's correspondence with you. I assume you've started work on this book? May I see the chapters you've already written?"

Bingo. He'd zeroed in on the place I didn't want him to go. "There aren't any fully written chapters as yet. As I said in the email, your father passed away before we could begin the interviews."

"You never met him?" His eyes brightened, and the 100,000-volt smile that followed was totally worth waiting for. "Naturally, I assumed that—forgive me, you look exactly like the sort of person I would have expected him to employ. However, if you never met my father, you don't realize how extremely lucky you are, Miss Layne."

"Well, actually, I—"

His cell phone chimed, but he ignored it. "Please tell me about this book. Who have you interviewed so far?"

"No one."

He raised an eyebrow quizzically. "Who were you *planning* to interview?

"No one."

"*¿Estas loca?*" The smile disappeared, and he pushed his chair back defensively, as if my brand of crazy might be contagious. "You intended to write an entire biography about a public figure without doing any research at all?"

"It wasn't a *biography*. It was a *memoir*." I tried to keep the testiness out of my voice. It didn't help that I agreed with him. Perfectly innocent trees would have perished for a hard-cover manifesto that portrayed Charles-Henri Banville as a non-toxic lifeform. "A *memoir*," I told him, "is not an objective account. It's simply Charles-Henri Banville talking about himself."

"A book that tells everything from his point of view? Everything he did? Everything he did to other people?" My host shook his head. "That's not what I need."

"That's all there was in the contract."

"Your *contract*, if I understand correctly, was about taking the lies that man told as the truth? If I knew another writer..." He paused. "But I don't, and unfortunately I have very little time. My lawyers will draw up the new contract and send it to you."

He didn't ask me if I wanted the job, but since I did, I saw no reason to make a fuss. He reached for the bill just as I slapped my voice recorder down on the table.

"You want research?" I asked. "Let's get started."

Chapter Eight

"You want to interview *me*?"

"You're a key figure." I pulled a notebook from my purse because I never depend entirely on recordings. "Where are you from?"

"Madrid."

"Never been, but I hear it's pretty." I pressed the record button. *"April 28, 2017. Café de la Paix. Charles-Henri Banville Jr."* I made him wait while I played that back, noticing that he flinched at the sound of his name. "Were you born in Madrid?"

"I don't know why that is of any importance, but yes, I was born in Madrid. On August 17, 1980, to be exact."

"1980?" I repeated, mentally ticking off the months on my fingers. "He was still married to Delphine Carroll in 1980. The divorce papers were signed in"—I thought for a minute—"mid-June 1980, which would mean that…"

"There was enough time for him to marry my mother, Carmen Esperanza Ortega, before I came into the world. I may have underestimated you, Miss Layne." He sat back and narrowed his eyes. Some people look like lizards when they do that, but it just made him look sexier. "You appear to have done your homework after all."

Trying to smother a smug grin, I wrote *Carmen*

Esperanza Ortega down in my notebook. "Was your mother an actress?"

"No, she was the niece of the cleaning lady, and she was only sixteen years old. My wretched excuse for a father forced himself upon her while his wife was in the hospital miscarrying his child."

"But they got married?"

He snorted. "He was signing for his first movie in California, and what he'd done to my mother, in America it would be called a statue, statue...*como se dice?*" He raked his fingers through his hair. "A statue..."

"Statutory rape?"

He nodded. "They married secretly, and she was shipped off to Spain with a wedding ring and a warning never again to contact Charles-Henri Banville. *La pobrecita,* she still thought she loved him, so she cursed me with his name."

"I understand." There was a whole lot more that I didn't understand, but I plodded on. "How have you stayed out of the spotlight for all these years with a name as famous as that?"

"In Spain, we also take the name of our mother's family." He plucked a business card from his wallet and laid it on the table. *Professor Carlos Ortega, Universidad de Madrid.* "My birth was registered as Charles-Henri Banville y Ortega, and while the full name appears on my passport and legal documents, I have chosen to live my private and professional life as Carlos Ortega."

He slipped several euro notes under the sugar bowl. "Unfortunately, I have no more time for these questions today. The funeral exhausted my mother, and I am taking her back to Madrid in a few hours. Please review the new contract and make a complete outline of the book, with the names of everyone you plan to interview, before our next meeting."

"I'm free all next week," I said, opening my date book.

"I return to Paris on Thursday. You have forty-eight hours."

Chapter Nine

I was in the publishing business again, but what kind of whacked-out book did my new client have in mind? Daddy's requirements were crystal clear: a fluffy piece of propaganda that would make him look like a saint. Judging from our conversation, Carlos Ortega wanted a hatchet job on the Great Satan. Nobody was in the market for a fair and balanced record of Charles-Henri Banville's life on earth.

I gathered my notes and left the Café de la Paix before realizing that I was ravenous. The bistro next door, the Entr'Acte, had real-people prices, so I treated myself to a *croque monsieur* and a glass of fruity Beaujolais. Now that I had a job again, I could afford it. Besides, I told myself hopefully, if Carlos honestly wanted research, he might be more openminded than he appeared. Maybe I'd finally get my chance to write a real biography.

I left the bistro in a mellow mood, which only got better when I found a hand-delivered envelope from Banville's lawyers taped to the mailbox at home. When I looked at the numbers and calculated the euro-to-dollar exchange, it looked like my fee had been raised to $20,000.

But there was a lot of fine French print as well. Fortunately, I had a Parisian legal eagle on retainer, or at least on my futon, in NYC. I texted Marie-Christine and asked if she'd take a look at the contract. I got a positive response, so I scanned the paperwork and sent it off with my questions.

That accomplished, I organized my Banville timeline into chronological chapters and dug into genealogy websites. The actor came from a long line of dairy farmers in Normandy, which probably explained his strikingly Scandinavian appearance. The northern French coastline had been plundered by Viking warriors throughout the Middle Ages, so there were more blonds than average in the Normandy region.

I keyed in all the actor's movies, plays, TV shows, and awards into the outline along with the movie sites that listed the cast, director, and designers for his films. Then I made a separate file for talk show appearances since those would be my major source for direct quotes. I switched off the laptop and fell into bed at midnight.

I awoke the next morning to an email from Marie-Christine.

The contract pays all expenses related to research, but publication rights belong to the estate. PS: The basement in the building across the street was raided last night!!! New York is so exciting!!!

I wrote back with my thanks and told her I was glad that the city was living up to its reputation. Then I doublechecked the A-List of potential interviewees and their whereabouts. Delphine Carroll was touring France with a nostalgia revue of 1980s popstars. The model Ingrid Svenson was rarely out of social media range. Actress Charlene Trent could be contacted through her Los Angeles management.

I devoted the rest of the day to Charles-Henri's education. I found the address of his high school in

Normandy. He'd also spent several months at Paris's prestigious Cours Florent drama school until getting expelled for bad attitude. The academy's communications officer, rather reluctantly, said she'd see if any of his former classmates would agree to interviews.

My list of bad character references kept growing. After checking news reports about the yet-to-be-released *Adieu Marseille* that the actor's agent had mentioned, I added its producers and costars to the "We-Hate-Banville" club. At six pm, just as I finished printing out a twenty-page general outline, my client texted that tomorrow's meeting would be at the Café de la Paix at eleven the next morning. Pouring myself a well-earned glass of white wine, I began to research the part of the story that was of most immediate—and personal—interest to me.

Namely, the part of the Banville saga that began in a Madrid maternity clinic on August 17, 1980...

Chapter Ten

Carlos Ortega took his time perusing the outline I gave him, making tiny notes in the margins like a schoolteacher. Of course, he *was* a teacher, or rather, an assistant professor. He'd graduated from the University of Madrid in 2002 with a degree in medieval history and had joined the faculty a few years later. Despite my best efforts, that was all I could dig up on the first thirty years of his life.

A few years ago, however, his name and face started showing up regularly in the Madrid press. I found a four-year-old picture of him with a megaphone at a rally of *Indignados*, the Spanish "Occupy" movement, in *El Pais,* Spain's major newspaper. There was a picture of him dancing with the newly elected populist mayor of Madrid at her victory party. Plus a blurred newspaper photo, taken two years ago, of a disheveled and proudly defiant Carlos Ortega leading a posse of protesters as they were escorted out of a government building by the police.

What can I say? Carlos was one of those guys who look incredibly hot in handcuffs. I tweeted that picture off to Abby who responded enthusiastically. *Spanish Robin Hood!* she responded. *Better yet, single, 36 years old, and a Leo. Perfect for you!*

Right now, Mr. Perfect was frowning as he lined up the pages neatly and laid them on the table. "You haven't found any other trace of the family in Normandy?"

"His parents were dairy farmers and, when they died, no one else claimed their property. Your father was their only son."

"Finally! Some good news for a change."

My face must have registered surprise because he wiped the smile off his face quickly and crossed himself piously. "If his ancestors were simple peasants who worked the land, may they rest in peace."

Weren't those simple peasants *his* ancestors too? My client obviously wasn't going there, so I added his last comment to the many things that didn't quite add up about Carlos Ortega's family values. I flipped the page to the list of contacts. "Giorgio Morelli is in town, and that is excellent news. I've already left a message at his hotel."

Carlos was frowning again. "Who is Giorgio Morelli?"

"He directed your father in three of his top-grossing films. He'll provide invaluable insights on his acting technique."

"I couldn't care less about his acting technique." Carlos applied his red pen to my interview list, putting checks next to some names and crossing out others. "This one," he said, drawing a little star. "Start with her."

I craned my neck around to see who'd caught his interest. *Ingrid Svenson*? "Honestly, that doesn't..." I bit off "make sense" because the customer's always right, even when he's dead wrong. I switched to what I hoped was a placating, understanding sort of voice. "Ingrid was one of your father's many, many girlfriends, and I'll certainly speak with her eventually, but Giorgio Morelli is only in Paris until Sunday. He's got to be the priority right now."

Carlos shook his head. "No, I'm telling you that Ingrid Svenson is the priority. Begin with her."

"Believe me, I'll be treating your father's personal life in depth, but his acting career will be a large part of any serious biography."

He was silent. Too silent.

"This *is* a serious biography, isn't it?"

"Of course, it's serious." Carlos waved for the waiter. "Perhaps you desire a *croissant* with your coffee?"

Actually, I desired *lunch*. The French couple at the next table were digging into roast chicken with mashed potatoes, and it smelled absolutely heavenly. My client wrinkled his own nose in amused disapproval. "In Madrid, we would never eat lunch before three in the afternoon. It's more civilized."

I wasn't sure my rumbling stomach could handle that much civilization. "Any reputable publisher will want the career angle covered in detail," I persisted. "Banville was known as a method actor. He learned fencing from an Olympic champion when he starred in *Les Trois Mousquetaires*. For the movie about Pierre Curie, he spent hours in scientific labs. He lost twenty-five pounds for the movie about WWII prison camps."

"Who cares what that *hijo de puta* ate for dinner? Listen to me, I'm telling you to forget about the cinema."

"You want a movie star biography without any movies in it?" Sad but true—the guy from Discount Carpet City, who insisted on two full chapters about nylon area rugs, was my sanest client so far. "Maybe you had better explain what you want from me. It doesn't sound like a traditional biography."

The waiter deposited two coffees and a breadbasket on the table and hurried off.

"I am instructing you to begin your inquiries about this biography with Ingrid Svenson. Do you have a problem with that?"

"Of course not," I said, mentally crossing my fingers behind my back. "What exactly do you want to know about her?"

"Everything that pertains to her relationship with Charles-Henri Banville." He pulled a colored photocopy of a *Gala* magazine cover from his briefcase. It showed Ingrid Svenson on a red carpet with two blond blue-eyed adolescent boys. "Those boys look very much like him, don't they? Much more than I do. It's very possible that they are his children."

"There are DNA tests for that," I pointed out.

"Ingrid rejects all modern medical technology," Carlos said as he refolded the photocopy. "For someone with 500,000 social media friends, she has a curiously medieval vision of the world."

"Have you thought about hiring a detective?"

"Why should I hire a detective? I have you."

Chapter Eleven

Ingrid Svenson's location was easy to pinpoint thanks to social media. I even knew what she'd eaten for breakfast this morning at a posh spa in central France. (*Granola, low fat vanilla yogurt, and pineapple slices.*) Thanks to the health properties of its fizzy spring waters, Vichy made its resort debut as an R&R destination for Julius Caesar's troops. The Swedish supermodel had signed on recently as the "face" of the spa's celebrated anti-aging creams.

I spent the first hour of the train ride to Vichy transcribing last night's phone interview with Giorgio Morelli. So what if my new "client" wasn't interested in movie anecdotes? His ideas about this book were just as narrow and self-serving as his father's. With luck, I could dig up enough "Daddy Dearest" dirt to quench his thirst for vengeance and still have more than enough material to write a "real" biography on the side.

Morelli had lots of fascinating movie lore, but I was particularly interested in his memories of Charles-Henri Banville on the set of *Le Jardin du Mal* in May 1980. "Always drunk, always late, even more impossible than usual," recounted Morelli.

Now that I knew that Charles-Henri was balancing a pregnant pop star wife, a pregnant teen-age maid, and his first Hollywood contract, that was hardly surprising. It was an enormous amount of pressure for a guy who was prone to throw tantrums over parking tickets. I filed the info as deep background and got back to Ingrid Svenson.

Her "official" bio said she was twenty-five when she met the fifty-year-old Charles-Henri Banville in May 2000. I suspected that she'd shaved a few years off, but as she couldn't fudge the age of her twins, she'd be at least forty today, well past her "sell by" date for a model.

But in fact, as spokeswoman for this new face cream, Ingrid was doing better than ever. An internet search through past *Vogue* and *Elle* covers showed that her career took its biggest hit right after Charles-Henri rejected her during her pregnancy. She'd had a tough time ditching the baby weight and lost her agency contract in the process.

She'd petitioned for child support during those hard luck years, but given her resistance to medical tests, I assumed it was easy for Banville's lawyers to block her requests. I also found some snide Banville interviews in which he implied that Ingrid had been sleeping with the phonebook all through their liaison.

I'd booked the cheapest single room available at the elegant spa. There were less expensive lodgings in town, but I was counting on running into Ingrid "casually" at the granola bar or, even better, while we were both sipping herbal tea in one of the fancy "relaxation" rooms that I'd seen on the website. I was practically drooling over the spa options. All expenses paid in relation to research, right?

The fly in the massage ointment? I wasn't sure that I approved of my client's motives. The relief on his face was nearly palpable when I couldn't turn up any living relatives in Normandy. And what was the one thing that set Ingrid apart from all the other featured females in Charles-Henri Banville's checkered love life? Her two children.

Two children who, if they shared Banville's genes, could claim a big part of the actor's estate.

The estate was well worth a fight. If Charles-Henri Banville was sloppy in his personal life, his financial savvy was spot-on. The actor owned an expensive, five-room apartment in Paris, a vineyard in Burgundy, a vast art collection, and a fleet of vintage sportscars. Now that Señor Robin Hood was about to join the one per cent, it looked like he was too cheap to share the loot with a couple of Swedish half siblings and a few "simple peasants" in Normandy.

It shouldn't have disappointed me so much, but it did.

Chapter Twelve

Vichy was already a popular resort in the 1700s, but according to the internet the town's glory days date from 1861 when Napoleon III began "taking the waters" as a health cure. His planners laid out parks and built fancy housing, a new train station, and a marshmallow-white casino where super-rich industrialists and aristocrats could gamble their fortunes away during the tourist season.

As I wandered down streets lined with the grandiose mansions built by rich and famous Europeans back in the day, I realized that Vichy was exactly the kind of flashy playground which would have appealed to Rhett Butler and Scarlett O'Hara. They would have scheduled their second honeymoon here if their romance had lasted that long. I almost wished I had a time machine to see what the town was in the age of gaslights.

As if on cue, two steam-punk babes in hoop skirts flounced out of a candy store and climbed into a horse-drawn buggy. I stopped short. Was I hallucinating? "What...?" was all I could say as I pointed to the carriage in shock.

"Every year, in the springtime, there is a festival weekend," said an elderly gentleman whose honey-colored spaniel sniffed at the rollers of my suitcase so eagerly that I wondered if I'd wheeled it through a puddle of steak sauce. "We dress in historic clothing and have a costume parade through the center of town. There will also be a gala dancing party tomorrow night."

"*Merci*," I murmured.

The man nodded and tugged on the leash. The dog, immediately losing interest in my suitcase, raced toward a flock of pigeons, dragging his owner behind him. "You will enjoy the festival," the man called over his shoulder.

I'd already started enjoying it. I whipped my phone out fast enough to snap a picture of a man in a gold-trimmed military uniform—complete with sword—and a lady in a two-tone burgundy hoop skirt outfit with a matching lace parasol. "*Street fashion in rural France,*" I texted Abby.

The hotel was a giant white mega-complex on the edge of town. "You were extremely lucky that we had a last-minute cancellation," commented the receptionist as I checked in. "This is a very popular weekend, and all the rooms have been booked months in advance."

My room was worth booking *years* in advance: fifty shades of royal blue; a pair of ultra-soft twin beds; picture windows overlooking a vast swath of greenery; and a state-of-the-art bathroom with a walk-in shower that was bigger than Marie-Christine's kitchen.

I had little to unpack except my laptop, which I promptly plugged into the wall socket to recharge. I checked my phone to see if Ingrid Svenson had tweeted anything newsworthy in the past fifteen seconds. "*Photo shoot in the park! Perfect weather!*"

I'd already sent an interview request to Ingrid, but I was certain that my email would languish in the spam file of her manager's assistant's intern until sometime next week. However, my client insisted that this interview was urgent, so it was time for me to take a stroll in the park.

"Which park?" asked the cheerful concierge as he spread a map of Vichy across the reception desk. "We have nearly 580 acres of parkland in Vichy."

Whoa...this town would be paradise for my father, who lived for landscaping. But for me, all that park was a problem. I shifted to Plan B and parked myself on the sidewalk terrace of the café across the street from the hotel. As long as Ingrid wasn't one of those paranoid celebrities who sneak through service entrances in disguise, she'd be tough to miss from this vantage point. I ordered an herbal tea and settled in for a stakeout.

Luckily, I'd bought a handful of Vichy postcards at the train station. Three of them sported adorable, gray-striped tabby cats playing roulette at the casino; the other two featured Persian kittens at the Art Nouveau opera house. You've wondered who buys postcards like that? Me.

Absorbed by supermodel surveillance and kitty-kitsch, I paid no attention to the other customers. It wasn't until a slight breeze wafted one of my postcards to the pavement that I noticed the teenage boy sitting at the next table.

It was Lars.

Or maybe it was Erik.

At any rate, it was fifty per cent of Ingrid's Swedish twin team. He was tranquilly slurping cola through a striped straw and devoting all of his blond, blue-eyed attention to a Nikki Minaj video. I'd have no chance of building a cordial interview relationship with Ingrid if she thought I was stalking her kids. Luckily, I'd already paid for the tea, so I packed up my postcards, pocketed the receipt, and prepared to make a quick getaway.

But it was too late. Heading right toward me, at a slow and stately swivel-hipped catwalk crawl, came Ingrid Svenson, surrounded by a posse of paparazzi.

"*Oh shit! Oh shit! Oh shit!*"

But surprisingly, that wasn't a voice in my head. It came from the boy sitting next to me, who whispered those words over and over and over in nearly unaccented English.

Chapter Thirteen

"You've got to help me." He slid the cola bottle over to my table and appropriated my empty teapot and cup. "Mama doesn't like me to drink soda."

Mama had already spotted us. I mean, she'd already seen Eric/Lars and was waving to him enthusiastically. I couldn't run away now. I was already in Ingrid's sights, and I was going to have to talk to the woman sometime. It wasn't like I could wear a mask when I did the interview.

"Darling Lars," said Ingrid, sweeping down on him and giving him the kind of professional air-kiss that didn't smudge her makeup. "Where is Erik?"

"He's at the pool," said Lars. "I just came here to have a cup of tea and do my English homework."

Ingrid beamed at him. "Green tea is so much better for your skin than carbonated drinks filled with sugar and chemicals." She eyed "my" soda bottle disapprovingly. Lord, her peach-tinted skin was perfect. Not a wrinkle, not even the hint of a blemish. If that's what Vichy face cream did for the complexion, I was going to stock up on the whole line.

"Miss Svenson, I'm Melody Layne and..."

Ingrid's wide blue eyes narrowed to icy Nordic slits. She was one of those people who looks even more gorgeous than usual when she gets mad. And she was sure looking gorgeous right now.

"Melody Layne? Aren't you the one who's writing a book about that monster?"

"You're writing a book about a monster?" asked Lars, looking at me with new interest. "Like Voldemort or Godzilla?"

Ingrid pulled her hotel keycard from her snakeskin clutch. "Lars, darling, would you go to my room and bring me my blue sweater? Then you can tell me what you learned with your English homework."

He stood up and looked at me anxiously. I smiled to let him know his secrets were safe. Music is an excellent way to absorb Anglo-Saxon culture. After he left, Ingrid slid into his chair.

"Miss Svenson, your son just happened to sit down next to me. I didn't ask him any questions at all."

"That's good because neither of us have anything to say about Charles-Henri Banville. That evil man means nothing to us."

"Why did you attend his funeral?"

"Who wants to miss the party of the season?" Ingrid smiled. It wasn't the kind of smile that sells expensive face creams. Not unless the secret ingredients include arsenic, hippopotamus poop, and radioactive waste. "If you ever met Charles-Henri Banville, you'd know that the world is a much better place without him. I was happy to see the last of him, but I certainly wasn't the happiest person there."

"Who would that be?"

"Why, the person who put him in that coffin."

"No one put him in a coffin. It was an accidental drowning."

"Perhaps it was." Ingrid brushed a glossy strand of white-blonde hair behind her delicate, shell-shaped ear.

"At any rate, it was providential. Your message said you had been hired to write this book. Who hired you?"

"His son."

"*His son*? That's ridiculous. Charles-Henri never had any children."

"There was a secret marriage to a young Spanish girl in 1980."

"There was?" Ingrid bared her perfect teeth, and for a moment she reminded me of Purrboy when he got ready to pounce on his catnip mouse. "That evil, evil, *evil* man fathered a son that he accepted as his own? I see. But if so, that means..." Her turquoise eyes shot those ice-blue Scandinavian death rays at me again. "That means that this miserable Spaniard employer of yours thinks he's the sole heir to the Banville fortune? And he's worried that my poor innocent boys pose a threat to his inheritance?" She spat out a string of Swedish words that I rather hoped she wouldn't translate. "Is that what's going on?"

I didn't contradict her because that was exactly how I saw the situation shaping up.

"I will make an important announcement at the Gala tomorrow night," she said. "An announcement that will have enormous financial impact on the future of my sons." She opened her purse and extracted a cream-colored envelope addressed to *Greta and Olaf Svenson.* "My brother and his wife had to cancel, so there are two extra seats at my table. Your greedy Spaniard will learn something of interest if he attends." She flashed that ice-cold smile again. "But of course, you both must wear historic costumes, or it won't be my fault if you are not admitted."

Chapter Fourteen

"Not good," I muttered to myself as I watched Ingrid sashay across the street to the hotel, pausing only to wrap her arms around Lars as he exited the revolving door with her blue sweater.

I'd made an enemy out of Ingrid, and I hated that feeling. Self-employed, single mothers automatically win my respect. Ingrid had been treated badly, and she was doing her best to protect her children. If I wasn't working on this damn Banville book, we might have been friends.

I slit open the envelope and found two VIP passes to the Gala dinner dance. The hitch was the dress code. How the hell was I going to get a hoop skirt by tomorrow night? Would the hotel concierge be able to help me?

Ingrid was no airhead, I mused as I slid the passes back in the envelope, but she wasn't as sharp as all that. She hadn't noticed the faint smudge of my lipstick on her son's teacup. Which made me think...

I stared at the soda bottle in front of me. I've watched enough CSI to know that you can get DNA trace from just about anything that makes lip contact. Whose side was I on here?

The sexy Spanish skinflint who was paying me?

The Swedish super-model who hated me?

The dead creep who hired me in the first place?

My side. That's whose side I was on. Trying not to overthink the ethical issue, I slipped the straw into the paper bag from the postcard store. I wasn't exactly sure what I was going to do with it if I did anything at all. However, at this stage when it came to information, I felt it was better to have than to have not.

Back at the hotel, the debonaire concierge was ever so sorry. My request, he explained, was impossible. Every suitable ballgown in the vicinity was already taken. I wondered if I could pull off an arts'n'crafts solution. If I found a really big skirt and a hula hoop, could I superglue them together into something that would look convincing? Probably not. A soothing hot shower, room service, and an early night…that was all I wanted from life at this moment in time. I'd worry about the costume tomorrow.

However, I still had one more task on my list before I could relax. I had to invite Señor Scrooge to the prom. Carlos answered on the second ring. I filled him in on my close encounter with Ingrid and relayed her message that he might learn something of interest at tomorrow's gala.

He was surprisingly cooperative. "Very good. I'll take the train from Paris tomorrow. What time does this event begin?"

I checked the passes. "Eight-thirty. It's dinner and dancing."

"Dancing? I love to dance. I'll pick you up at the hotel at eight."

"Not so fast," I told him. "This is a costume party."

"It's a costume party? Like …*como se dice?*…your Halloween? We are supposed to dress like vampires and ghouls?"

"Not exactly. The theme for the party is 1865."

"Second Empire?" I detected some amusement in his voice now. "Of course, it would be Second Empire. Napoleon and Eugénie vacationed at Vichy."

"I thought it was Napoleon and Josephine."

"No, Melody, that was Napoleon Bonaparte. This is his nephew, Louis-Napoleon, who declared himself emperor in 1851."

"Of course." I decided to cut him off before he launched into history-teacher mode. "I'm not having much luck finding a costume for myself but, according to the concierge, men can get away with a formal evening suit. You might find something suitable in your father's closet."

"Even if I could bear to touch something of his, it wouldn't fit. I'm much taller than he was."

"I suppose so. You're certainly broader in the shoulders."

There was a pause. "How would you know that, Melody? You told me that you never met him."

"I never had a chance to interview him for the book, but I had dinner with him in New York." I shuddered at the memory of the actor's boozy breath and hands-on approach.

"A very intimate dinner? With a lot of wine?" There was another long pause. "And it was after this dinner that he offered you the job?"

"Well, yes, in a sense, but…"

"Don't worry about your clothes, Miss Layne. I'll rent something for both of us in Paris. What is your size?"

In America, sizes start in single digits: 2, 4, 6, 8 etc. I'd seen clothes on the racks in France with numbers in the 30s and 40s, but I hadn't tried any on yet.

"I'm not sure."

Exasperated sigh. "Well then, tell me your height and weight, and the people in the shop will work it out."

I treat those numbers like state secrets, available only on a need-to-know basis but, damn it, Carlos Ortega needed to know. "Five feet eight inches and 135 pounds," I replied as cheerfully as I could, shaving off five pounds purely on principle.

"Fine. I'll bring your costume to the hotel tomorrow."

Chapter Fifteen

I brought my laptop down to the dining room the next day, half hoping for an Ingrid sighting at the granola trough. No such luck. She posted a picture of herself having breakfast in bed just as my coffee was served. I spent the rest of my Saturday morning earning my fee by emailing interview requests to the rest of the Banville contacts on my list.

After lunch, I took a well-deserved break for tourism. I caught some of the parade and snapped dozens of pictures of ornate villas modeled after Gothic citadels, Byzantine palaces, and gingerbread Swiss chalets. I filled my empty bottle with some of the miracle water that bubbles from the Vichy springs. My guidebook claimed that it cures everything from arthritis to zits. If this stuff did a number on writer's block, I could become addicted.

Since most of the women swanning around town in their hoop skirts wore their hair in elaborate upsweeps, I invested in bobby-pins, a fake tortoise-shell comb, and a can of "extra-hold" hair spray. I figured I'd need at least an hour of DIY in front of the bathroom mirror to approximate an 1860s 'do. When I got back to the hotel at four pm, the receptionist handed me a large silver garment bag and told me that Monsieur Ortega would be waiting in the lobby at eight.

I'd been hovering on the edge of fairytale

anticipation mode all day, but full-blown Cinderella fever took over as the elevator doors closed. I was in a five-star hotel, I was going to an actual ball in a princess dress, and my escort, who was bound to be the handsomest guy in the room, actually *liked* to dance! Maybe he'd even know *how* to dance. This might be the best night of my life.

My major stress was still about the dress. While reassuringly heavy, the garment bag was disturbingly skinny. Carlos, after all, was a guy. Maybe he figured that one vintage dress was as good as another? What if he'd rented me a 1920s flapper costume or a Greek toga? I was pretty sure they wouldn't admit me into this nineteenth-century bash unless my dress had "nineteenth century" written all over it.

I heaved a giant sigh of relief when I unzipped the bag. The dress was perfect for an 1860s rave. It looked just like the gowns in the event's publicity pictures that were taped up all over town. Gauzy, off-the-shoulder cap sleeves were tied with slim, purple satin ribbons. The skirt was fashioned from yards and yards of iridescent mauve taffeta accented with darker lilac fringe.

The low-cut lavender bodice had corset-like strings in the back, making it conveniently one-size-fits-all, but I spotted a major infrastructure problem right away. There weren't any hoops for the hoop skirt. I shook the garment bag in frustration until a flat white packet, about the size of a FedEx envelope, tumbled out. When I cut through the tape with my nail file, a puffy cone of white gauze popped out like a genie from a lamp. I had my hoops. I was saved!

After a long, luxurious soak in the Olympic-sized

bathtub tinted with bright blue bath salts, it was time to get started on my hair. That took longer than I'd bargained for, and it was nearly half past seven when I fastened the waist strings on my hooped petticoat and slipped into my dress. Now…who was going to lace it up for me? I peeped into the hotel corridor and waved to a maid who had begun her turn-down service.

Rosemarie turned out to be the Pablo Casals of corset strings. I tipped her heavily and stared at my image in the mirror in consternation. There were several square miles of fabric in the skirt, but the top part of the dress was barely there. In fact, the neckline was playing touch-tag with the waistline, and my bust was literally busting out of the balcony. Most bikini tops cover more skin.

I shook the garment bag again. There had to be something else in there. A scarf? A shawl? But there was nothing. *Nothing*! How was I supposed to wear this in public? I rummaged through my carry-on, praying for a miracle. What I *needed* right now was a pashmina with a pearl-beaded fringe. And I had one of those. It was folded up in Marie-Christine's dresser in Paris.

What I *had* with me was a Garfield night-shirt and Hard Rock Café tank top. A quick search of the hotel room turned up nothing in the textile department except triple-ply bath towels. There was a lace doily under the phone on the bedstand, so I tried tucking it into my cleavage. The effect was comical, the equivalent of pasting a band-aid over the Grand Canyon. I still looked like a waitress in an 1860s brothel.

Carlos Ortega was picking me up in ten minutes, so I pulled myself out of panic mode. None of the hoop skirted ladies I'd seen in town today wore anything half as skimpy, but they hadn't been dressed for evening either. Obviously, this had to be the way that women dressed for parties back in Napoleon's day. I practiced sitting down and standing up. Despite the hoops, it was easier than I expected. Everything would be just fine as long as I didn't breathe heavily, eat more than one cracker, or—heaven forbid—need to visit the restroom. The skirt itself was wider than most toilet stalls.

At five minutes to eight, I sailed into the lobby. "Sailed" is the right word too. You can't simply "walk around" in a ballgown that takes up this much floorspace. The only options are "waltzing across a dance floor" or "floating on a cloud." My denim jacket spoiled the effect, but the night was cool, and catching pneumonia was not on my "To Do" list. Tonight, I was going to a ball with the handsomest man in France. Tonight was all about feeling like Cinderella.

Chapter Sixteen

The hotel lobby was filled with glittery women decked out in beribboned evening cloaks in rainbow shades of gold, crimson, sapphire blue, and emerald green. A few wore sparkling tiaras, and several carried jeweled fans. Most of the men wore black or charcoal-gray evening suits, and Carlos Ortega was no exception. I spotted him right away and floated across the floor in his direction, noting that he wore a top hat, silk tie, and black tails with remarkable ease for a rabblerousing leader of the proletariat.

"You look quite elegant," I said.

"And you look exactly like Marguerite Bellanger."

I had no idea who that was, but I intended to do an internet search on the babe in question as soon as possible. I certainly hoped she was beautiful. My escort and I joined the procession that was heading toward the party.

"What exactly were Miss Svenson's words?" he asked.

I'd almost forgotten that we were attending this gala for business reasons. "She said you would learn something of interest relating to her sons' financial future. No other details."

"I don't see why she couldn't express that in an email instead of making me trek all the way to the hinterlands for this ridiculous dance."

Ridiculous dance? I looked at him, but his perfect profile revealed nothing. "But I thought you liked to dance."

"With my *friends*. I like to dance with my *friends*." A flicker of irritation crossed his brow. "Since I'm coauthoring a book about Empress Eugénie, this trip isn't a total loss. Eugénie de Montijo was Spanish, of course," he continued. "She loved spa towns, although she detested Vichy."

"Why?"

"One day, as Eugénie walked through the town with the emperor, the dog that belonged to his mistress broke its leash and ran to the emperor like a dear old friend. That was enough for the poor empress. She left Vichy the very next day." Carlos frowned. "The mistress was a well-known prostitute named Marguerite Bellanger."

Wait…wasn't that the name that he just…?

"Aside from his flamboyant taste in architecture, there's nothing nice to say about Napoleon III on a personal level," he continued.

"He must have been kind to animals," I muttered. "The dog apparently liked him."

Carlos snorted. "Perhaps there's a ray of sunshine in the darkest heart that only bloodhounds can detect. I certainly hope so," he added as we climbed the stairs of the Palais des Congrés, "because if not, this idiotic book will be a waste of time and money."

Idiotic book? "Is there something wrong with the book? Do we need to discuss something about our contract?"

"Not now, Miss Layne," said Carlos. "You did remember to bring the tickets, didn't you?"

I fished them out of my bag and handed them to a man dressed like an imperial grenadier. "Welcome to the Emperor's Ball, Monsieur and Madame Svenson." He flipped through the pages of the guest list and put an "x" next to our assumed names. "You'll be dining at table twelve in the VIP section. The coat check is directly to your right."

Chapter Seventeen

I definitely did *not* want to surrender my coat. Not when what was underneath would make Miley Cyrus blush. Especially not when my date/boss was treating me like the dirtball from hell all of a sudden. My book was "idiotic"? He only dances with "friends"? He thought I looked like some bygone prostitute, too. What brought this on? He'd seemed fine on the phone yesterday.

Unfortunately, there was no way I could get away with wearing a jeans jacket at this clambake. I could already hear the Champagne corks popping and the strains of the waltz played by the live orchestra. I was in one of the rare places on the planet where vintage denim doesn't make fashion sense.

Carlos hung back with the menfolk whose evening wear did not need to be checked while I was guided toward the coatroom with a bevy of other hoop skirted babes. Their dresses will be just like mine, I told myself. When they slip off those embroidered capes, their dresses will be just like mine.

Wrong.

Their dresses were *similar* to mine, at least from the waist down. Upstairs, it was a different story. Their tops were PG and mine was totally X-rated. The elderly woman next to me pursed her lips disapprovingly and shooed her bug-eyed grandson away from me.

Did Carlos choose this dress for some unsavory voyeuristic purpose of his own? Or was it simply a careless mistake? Too many guys don't have clothes sense. I could see my father picking this outfit off the rack for me or Abby simply because he loved the colors of lilacs and hyacinths. I figured I'd know what Carlos had in mind when I turned around and saw the look on his face. Why was the cloakroom guy taking so long to bring me the claim check?

Ah. When he pressed the coat check into my hand, it had a phone number written on the back. Oh dear. I turned around and focused all my attention on reading my escort's face. Would I see a surprised look? A lecherous look? An admiring look? What I caught, or what I *think* I caught given that his face was as expressive as an Easter Island monolith, was satisfaction.

Satisfaction?

Was Carlos as sick as his dad? How was I going to get through a whole night in this dress? I considered reclaiming my jacket and running away. The problem with that? I still wanted this job. What was the downside of sticking it out? Not much. I could face the fallout if "French Slut" photos of me circulated on social media. It wasn't like I knew anyone here. As a matter of fact, they weren't going to know me either, thanks to the gilded name tag clipped to my overexposed décolleté that identified me as Greta Svenson.

"Do you like the dress?" asked Carlos as he took my arm and led me to the dining room.

"It's perfect," I hissed. "What a lovely choice."

Ingrid, a vision in sky-blue satin with navy velvet

accents and a hyper-demure neckline, presided over a very large round table seating sixteen. Carlos and I were shown to our places directly across from her. We were too far away for casual conversation with our hostess but not completely out of range if she started a food fight. I stared at the poppyseed dinner rolls already in place on the gilt-edged bread plates. They looked kind of hard.

We were barely seated before the speeches started. A gentleman who was dressed up like Napoleon III rambled on and on in French. Carlos, seated to my right, chose to read and reread the menu that was placed on his plate. However, my porno-bodice captured all the attention of the man to my left, who quickly introduced himself as Richard Davis, Ingrid's talent agent.

Holding his empty flute for the waiter to refill, he slipped the other arm around the back of my chair. Leaning in very close, eyes fixed on my cavernous cleavage, he whispered, "You ever thought of modeling?" If Carlos was functioning as my "date" this evening, he might have helped me out. But no, he pointedly ignored the situation, seemingly the only person in the room who was listening to the speech with full attention.

When the applause died down and the waiters began serving plates with lobster in cream sauce, I jumped on the opportunity to disengage from Richard. I turned to Carlos. "Since we have some time now, it would be great to have your impressions of your father."

"That won't take long. I only met him once."

"Can you tell me about it?"

Carlos lifted his wine glass but put it down before tasting it. "I attended a private French-language school in Madrid with entrance fees that were far beyond my mother's means. She told me that I'd won a scholarship, and since my classwork was very good, I believed her. I believed her until..." He speared a chunk of seafood with his fork and lifted it to his lips. "This is really quite good."

"You believed her until...?"

"I won a school prize for English when I was eleven. The medal was inscribed to Charles-Henri Banville. I didn't understand how they could make such a mistake. My name, after all, was Carlos Ortega. When I complained, the school's director showed me my files. It was quite a shock to learn my full legal name and that a Frenchman named Charles-Henri Banville was paying my school fees."

"Your mother never said anything about him to you?"

"She still doesn't, but after that day I saw his name—or rather 'our' name—everywhere. On posters, at movie theaters, in the newspapers, in magazines."

"What did you do about it?"

"*Nada.* I did nothing." He sipped his wine. "No, that's not completely true. I went to see his movies secretly, and I never told my mother. As a search for a father figure, it was rather confusing. He always played the heroic man of honor on the screen, but it didn't seem like he'd been a hero for my mother. However, with the blissful ignorance of youth, I was sure I could bring my family together. What a fool I was."

"What did you do?"

"Seven years later, I was graduating at the top of

my class, and I had an exquisitely beautiful girlfriend, Paola Ruiz. Feeling sure that he would proud of me and happy to reunite with my mother, I sent him an invitation to the ceremony."

"He didn't show up?"

"Oh yes. For some reason, he showed up, very drunk. He barely noticed my mother—she was probably too old and too plain for his taste—but when he left that night, he took my Paola with him. He sent her back from Paris a few weeks later, slightly used, with a new wardrobe." He shrugged. "When I read in the papers that he was dead, I couldn't even pretend to be sad. I think that concludes your interview with me. With whom will you be speaking next?"

"I'm waiting for replies, but in the meantime, it would help to see any letters or photos he might have kept."

"A sensible idea. I have no idea if he had anything like that, but I can ask the lawyers to give you a key to his apartment."

The waiters cleared the table and brought plates of chicken with green beans and puff potatoes.

"In fact," I began, "if there's a…"

But Carlos had already turned his attention to the woman on his right who introduced herself as Ingrid's Aunt Liv. They chattered away about the state of the European Union while I was left to cope with Mr. X-Ray Vision. "I meant it about the modeling. You're remarkably ink-free," he said, staring at my nearly naked torso approvingly. "Tits without tats are a rarity these days."

Thankfully, everyone else at Ingrid's table, with the exception of the twins who stared across the table like I was the answer to all their teenage dreams, treated my dress with equanimity. Swedish people, I learned gratefully, share an easygoing attitude toward partial nudity at the dinner table. If Carlos set out to make me feel uncomfortable, his plan had backfired. But why would he want to make me uncomfortable in the first place?

When there were plates of lemon truffle cake and fresh flutes of Champagne in front of everyone, Ingrid tapped her wineglass with a silver spoon and rose, arm-in-arm, with the silver-haired gentleman who'd been sitting next to her. Lars and Erik hastily stuffed their phones in their pockets and stood at attention on either side.

"I have some very happy news for my friends and for my family, and I think it will please others—" She paused and fixed her ice-blue gaze on Carlos and me. "—at this table as well. Sir Andrew Beechwood and I are to be married next month, and he is adopting my darling twins, Lars and Erik."

Richard Davis whistled under his breath. "Ka-ching, ka-ching."

I looked at him blankly.

"Beechwood International Resorts."

"How wonderful!" cried Ingrid's Aunt Liv.

"Congratulations!" shouted someone from the next table.

"A toast to the future family!" called another.

A small crowd was clustering around Ingrid, Andrew, and the boys in an orgy of hugs and kisses. I was surprised when Carlos stood up to join them and even more surprised when he and Ingrid moved away from the others and spoke privately.

"With all that guy's loot, she'll never need to work again," groaned Richard, tapping furiously on his cellphone. "Frankly, Ingrid's our cash cow. This'll be a huge loss for the agency. I wish she'd never met him."

I wished I knew how to lipread. Whatever was going down with Ingrid and Carlos seemed surprisingly warm and courteous. Where were the insults, the brass knuckles, the baseball bats? They even shook hands as though cementing a deal. Carlos made a sign for me to join them.

"It will be faster if you send your questions to my private email instead of the agency," said Ingrid, handing me a card. She opened and closed her jeweled fan and rapped it against Carlos's shoulder. "You're not at all like your father, Mr. Ortega. I hope you find what you're looking for." With a flounce of her sky-blue ruffles, she returned to her sons and her future bridegroom.

"What *are* you looking for?" I asked him as we walked to the coat check a few minutes later.

"If I told you," he said, "you'd never be able to find it."

Chapter Eighteen

I enjoy a treasure hunt as much as anyone, but it's tough going when you don't know what you're looking for. Maybe it was impossible to expect a straightforward answer from someone with Charles-Henri Banville for a father. However, it wasn't the mysterious side of Carlos that made me toss and turn most of the night. It was the new chilliness in his manner. He'd bestowed those engaging little smiles, the ones that made my heart flip-flop at the Café de la Paix, on every woman at our table except me.

As I wrestled my gown back into its garment bag the next morning, I wondered if my sensitivity to his moods could be chalked up to loneliness. Back in New York, I had an active social life filled with my sister, my friends, and my cats. I was manless in Manhattan after Eric left, but I got by fine without him. In a city that never sleeps, it's hard enough to doze off for a few hours, much less find the time to snuggle up with another workaholic.

Paris, on the other hand, was the City of Love, and I hadn't even had a kitten to cuddle since my arrival in France. In romantic France, I felt like the only high school kid without a date for the prom. However, it was dumb to fantasize about the one and only man I'd met in Paris. Carlos Ortega was my one and only client, and as such had to be treated with kid gloves. If he wanted cold, I'd take my clues from Frosty the Snowman. Besides, France was full of people with much smaller chips on their shoulders. Carlos had good reason for packing those chips—that story about his high school graduation almost broke my heart—but he didn't need to take it out on me.

Last night, as Carlos Ortega politely but coldly escorted me to the hotel, he said that he was taking the 11:45 train to Paris. So was I, but given his attitude, I decided not to mention it. Why not let Fate handle the details? If we met at the train station, great. If we didn't, that was great too.

Fate, however, decided to take a pass on the train situation. As I was checking out, the concierge waved to the bellboy, who took a garment bag that matched mine off a brass rolling rack. There was a scribbled note taped to the plastic. *Called to Madrid urgently. Please return the costumes to following address. C. Ortega.*

I used the solitary Sunday train ride to email some follow-up questions to the newly cordial Ingrid Svenson. I also checked on the location of the theatrical rental service. It was in Vincennes, a suburb east of Paris, which was easily accessible by the subway. I planned to get that errand out of the way first thing Monday morning.

I was back in Paris before dinnertime, so I picked up some groceries at the minimart and settled down for a quiet Sunday night of crackers, camembert, and Chardonnay. Surfing the channels on the TV turned up a surprise: three episodes of *Lie to Me* dubbed in French. I fell into a deep sleep midway into the second episode, wondering why my client was being so coy about his motives. He might not be lying, but he sure wasn't telling me everything.

The sun was bright and the sky a cheerful shade of turquoise blue as I entered La Maison Ducrocq, a sprawling wardrobe warehouse, at 10:30 on Monday morning. Madame Ducrocq, a buxom woman with a rather large wart on her chin, relieved me of the garment bags in short order and began going over the costumes like an FBI forensics specialist.

"When he told me that he was renting these for a dinner party, I nearly said no," she told me as she examined the bodice of my lavender dress with a magnifying glass. "Our clientele is professional, and even a tiniest splash of *beurre blanc* on satin or silk moiré fabrics can be a disaster. But he was so charming, I couldn't resist him. And when I photocopied his passport for the deposit and saw that he was the son of Charles-Henri, well, then he was like family. Those costumes that Charles-Henri wore for *Splendeurs et Misères* three years ago? All mine...and they were in perfect shape when he returned them, may he rest in peace."

"I couldn't help noticing," I said, "that my dress was more revealing than many of the others at the ball."

"*Eh bien*. I didn't have very much in your size at such short notice," said Madame Ducrocq, running her hands over the velvet ribbons on the sleeves. "There were two more modest ones available, but this very, shall we say, *provocative* gown was designed for one of the prostitutes in *Splendeurs*. Carlos said it would be perfect."

"He chose this horrid dress specifically for me?" My voice rose to a screech that nearly hurt my own ears.

"It's a very, *very* beautiful dress," said Madame reprovingly. "One of the most expensive in my collection.

"Did he say *why* he chose this particular dress for me?"

Madame Ducrocq wrinkled her brow. "He said you were a very close friend of his father. An intimate friend, that's what he said. An intimate friend. I assume that's why he wanted to make sure that you had a very special costume."

An "intimate" friend? As in "lover"?

Somehow, I managed to get the receipts exchanged, retrieve the cancelled check that Carlos had left as a deposit, and get out of the building without exploding.

Dammit, I'd been slut-slammed 1860s style! What on *earth* gave Carlos Ortega the idea that I was an "intimate" friend of his dirtbag dad? Did he think I'd slept with him to get this job? I jammed my subway ticket into the turnstile slot. How *dare* he?

By the time I got to the Nation subway station where I changed trains, my boiling rage had cooled to a furious simmer. What could have given him that idea? What exactly had I told him about his damn father?

Just the truth.

That I'd never interviewed Charles-Henri Banville.

But then?

But *then* I told him I'd met his father for dinner, hadn't I? I told him that when I invited him to Vichy, and that's exactly when he got all cold and distant with me.

I could kick myself. Carlos wouldn't need a crystal

ball to figure out that his dad had treated me like the main course at that dinner. In fact, if Banville hadn't been distracted by a better offer, I'd have run for the exit and kissed my first celebrity memoir goodbye. As a career move, it wouldn't have been brilliant, but it was a million times better than kissing a creepy-crawly lecher like Banville.

Carlos Ortega thought I slept my way into this job? He'd believe the worst about me, just like that? Given what he knew about his father, I couldn't blame him.

But I did.

I really did.

Chapter Nineteen

The rest of my workday contained nothing but good surprises. Jenna Bardet, the VJ who'd been fired from her job after accusing Banville of harassment, sent me a text suggesting we meet for lunch the next day in the Marais. Perfect! I wrote down the address and confirmed for one o'clock.

Then I got a long, rambling email from Ingrid. What had Carlos said to her to make her so cooperative? She wrote about her childhood in Stockholm and her first modeling contracts, which was good background but not truly relevant to my project. I scrolled down to the part that interested me.

I had finished the Pirelli calendar and was considering offers from two rival lingerie companies when I met Charles-Henri. He told me he could get me a role in his next movie.

I was thrilled and canceled a major photoshoot after he invited me to Chamonix for a party weekend. But when I arrived, there was no party. Just the two of us in a freezing hut far away in the Alps. He kept sitting outside in a tee shirt, shivering and asking me to tell him everything that Swedish people know about snow.

I told him Swedish people don't sit in the snow in their tee shirts. He said he needed to learn about cold for his next movie which took place somewhere in the Arctic. He kept telling me there was a role for me.

Later, I found out that the part had already been promised to another actress.

He told me there would be another role, and I neglected my career to follow him on location again. One day, when I visited him in his trailer, I found him in the bed with his costar. He told me he needed to experience sex with her so that he could play the role of her lover correctly.

I was bitterly unhappy. I went to a bar near the movie set to cry. Two months later, however, I found out I was pregnant. Charles-Henri was very cruel, insisting that my babies were not his. Today, however, I am happy at last with my wonderful fiancé and my two beautiful sons.

So here is the one thing I can tell you about Charles-Henri Banville: He was a dedicated actor, always doing research for his roles.

I hope this helps.

I sat back and stared at the printout. It didn't help me very much at all. Why did she tell that awful story about the way Banville cheated on her and then shift gears to inform me that he was serious about his acting roles? That was not exactly a revelation. You don't get to be one of the world's most bankable movie stars without being a professional.

She'd neatly sidestepped the paternity issue as well. She'd been ready to sue Banville for child support at first, then dropped the charges and refused to follow through. Had Banville been right after all? Were the kids somebody else's?

I pulled her card out of my purse. While she'd offered to help, she hadn't exactly invited me to telephone her, but what the hell? I decided not to overthink the question and dialed her cell. Heritage issues were apparently very important to Carlos, and right now I needed to impress him.

Ingrid answered on the third ring. I told her how much I appreciated her email, then eased into the slippery Lars/Eric trail.

"Of course, I thought they were his at first," she said. "I honestly believed he was in love with me. When I found him in the trailer with that woman, I was so shocked that I ran to the nearest bar in tears. That's where I met Hans, the set designer. He told me that Charles-Henri had seduced all the women on the set, including his assistant and the associate producer. I was so broken-hearted that I spent that night with Hans."

Ingrid sighed. "It's hard to keep secrets on a movie set, and Hans must have talked about it. After that, Charles-Henri told everyone I'd been unfaithful throughout our relationship. That was not true," she added. "It was just that one night."

It finally made sense. "So that's why you've refused DNA tests for your sons? You're afraid they aren't Banville's?"

"No," said Ingrid. "I am afraid that they are. Who would want such an evil father for their children? A man who refused to even consider that they were his? If there was the slightest chance that they were not Banville's, I wanted to believe it."

"What about Hans?"

"What about him?" asked Ingrid. "A man who bragged about sleeping with me to everyone on the set is not much better than Charles-Henri. I never contacted Hans again. Look, I have told you the truth about Charles-Henri. He worked very hard to be a great actor, even though these memories are painful to me. I have fulfilled the promise I made to Carlos Ortega. Please give him my regards and tell him that this is the best I can do. From now on, I want to forget the past and plan my wedding in peace."

The telltale straw I'd swiped from Lars/Eric was still wrapped in its plastic bag in the side pocket of my carryon. I retrieved it and tossed it in the garbage. For better or for worse, Ingrid's secrets would be safe with me.

Chapter Twenty

Jenna Bardet had such flaming copper-colored hair, and so much of it, that she shone like a lantern even in broad daylight. Her smile was even brighter as she waved to me. I threaded my way to her table, trying my best not to knock over any of the towering flower vases or fragile, glass-topped dessert trollies.

"I was so excited when I got your email," she gushed. "It's about time that someone wrote a book about that snake. You said that his son hired you to tell the truth about that man?"

"Um, yes." I scanned the menu nervously, searching for the cheapest thing that wasn't made with pig's ears or cow brains. In this case, it was an appetizer of truffle-potato soup that cost almost fifty bucks at the current rate of exchange.

"Don't worry," said Jenna, sensing my dismay, "this is on my expense account." She made eye contact with a wine steward across the room who was holding a bottle of Champagne. He materialized at our side an instant later with two flutes of bubbly on a silver tray.

"To Charles-Henri Banville," said Jenna, lifting her glass. "Let's hope the flames in hell are bright enough for him to read this book."

We clinked glasses cheerfully. "Would you mind if I ordered for both of us and we taste each other's plates?" asked Jenna. "I'm testing this restaurant for a food guide, and I want to try the shrimp with anchovy sauce and the grilled lamb chops with sautéed spinach."

I gave her a thumbs-up, and after an animated huddle with the headwaiter, Jenna turned her attention back to me. "I expect you want to hear how Charles-Henri Banville got me kicked out of my cable job?"

"Please," I mumbled through a mouthful of one of the delicate cheese-filled pastries that showed up on the table with the Champagne.

"It was my first celebrity interview in France, so it was a huge break. When I got to the hotel, Banville left a message that I should go to his room while the cameraman set up in the bar. When I got to the room, he was in his bathrobe. And then, goodbye bathrobe." Jenna broke off. "I won't give you the details while you're eating, but for a warty old guy he had lots of upper body strength. He ripped my jacket right off my back as I ran for the door."

"How did the station react?"

"The station believed Banville when he said that I was a pathetic kook who tried to seduce him." Jenna skewered a shrimp and plunged it into a dish of cocktail sauce. "Later I found out that Banville had specifically requested a young female journalist. My station manager set me up, refused to back me up, and then fired me for not getting the story."

"Triple whammy," I murmured.

"Quadruple whammy. The jacket was ruined."

"*Mousse de morilles parfumé aux truffes,*" whispered the waiter as he slid two tiny shot glasses filled with foam topped with chopped herbs in front of us.

"I had my own close encounter with Banville in a

New York restaurant," I told her. "He was all over me until another woman came by and dropped her lingerie on his lap."

"That's the problem, isn't it?" said Jenna. "When guys get used to that sort of come-on, they think they're irresistible. Does the son have the same attitude?"

"He thinks that I'm a slut who used sex to get the book contract." I filled her in on the dress debacle, and Jenna disappointed me by bursting out in laughter. "It wasn't funny," I said, glaring at her. "He dressed me up like a period porn star."

"Both those Banville boys are complete losers, aren't they?" said Jenna, wiping her eyes with her napkin. "Daddy's a perverted predator, and sonny-boy's a puritan crackpot. Nothing in between. However, if you want this Carlos creep to keep signing your paychecks, you had better clear the air as soon as possible. He may be a coldhearted bastard, but work is work. You don't have to like the guy."

"I did like him at first. I liked him a lot."

"Then that's all the more reason to clear things up quickly," advised Jenna. "Sometimes things that seem like setbacks work out for the best. If Banville hadn't got me fired, I wouldn't be working for a food guide. I like this job much more than the cable TV celebrity gig." She waved at the white linen tablecloth, ornate silverware, and crystal wine glasses on the table. "I'm eating and drinking like this every day...and getting paid for it. The world, you might say, is my oyster."

As if on cue, the waiter showed up with two lavishly appointed plates.

"To your oysters," I said lifting my glass.

"And to yours," said Jenna with a wink.

Chapter Twenty-One

Jenna and I made plans to meet next week, but just for fun. There wasn't much more she could tell me about Banville, and when you came down to it, there wasn't much that anyone was telling me that I didn't already know: The guy was a brilliant actor and a first-class... Well...my French vocabulary was getting a whole new slew of nasty swear words.

If Charles-Henri Banville were alive, he'd emphatically proclaim that he *wasn't* a (French expletive deleted) jerk. However, as he was sidelined in the hereafter, this biography faced a serious cheerleader shortage. All the women I'd met so far detested him, and it wasn't just the women. Tony Major loathed him, and Giorgio Morelli described him as a nonstop nightmare on the set. His only son, Carlos Ortega, was packing an industrial-strength Oedipus Complex. The producer of his latest film, *Adieu Marseille*, couldn't get enough curse words into our ten-minute phone conversation.

The late afternoon sunshine streamed into the kitchen windows of Marie-Christine's apartment as I stared at the printouts of the interviews I'd done so far. I didn't see any logical way to pull this book together without using Banville's movies as the glue, but Carlos insisted he didn't want any acting anecdotes. What did Carlos the Sphinx want anyway? *"If I told you what I wanted, you wouldn't be able to find it?"*

Big help.

Another weird thing: He never mentioned *anything* about his publishing plans. I assumed he intended to self-publish, which was good because I didn't think a movie star bio without movie lore had much of a chance. But what was his motivation for going to all this trouble in the first place? I'd had several clients who commissioned a book as a memorial to their dear departed loved ones, but that wasn't the case here.

My first impression, that Carlos wanted to use my research to prove his sole claim on his father's estate, fizzled when he made a peace pact with Ingrid. He didn't seem petty enough to want a catalog of his father's sins for revenge either. Something was going on with Carlos, but it probably didn't have much to do with books. My client, the international man of mystery.

Part of me still wished that Carlos was more than "just" a client. Today was the first day that spring really felt like spring. The Parisian weather had finally pushed those black down jackets to the back of everyone's closets, and the graceful trees that lined the streets were in full bloom. My personal sap was rising too, but it had no place to go. Abby had already sent me three emails about beets that I hadn't answered. Part of my lovesickness could be written off as Feline Withdrawal Syndrome. I truly missed those furry little critters who used to warm up my bed each night.

Now, however, I was fantasizing about a partner who didn't cough up hairballs on the pillow after cuddling with me. Carlos Ortega was the only man I'd met in Paris, and right now he'd classified me as one his father's conquests and consigned me to the trash bin. As Jenna said, I'd have to set him straight and as soon as possible.

How would I do that? The situation was almost as complicated and convoluted as one of Charles-Henri's movie scripts.

Maybe I could think of it as a movie screenplay?

Take 1: *Carlos, nothing happened between your father and me.*

That was okay, but should I be more specific?

Take 2: *Nothing happened between your father and me that wasn't strictly professional.*

Wait…since his dad was a professional womanizer, that wouldn't fly.

Take 3: *Carlos, I'm not that kind of girl!!!*

Take 4: *Except with you! Take me, take me, take me!*

Forget it. I'd just have to wing it the next time we spoke. My email pinged. *Carlos?* No, it was Charlene Trent's Hollywood manager. Banville's last-known fiancée was coming to France for the Cannes Film Festival and would be happy to meet with me there.

What luck! I did an internet search for the dates for the Festival. First week of May? Perfect timing! In just a few weeks, I'd be catching the rays with movie stars on the French Riviera. Maybe I hadn't found true love, but the sightseeing perks on this project couldn't be better. I dashed off a reply when the phone rang. *Carlos?* Perfect timing again.

"*Allo*?" asked a deep, masculine voice.

I guess my anger had been building because I let it all out now. "Listen up," I told him. "I have never, *ever* slept with anyone for a job. And I want you to know

81

that goes double for your father."

There was complete silence on the other end of the line.

"*Mon dieu*," came the reply at long last. "At thirty euros an hour, I hadn't even considered the possibility."

My heart sunk. "This isn't Carlos Ortega?"

"*Mais non*, my name is Bertrand Olivier. I'm calling about the English lessons."

Chapter Twenty-Two

Mornings—all mornings—always make me feel happy and hopeful, and this one was no exception. Coffee brewed, orange juice squeezed, and I was ready to face the world with a smile. I'd put a temporary moratorium on those *pain-au-chocolat* pastries, buttery little calorie-bombs that I loved way too much, except for special occasions. And since I gave myself the power to define those special occasions, like "Forgive Yourself for Making a Fool of Yourself on the Phone Day," I planned to pick up one of those delicacies at the bakery and enjoy it with my second cup of coffee at the café.

I was also happy that I had a little cash coming my way as well. After a very embarrassing conversation last night, I'd scheduled a two-hour English class with Bertrand Olivier for tomorrow afternoon.

Today, however, was my first French road trip. Rouen, the cathedral city not far from Charles-Henri's birthplace, was one hour from Paris by train, and I'd made a lunch date with Jacques and Véronique Poinot, a retired couple who'd been to grade school with Charles-Henri. I didn't expect they'd tell me that Charles-Henri had shared his lunch money with the other kids. The way things were going, I'd probably find out that he'd stolen the exam results and humped the math teacher during recess.

I'd already emailed my restaurant expert asking for a good eatery in Rouen, and Jenna replied instantly with a name and address. *"Take them to La Couronne. It's traditional, and everybody adores it."* Apparently, Jenna was right about everyone loving "The Crown." Jacques and Véronique were delighted with my choice and even said they'd take care of reserving a table for three at one o'clock.

At 10:45, I boarded my train at the Saint Lazare station. In theory, I'd arrive more than an hour ahead of time, but, like all recovering Amtrak passengers, I consider train timetables to be works of fiction. Imagine my surprise when the train left precisely on time. It was also clean, quiet, and comfortable. I opened my guidebook to prepare for a little pre-lunch tourism.

My college roommate, who'd majored in Art History, had three different posters of the Rouen Cathedral that Monet had painted, so that was the "must" for any free time I had after lunch. Even in reproduction, it was magical to see how the Impressionist's skill had captured the façade's different hues as the weather and time of day changed.

When I glanced up from my guidebook thirty minutes later, we were already in the countryside. From then on, I was glued to the window as the train sped by lush pastures where contented cows and sleek horses grazed. I was almost disappointed when the landscape melted back into stone-hewed, manmade vistas as we approached Rouen.

Just five minutes after getting off the train, I found a city constructed with half-timbered homes straight from the fairytale catalog. Charmed by the spectacle, I put the cathedral visit on hold as I wandered toward the restaurant, marveling at the narrow houses with the dates of their construction—like 1535—carved over the front doors.

The restaurant, a handsome timbered building overlooking a cheerful farmer's market, was even older than that. "La Couronne has been operating as a tavern since 1345," said the waiter as he as he took my coat. 1345? I had to make him repeat that. "Absolutely," he replied. "La Couronne was already one hundred years old when Joan of Arc was here."

I quickly discovered another reason why Jenna's choice was inspired. The walls of the restaurant were covered with autographed pictures of the celebrities who'd dined there: Brigitte Bardot, Jean-Paul Belmondo, even John Wayne. The waiter was showing me to a table next to black-and-white poster of Audrey Hepburn when I had a flash of inspiration.

"Are there any pictures of Charles-Henri Banville?"

"Of course. He came here often." The waiter led me upstairs to a table by the window. "Will this be all right?"

"*C'est parfait,*" I told him. I took the seat under a Kodachrome headshot of Charles-Henri that was signed and dated November 18, 1972. He was wearing a dashing wide-brimmed hat with a plume. Was that when he played D'Artagnan in *Les Trois Mousquetaires*? I thought so, and I wondered if Jacques and Véronique were the kind of fans who would know for sure.

They showed up a few minutes later, a gray-haired couple with a shy demeanor. I noticed that the cuffs of Jacques's tweed jacket were frayed when we shook hands and figured that Véronique must have bought her shirtwaist dress when I was about five years old. They were definitely country mice, and when the waiter buzzed by to ask if we'd like a Champagne cocktail to start with, they looked at me like hopeful cocker spaniels who were too polite to beg for treats from strangers.

"Of course," I said, and they beamed at me. Although I'd only been in Europe for a few weeks, I'd grasped the overwhelming importance of food issues for the French and understood that there would be no serious conversation about Charles-Henri Banville before the menu was fully perused. I'd been given an English translation, so I had no trouble following the intense discussion that Jacques and Véronique were having over each option. Jacques leaned over several times and pointed to different parts of my menu to make sure I understood all facets of the spinach versus asparagus debate.

"Their *sole meunière* is famous," said Véronique.

"That sounds wonderful," I said. "Would you order that for me?"

"*Sole meunière, trois fois*," said Jacques when the waiter returned. When the cocktails arrived, Jacques chose a bottle of white wine to go with our fish. After we toasted Charles-Henri, whose estate was paying for our lunch, we got down to business.

"He was a very handsome man in his day, wasn't he?" Véronique gestured to the autographed headshot above my head.

"If you like blonds," shrugged Jacques. Judging from the salt/pepper ratio of his shaggy mane, his own hair had been very black in his youth.

"What do you want to know about him?" asked Véronique.

"Anything about his childhood. What was he like?"

"No one was surprised when he became an actor," said Jacques. "He was always imitating people. He did that very well, but it wasn't always kind."

"It wasn't kind at all," said Véronique. "Remember Jean-Marcel, the little boy who stuttered? He made him cry more than once."

"He memorized things quite easily, so he did quite well in class," volunteered Jacques. "Otherwise…" His voice faded.

"I brought our class picture from our *lycée.*" Véronique unrolled an 8x10 picture. "We were all, I think, fifteen years old."

It wasn't hard to pick out Charles-Henri. I'd already met his modern-day doppelgangers, Lars and Erik Svenson. In the slightly faded picture, Véronique sat in the row in front of him. She was the prettiest girl in the class, a teenage dream with dark, wavy hair. I wondered if there was a little bit of backstory with Charles-Henri, but I decided not to ask.

As if by mutual agreement, our conversation moved to neutral but passionate topics like wine, music, and food when the sole arrived. It wasn't until we were finishing our luscious Grand Marnier soufflés that I broached the Banville subject again.

"Had you seen him recently?"

"No," said Véronique. "Three years ago, the village schoolhouse was struck by lightning. It was rebuilt, but the insurance didn't permit us to add a stage for student assemblies. We thought that Charles-Henri might be interested in something theater-related, so the town council wrote to him and asked if he could appear at a local fundraiser."

"He answered that he had no time for backwoods nonsense," added Jacques. "We backwoods people would have been happy if he just sent a check, but he didn't have time for that either."

"He was a great actor but not a generous man," concluded Véronique bitterly. The look in her eyes confirmed my suspicion that there was some afterschool drama concerning Charles-Henri. "Not a nice person at all."

Over coffee, Véronique and Jacques supplied a few more anecdotes about Banville but nothing too earthshaking. He'd been very ill with measles when he was eight. He borrowed Véronique's cousin's bicycle and didn't give it back for weeks when he was eleven. He'd starred in the high school play as Rodrigue in *Le Cid*. Véronique was almost sure that she had some pictures of the play, and possibly a program, in a box in her attic. She promised to call me if she found them.

On the five o'clock train back to Paris, I knew my next trip to Rouen would be purely for pleasure. There wasn't much left of the Normandy that Charles-Henri knew, so my work was finished. The 1930s schoolhouse that Banville had attended had burned down and, according to Jacques and Véronique, the new owners of the Banville dairy farm had razed it and replaced it with a modern brick structure.

I'd made significant progress on the Carlos-approved interview list, but the book would be mighty thin without the movie anecdotes that Carlos claimed that he didn't want. The only major players who hadn't returned my calls were Banville's ex-agent, Marius

Dubrovski, and the actor's first wife, Delphine Carroll. Delphine's pop revue was scheduled for five concerts at Paris's Olympia theater in a few weeks, so I'd take my chances with the venue's press office.

Ping went my phone. Email from Carlos. Meeting tomorrow, eleven am, but at a different café. The address was on the Place Victor Hugo. I looked it up. It wasn't far from the Arc de Triomphe in an area of town I hadn't yet explored. I emailed "yes" and budgeted time for a relaxing avocado skin masque when I got home. I wanted to look sunny and fresh-faced when we met. I certainly didn't want to look as pissed off as I felt.

Chapter Twenty-Three

I arrived at the café ten minutes early, but Carlos was already there, with an empty cup of coffee, a basket of croissants, and copies of *Le Monde* and *El Pais* spread across a large table near the window. As I slid into the seat across from him, I noticed that he looked rather tired, although I had to admit the faint shadows under his eyes weren't entirely unbecoming. If his day hadn't started well, that was too bad for him. I planned to make it worse.

"You owe me an apology," I stated.

"For what?" Carlos looked up in surprise. "For not returning the clothes? Didn't I tell you that it was an emergency situation? My mother had a severe nervous crisis and worried herself into such a state that she couldn't walk." He pushed a rebellious lock of raven hair away from his forehead, but it swooshed right back. "I have no need to apologize for anything."

A waiter swung by just long enough to take my order for a *café au lait* and a second espresso for Carlos.

"Yes, you do, but first we have to set a few things straight about my meeting with your father. He made some very crude, sexual advances towards me…"

"¡*No mas, por favor*! I told you already, Melody. I do *not* want to know any of the details."

"There *are* no details, Carlos. He left the restaurant

with another woman."

"What?"

It was rare, and somewhat gratifying, to see Carlos at a loss for words. "Another woman came up to the table, dropped her underwear in his lap, and he took off with her right away."

"He preferred another woman instead of you?" Carlos sat back in his chair and rubbed his forehead. "*Madre de Dios*, there is no accounting for taste. But would you have gone with…no, I am sorry. I suppose that isn't my business, forgive me."

"Rest easy, Carlos. I wouldn't have gone anywhere with your father. Your father was a…he was a…"

"…pig?" asked Carlos. "Don't worry. He's been called worse by many people."

"I wouldn't call him a pig. Pigs are kind of cute."

"You're right." Carlos flashed me half a smile, so fleeting that I barely saw it. "He was not a cute pig. He was a bad man. A very bad man. And when I think that I'm his son, that his horrible blood runs through my veins, I'm always worried that there might be something in me that's the same."

"Carlos, that's ridiculous! That sort of thing isn't inherited. Look at my father. He's a brilliant landscape gardener, and while he's taught me a lot, I don't share his magic touch with greenery. When my father talks to the trees, the trees *answer*."

"Does your mother share that gift with plants?"

"My mother?" I chose a croissant from the basket. It was getting too close to lunch for me. Would I wean Carlos off his Spanish meal schedule or would I eventually adapt to midnight suppers? "My mother had other plans for herself. She wanted to see the world, and she met an airline pilot who made that possible. They got married in New Delhi a few years ago. I think she's in San Diego, at least that's the last I heard."

"*¿Es verdad?*" Carlos looked at me in dismay. "Melody, you don't even know the city where your mother lives?"

"She never misses a birthday present, but she's made her own life, and that's her right. My family consists of me, my sweetheart of a father, and my sister Abby. The three of us, we've been just fine without her for the last ten years."

"My heavens," said Carlos, "what a strange pair we are. I had an absent father whom everyone hates, and you have a sweet, responsible father who is even respected by plants. You have no contact with your mother and I...well...perhaps I have too much contact with mine. Sometimes my mother, she is..."

His phone rang. *Despacito* instead of opera. Carlos was jazzing up his act.

"*Si, si, Mama.*" He listened to a flood of Spanish. "*No, Mama, no hay problema en el aeropuerto, Mama. Si Mama, ti quiero. Hasta esta noche.*"

He groaned as he replaced the phone in his jacket pocket. "She's convinced there's some kind of strike at the airport. There is no problem. I know that because I checked after the last three times she called, but I better not miss that plane. I'm glad we were able to talk and clear things up." He gestured for the bill and reached for his wallet.

"Not so fast," I said. "You still owe me that apology."

"What on earth should I apologize for?" He sat back down and stopped counting out the euros in his hand. "Everything's cleared up, isn't it? There's nothing more to discuss, no?"

"There's a little matter of that dress you rented for me."

Carlos flushed. Not quite as red as I blushed when the maid laced me into that nineteenth-century hooker outfit, but almost. That was gratifying too.

"The dress?" he asked, with just a slight smile. "That dress was quite appropriate for the period of history."

"What there was of it."

"Melody, Melody...perhaps, in retrospect, I may have jumped to a conclusion..."

"I'd say you pole vaulted to a conclusion."

"But not without justification," he countered. "You are definitely my father's type. Young, blonde, beautiful..."

I stopped listening for a heartbeat. *Beautiful*!

"...and your French, while adequate, is far from perfect. By all accounts, my father had a weakness for women who couldn't understand most of what he said."

"I think he preferred to use body language." Remembering those hands, well-oiled after having sopped up all of the butter sauce with his bread, I shuddered in spite of myself. "Honestly, Carlos, why didn't you sew a scarlet letter on that dress? You made me look like a tart!"

"You were a very beautiful tart." He held out his hand. "And I must admit, it gave me considerable distress to see the effect that your dress had on that horrible man sitting next to you."

"Richard?" I said. Carlos had noticed after all! "By the way, Richard works at Ingrid's talent agency. He offered me a modeling contract."

"He did? I hoped you turned him down."

"Perhaps." I was still digesting the fact that Carlos called me "beautiful" twice. I couldn't wait to tell Abby and Jenna.

"Well, I'm sorry for the dress. I will try to atone for it. Now, before you take off for Milan to begin your career as a supermodel, may we talk about the project? Were you able to learn anything new in Normandy?"

"Two of his old schoolmates confirmed that your father was interested in the stage from a very young age. They also said that he was gifted at memorization and did good imitations."

"Did they like him?" Carlos asked.

"Not really."

"Just what I expected." Carlos leaned back in his chair and rubbed his eyes. "What about Ingrid Svenson? Has Ingrid been in touch with you yet?"

"Yes, and she says that your father didn't treat her very well. She wants no part of his estate for her sons."

"She told me all that in Vichy. Didn't she have anything more to say? Anything at all?"

"She shared two stories in which your father put concern for researching his roles over kindness to her. She insisted that he was very, very dedicated to his art."

"That was the best she could do? That's not enough, not nearly enough."

"Enough for *what*?" I asked. When was this guy going to clue me in on what I was supposed to be doing?

"Enough for…" Carlos paused. "I would like to tell you what I need, but I don't want to influence your research."

"It will save time if I know what you want from this book."

"The book?" He stared into space. "I don't even want a book!"

Now we were cooking with gas. Was Carlos finally getting around to giving me straight story?

"All right. It's very simple." He took a deep breath. "I need to know some good things about that *hijo de puta*. Find me one or two instances where he acted like a decent human being instead of a monster, write them up, and your contract will be paid in full."

"What for?"

"There's a private clinic in Switzerland that could do wonders for my mother, but I've never been able to afford it. We'll have the money as soon as the estate is settled, but my mother refuses to accept it unless she thinks the money came from a good man." Carlos groaned. "I thought people never spoke ill of the dead, but they're certainly making an exception for my father."

I caught sight of a *pain au chocolat* hiding under the croissants and snagged it. If Carlos expected me to find some sunshine in Charles-Henri Banville's sour, sex-offending soul, I needed a bigger sugar hit than the croissants provided. "You said he paid for that fancy school of yours? Doesn't that count?"

"Not for my mother. That condition was apparently built into the contract written up by my father's agent."

"Marius Dubrovski," I said. "When I find him, I'll try to find out if the school was your father's idea. Would that help?"

"Yes...no...maybe. Honestly, I don't know anymore, but it's certainly worth a try. Who else are you seeing?"

"Charlene Trent. She's coming to Cannes, and her agent made an appointment for me on the eleventh."

"Charlene Trent? That name seems familiar."

"She stars in those '*Beach Zombie*' movies."

"Really?" Carlos looked up from his coffee cup. "I remember those posters. Isn't she the woman with the extremely large…"

"That's her." If you did the math, Charlene was probably forty per cent silicon, forty per cent collagen, and twenty per cent hair extensions. I hated her on principle. "Your father was very close to Charlene. Of course, your father broke their engagement quite publicly, so it's possible that she may not have anything nice to say either."

"She has good reasons to hate him as well?" Carlos sighed. "I'm beginning to feel like Don Quixote, tilting at windmills, chasing after a hopeless cause. What about that first wife of his, Delphine Carroll? My mother must have lit a million candles for Delphine Carroll by now. She blames herself for the woman's miscarriage. A kind word from Delphine Carroll would go a long way."

"She hasn't replied to my messages yet."

"Didn't you say she's on tour? Perhaps she's not reading her email while she's traveling?"

"That's possible, but I've also been in touch with the publicity people handling the tour. It's rather strange that no one's got back to me." I stirred my coffee pensively. "However, that revue of hers is booked for five nights in Paris at the end of May. If I don't have any answer by then, I'll camp out at the stage door."

"She's interesting because she's the outlier," said Carlos. "As far I know, she's the only one in his harem who was French."

"Maybe not so French as all that," I said. "She was born Delfina Carolasanti."

"Italian?" asked Carlos, reaching for the check.

"I'm not sure, but I'll try to find out."

Now I knew what Carlos wanted from the book, it was time to let him know what I wanted: the right to proceed on an authorized biography. I drew a deep breath. "Carlos, after I deliver the book you've asked for, can I write an unbiased biography and try to sell it myself?"

"If you want to do that, please yourself. I couldn't care less." Carlos fished into his pocket for change and dropped a heavy gold keychain on the table along with the coins. "I almost forgot. Here are the keys you wanted. His apartment is on the avenue Foch, a few blocks away from here."

Glancing at his watch, Carlos announced that he needed to leave for the airport. I lingered in the café after he left, barely believing my good luck. To begin with, an uber-hot stud in Paris just called me "beautiful" twice in a row.

And even better, I was now writing an "authorized" biography with expense-paid access to major celebrities. Not a phony "memoir" or a fast'n'dirty "as told to" book for a minimal fee. This would be a book where I could sign my name and get all the royalties…if I managed to sell it, of course.

What if Carlos only cared about digging up some wholesome anecdotes? I needed "nice" as badly as he did in order to balance out the truckloads of "nasty" I'd been collecting since I started this project. When the waiter came around with the lunch menu, I ordered a *croque monsieur* and a glass of rosé. Carlos, bless his heart, probably thought that noon was still time for a late breakfast.

Banville's keys were fastened to a Gucci ring to which an ivory card with an address was attached by a paperclip. Two sets of numbers scribbled on the back were the door codes. Everything was great except that Charles-Henri was dead, and I hadn't liked him much when he was alive. While this was a priceless research opportunity, I wasn't really looking forward to touching any of the actor's belongings. I hated other people touching my things. Was I just projecting my feelings on his?

With so many mixed emotions flooding through me, I shouldn't have been surprised that I'd finished my rosé before the grilled cheese sandwich came. I ordered another glass.

This wasn't the sort of afternoon that I wanted to face cold sober.

Chapter Twenty-Four

The Avenue Foch has a big swath of trees and flowers down the middle, which gives it a superficial resemblance to Park Avenue. In New York, however, those prestigious residential high-rises sit securely on the sidewalk, guarded by doormen. The wealthy barons of the Avenue Foch prefer to hunker down in mini-fortresses shielded by heavy metal gates. The first five-digit code clicked me into an urban jungle of marble and potted trees. I could almost hear my father saying that those trees didn't get enough light, but I supposed they were changed regularly by the landscaping firm.

The second key gave me access to a magnificent hallway with a glossy mosaic floor, a curved stone staircase, and a gleaming brass elevator. The lace curtains parted on a small side door marked "Concierge," and a heavy-set woman with an impressive moustache opened the door and peered out.

"I'm going to Charles-Henri Banville's apartment," I said, waving the Gucci key ring to make myself look more legitimate. "I'm here to…"

"Third floor," she said, shutting the door before I could finish. She wasn't much of a watchdog, but then, she didn't look like the sort of woman that Charles-Henri squandered much of his charm on. Obviously, she didn't care if I was there to loot the place.

There was only one apartment on the third-floor

landing, and it took me a good five minutes of trial-and-error to get the four shiny deadbolts unlocked. When the massive door finally swung open, the queasiness hit me with a sledgehammer. I was in somebody else's house. Somebody I didn't like. Somebody who'd never invited me in. Somebody who was dead.

I'd never given anyone but my sister the keys to my New York lair until this apartment trade. When guests came, I barely let them rinse out a wineglass after dinner. I didn't have much, but it was all mine. Nobody but me touched anything in my place, and I'd never wanted to touch anything in anyone else's home either. The fact that I'd swapped apartments with an unknown French woman still amazed me. If it hadn't been the best job offer in my life, I'd have never done it.

I looked around the foyer and took a deep breath. For the moment, I was in neutral territory. This is where Charles-Henri would have signed for deliveries and paid off the pizza guys. I was cool. There was nothing to see but a rough-hewn wooden table, a framed Broadway poster of the *Père Goriot* musical, and an ornate Oriental vase with an umbrella sticking out of it. Nothing personal so far.

I pushed into the living room, reminding myself that even someone as neurotically OCD as myself wouldn't care who touched my stuff when I was dead. And some people didn't even have to die to feel that way. My sister Abby, for example. Every time she took a vacation, she rented out her apartment via website. Maybe Charles-Henri felt equally casual about his stuff. I stepped into the living room and looked around.

Money.

This place practically stank of it. Two sofas covered in soft, butterscotch suede straddled a glass-topped coffee table that was larger than a single bed. The royal-blue velvet drapes were edged with gold brocade. Thick Persian rugs adorned a parquet floor that had been polished to a mirrorlike gleam. The oil paintings on the wall looked like they'd feel perfectly at home in the Louvre.

But as far as personal items went, the room was a desert. No clutter, no photographs, no knickknacks. I crossed over to the black marble fireplace. The mantel was crowded with trophies—the Tony award for *Père Goriot*, the Golden Globe for best supporting actor, and a bunch of other statuettes from film festivals around the world. I liked the cute metallic teddy bear best with "Berlinale Film Festival 2009" etched on its belly. I remembered reading about that prize. Charles-Henri had scandalized the audience in Germany by sticking his hand down the dress of the actress who presented it before they were off-stage and off-camera.

Mirrored panel doors opened onto a dining room with a mahogany table that could easily seat sixteen. The small adjoining alcove had been converted into a library with floor-to-ceiling bookshelves. This was the first place that looked like it might yield paydirt. There was a foot-high pile of scripts stacked on the desktop, so I pulled up a chair at the dining room table, hoping for lots of hand-written notes in the margins. I flipped through one after another. Nothing. Either he hadn't read these scripts yet or he'd rejected them after the first few pages.

I hit the ultra-modern kitchen next. Like the living room, it resembled a photo from a glossy home magazine—enough polished granite to supply an upscale graveyard and shiny countertops that glittered with almost every stainless-steel culinary gadget on the market. I peeked into the cupboards and the fridge, and I found nothing to contradict my first impression of the actor as a rich bachelor who ate most of his meals in restaurants. Russian vodka, Red Bull, a jar of olives, and a few bags of gourmet-style potato chips. No perishables. Every surface sparkled. If Charles-Henri wasn't paying for a first-class maid service, he was a secret Susie Homemaker clone. It would be slim pickings if that was the only fun-fact I gleaned from this visit.

According to my research, he'd owned this apartment for twelve years. Even if he spent a good part of the year on location, he had to have left some stamp of his personality on the premises. This place looked like it had never been occupied. I headed down the hall. Here the polished parquet gave way to thick, dove gray carpeting which, thanks to the hours I'd spent at Discount Carpet City, I recognized as top-of-the-line, one-hundred-percent wool plush. I peeked into the first door: bathroom. Marble, marble, marble everywhere.

Here, however, there was some evidence that a carbon-based life form had resided on the premises. An extra-large turquoise bath towel had been flung over the shower door, and its mate was rolled up on the floor. Coincidentally, they were a perfect color match for the packet of bright blue pills on the countertop. The mirrored medicine cabinet was open, an invitation that most biographers would leap on, but I drew the line. I couldn't help clocking the prominently displayed turquoise sex pills, but his icky throat lozenges, sleeping pills, and laxatives were TMI for me. I pressed on toward the bedroom.

Oh, God…this part of the apartment was lived in.

And a total gross out. It was, quite literally, a bed of filth. Instinctively, I pulled back the foot that had touched the lint-flecked black carpet and wiped it against the doorjamb. In the center of the room, on a raised platform, the king-size bed had been ridden hard and put up wet, judging from the smeary stains on the black satin sheets. There was a mirror on the ceiling above it and a whole lot of art on the walls. These etchings weren't museum quality anymore, unless porn shops have museums. Hot-pink, fake fur pillows had been tossed to the floor. There were a few "toys" scattered across the bed that hadn't come from a Play-Skool catalog, and the whole room stank of musk. Charles-Henri must have burned patchouli sticks by the truckload in here.

The room spoke volumes but only about stuff I'd already guessed and didn't care to know about. No Banville bio was going to be squeaky clean, but this was too revolting to explore in depth. The maid service could deal with it. If they were smart, they'd wear hazmat suits while they were on this job.

I shut the door and headed back to the living room and sought refuge in the library alcove that adjoined the dining room. Books never fail to comfort me. If the bombs were falling, I'd probably hide in a library. A quick survey showed that Charles-Henri liked books too although he hadn't been keen on fiction. There was an entire shelf devoted to the French merchant marine, a section about the Catholic Church, at least fifteen books about boxing.

A biography of Neil Armstrong was jammed on top of the WWII histories. When the librarian in me returned it to the shelf with books about astronomy and space missions, something fell out of it—a plane ticket, first class, from Los Angeles to Paris. Was Charles-Henri the kind of guy who, like me, used any serendipitous piece of paper for a bookmark? If so, his bookcase might turn out to be a bonanza.

I grabbed a stack of books about the Arctic Circle. If he used these books to research his movie roles, these volumes would correspond with the period he was dating Ingrid and obsessing about snow.

Bingo!

The first item, wedged between Chapter Four and Five, was a restaurant bill dated December 2000, just about the time when Ingrid was (or wasn't) conceiving twins with him. Dinner for two in Grenoble, cheese fondue and lots of white wine, smack in the middle of the French Alps. Had diet-conscious Ingrid enjoyed the chocolate cake dessert?

Maybe she did, maybe she didn't. A few pages later, there was a lipstick-smudged cocktail napkin from the local Hilton with a phone number and a name, Anne-Marie. The next book turned up a stub from a Grenoble parking garage and a card with a date for a dental checkup.

After two hours, I knew where he shopped for clothes and what he usually ordered at restaurants (steak tartare and red Côtes du Rhône wine). Assuming he tipped well and signed autographs without complaining, the waiters and store managers might have lots of memories to share. I photographed everything and made notes of the books in which they were found.

At four o'clock, I called it quits for the day since Bertrand was meeting me for his first English lesson at my neighborhood café in an hour. I flipped through to the last book on the French resistance movement and extracted a piece of paper tucked into the back flap. It was just a single sentence in black block letters.

CHARLES HENRI, TES JOURS SONT COMPTES

Your days are numbered? I snapped a picture, tucked it back into the cover, and shivered. It was definitely, *definitely* time to go.

Chapter Twenty-Five

Bertrand said he'd bring a flower to the café, so I spotted him right away, a handsome, sixty-ish man in a leather jacket with a glass of red wine in his hand and a cellophane-wrapped rose sticking out of the water carafe. His gray hair was short, his goatee neatly trimmed, and he had a winning smile when he rose to greet me. I gave him a bonus point for choosing an indoor table. Sidewalk tables in Paris are invariably commandeered by cigarette smokers which make them very smoggy places to hang out.

"*Allo*, it is you!" he exclaimed when I sat down next to him. "The woman who refuses to sleep with me before she has even met myself! That is not," he said, "a very promising beginning on a French relationship."

"To a French relationship," I said since I didn't intend to take his money for nothing.

"To a French relationship." He flagged down a waiter and pointed to his glass. "You will have also? It is a pleasant Beaujolais."

"Yes, please. Tell me, why do you want to take English classes?"

"I have two childs," Bertrand told me, extracting a family photo from his wallet. "The oldest of him, he will be married in Australia. Now that I am *en retraite.*" He paused. "I have stopped of my work from my age. What is the word of that?"

"Retired."

"Now that I am retired one month from the police, I shall go for the wedding on Sydney and travel the back-out."

"Outback."

"Kangaroos," explained Bertrand. "I very much wish to see the kangaroos."

The waiter brought a glass of wine over, and we clinked glasses.

"And now tell me of you," Bertrand continued. "Listening comprehension is of great importance to me. What you are doing when you are not teaching?"

"I'm a ghost writer."

Bertrand pushed his chair away from the table almost imperceptibly. "You search for dead spirits? Like in the American movie?"

"I'm a ghost writer, not a ghostbuster. I write books for people who don't have the time or ability to write their own books."

Bertrand relaxed visibly and took another sip of his wine. "You see so many crazy people when you work of the police. For who are you writing this book?"

"Charles-Henri Banville."

"Charles-Henri Banville? But isn't he…"

"…dead? Yes, I'm writing the book for his son. He had a secret son." I had a sudden flash of inspiration. "Bertrand, did you deal with a lot of celebrities like Charles-Henri Banville when you worked for the police?"

"I have worked to protect famous people, yes."

"Do they often get death threats?"

"Movie stars and politicians attract the interest of many unstable personalities." Bertrand speared an olive with a toothpick. "They receive love letters, proposals to marriage, and yes, sometimes they receive angry messages inspired from hate."

"What do they do about them?"

"In general, little is done unless the messages develop into a stocking." Bertrand paused. "Why do you use that word for following people? Is it because stockings are worn on feet?"

"Following people is spelled differently." I wrote "stocking" and "stalking" on a page from my notebook.

"Then you have already resolved a mystery for me, *merci.*" Bertrand folded up the paper and put it in his pocket. "As I was saying, most celebrities ignore these threats unless they become very frequent and very specific."

"It wouldn't surprise you that Charles-Henri Banville received a death threat?"

"It would surprise me if he received only one death threat. There is a very dark side to fame as great as his."

"I'm finding that out," I said. "Bertrand, we really must do something about your prepositions." We got down to work, and two hours later I was sixty euros richer, and Bertrand had begun talking "to" me...not "on" me...or "from" me.

"We must have another lesson soon," he said as we gathered up our coats and umbrellas at the door because, once again, it was raining. The geraniums liked it, but I was bored with the daily April showers. "Next week, first of May, is a holiday, and I will be away, but shall we try the week after that?"

"I'm leaving for Cannes." I loved feeling like a jetsetter. "I'm going to the Film Festival."

"That will be a wonderful experience. Where are

you staying?"

"I've no idea, but I'm going to book a room tonight. Someplace central, at a decent price."

"In Cannes? For the Film Festival?" Bertrand opened his umbrella. "Good luck."

Chapter Twenty-Six

An hour later, I was pretty sure that I'd kick off my jet set career by sleeping on a park bench. I called all the Cannes hotels listed in Marie-Christine's Michelin Guide. Every single, double, and suite in every price category had been booked months before. Sometimes the desk clerks laughed at me for asking.

"What am I supposed to do?" I moaned to Jenna. "Buy a tent?"

"Of course not. You're going to look for hotels in nearby towns. Antibes, Cagnes-sur-Mer, Nice, even Monte Carlo. You'll just have to commute on the train into Cannes."

After zero luck in Antibes and Cagnes-sur-Mer, I finally scored a room at a pretty, Provençal-style inn called the Grimaldi in Nice, roughly 40 minutes from Cannes. By that time, I'd have settled for a vacancy in a roach motel, so it was an added plus that the website photos looked utterly charming. Of course, almost anyplace with palm trees and sunshine looked appealing to me right now. April in Paris, steady rain and fifty shades of gray sky, had not lived up to its reputation.

I made a reservation for three nights and spent the next two days in Paris trying to secure some interviews. However, by the time I buckled my seatbelt on the Air France shuttle to Nice on Thursday I'd had only limited success. Yes, I'd confirmed my appointment with Charlene Trent, but apparently no one else on the French movie scene wanted to take time out from their busy promotion schedules to chat about Charles-Henri Banville with an unknown American author.

The producers of *Adieu, Marseille* promised me a ticket to the screening and an invitation to a promotional breakfast with the cast. That was a major coup, although it was doubtful that Pierre Desportes, the actor who'd had his nose broken by Charles-Henri, would provide any of the feel-good stories Carlos wanted so badly. For the millionth time, I checked to make sure my voice recorder was tucked into the side pocket of my purse along with two packs of spare batteries.

It was love at first sight with Nice. The airport bus route followed the shoreline—white, sandy beaches and the turquoise Mediterranean—right into the center of town. And the small-scale boutique hotel outdid its own publicity pictures in charm. The concierge handed me a hand-delivered envelope containing my invitation to *Adieu Marseille* when I checked in. With a typically positive French attitude to amorous issues, the bed in my courtyard single was definitely wide enough for two people who didn't mind getting up close and personal with each other. It was topped with a bright scarlet throw. I could imagine using it as a cape, swirling it round and round to lure my elusive Spanish hottie to my bed.

The bed was nearly begging me to stretch out, stare at the ceiling, and milk that fantasy a little farther. However, I had work to do. After unpacking, I bought a sandwich at a street-side deli and headed for the train station. The next departure for Cannes was at noon, and I wanted to check out the lay of the land before my four o'clock meeting with Charlene at the Hôtel Martinez.

Did I say lay of the "land"?

That would be assuming I could see the sidewalk in Cannes.

Once I got away from the train station, people and cameras were jammed up against each other, elbow to elbow, rubber thong to sequined sandal. The main drag, *La Croisette,* was like rush hour on the subway except for the palm trees that loomed above the selfie-sticks. Real paparazzi—I assumed they were "real" because they were armed with fancy telephoto lenses instead of cellphones—perched a few feet above the crowds on fold-up plastic stools.

"What is going on here?" I whispered to a girl in a cartoon kitty tee shirt as I tried to inch my way through the tight scrum in front of the Hôtel Majestic.

"Bradley Cooper's in there. I loooove him."

"I would kill for that boy's autograph," announced a stout middle-aged woman in a gold lamé hoodie. The glint in her eyes made that sound entirely possible.

"I came *that close* to Sharon Stone yesterday," said Cartoon Kitty to no one in particular.

"Monica Bellucci's doing interviews on the beach later," murmured an Italian-accented voice behind me.

"Which beach?" asked several people at once.

I could see the sleek Art Deco marquee atop the five-star Martinez Hotel in the distance. According to the map from the Tourist Office, it was only ten city blocks away. Given the ground situation, that meant about 100,000 baby steps. I pressed on.

By the time I got to the Martinez, I needed a

shower in the worst way. I'd dressed for chilly Paris, and Cannes was summer-on-a-stick. At least two quarts of second-hand suntan cream had oozed into my black serge jacket. I sniffed at my pits surreptitiously. Thank goodness, my deodorant was holding up.

Trying to appear cooler and dryer than I felt, I approached the front steps. A man in black tie opened the door with an expectant expression on his face. I was already at the concierge desk before I wondered if I should have tipped him. Too late. I waited patiently, enjoying the air conditioning while the concierge staff ministered to a bunch of VIPs in white linen suits.

"I have a meeting with Charlene Trent," I told him when I'd worked my way to the front of the line. "My name is Melody Layne."

The concierge turned to his computer screen but not before I clocked his lascivious smile. "Ah, yes," he said a few seconds later. "Mademoiselle Trent is doing her interviews at the swimming pool."

Chapter Twenty-Seven

I was ninety minutes ahead of time, so I checked out the Wi-Fi in the lobby and made a pitstop in the elegant restrooms before doing some recon in the pool area. Charlene Trent reclined on a deck chair near the shallow end, clad in a pink-and-white checked bikini that left little to imagination...except what she did with the rejected bikini halves, since she sported a size 16 above and a size 2 below.

Her interview appeared to be wrapping up. The photographer knelt on the ground, packing up his lenses, and a lavender-haired minion with a hot-comb flitted behind the star, touching up stray strands of a streaked, honey-blonde coiffure that would drive the Lion King mad with envy. A tall girl in a *"Beach Zombies III"* tee shirt yawned behind her clipboard.

"One last question," said the journalist. "What will people say about you fifty years from now?"

"Ooh, I know what I'd *like* them to say," said Charlene with a dazzling white-on-white smile. "That I made the world a better place."

"Making the world a better place," said Clipboard Girl, rolling her eyes when the journalist moved out of earshot. "Isn't that a bit much?"

"Hey, it's only the truth," retorted Charlene. "Do you know anyone who's done more community service than me?"

I moved close enough to see that Clipboard Girl wore a nametag that said Taneesha Roberts. "Taneesha, I'll be waiting in the lobby. I have the four o'clock appointment. Melody Layne."

"Perfect timing, Melody," said Taneesha. "Scotland on Sunday's been held up." She penned an asterisk next to my name. "Charlene, this is the interview about the Banville book. You ready?"

Charlene lowered her sunglasses to get a better look at me. "Taneesha, honey, can you flag the barman? I'm gonna need a whole new pitcher of mojitos for this."

"The one you've got is half full," objected Taneesha.

"It looks half empty to me."

"Oh, for heaven's sake." With a shrug, Taneesha headed for the bar.

"This one's nothing but melted ice," Charlene said. "What do you want to know about Charlie-Poo?"

"Let me get my recorder set up."

"Uh-uh." Charlene placed an immaculately manicured hand over my recorder. "First we're gonna talk *off* the record. What exactly do you want to know?"

I took out my notebook. "Basically, everything. Where you met, your relationship, the good times, the bad times, the engagement, and of course, the, um, break-up."

"Gotcha," said Charlene. "We met at the Golden Globes. We were the only two people doing any serious drinking at our table, and afterward we went back to my place for a nightcap and cooked up the business plan."

"The business plan?"

"Let's call it an image swap. I needed European

exposure to break out of American Bimbo Limbo, and Charlie needed Hollywood since he'd been blackballed by everyone over here for his bad attitude. What delivers more feel-good press than a couple of boozehounds saying "I do?" We had a killer idea to go with it too, a mutual pledge to lay off the juice until the corks popped at our wedding."

I was amazed, both by the cleverness of the plan and by the fact that two notorious substance abusers devised it while totally sloshed.

"Charlene and Charles-Henri. The Cha-Cha Challenge." Charlene leaned back on her chair with a dreamy smile. "Every troll with a smartphone would be glued to our asses whenever we got within fifty feet of a Tequila Sunrise. His face plastered in every US magazine and my picture in all the European tabloids. Brilliant, right?" She sighed. "Well, it was brilliant until Charlie screwed the poodle and dumped me."

"Why did he do that?"

"Why did he bail on the wedding?" Charlene uttered a long and intense string of swear words that would have contorted her face unattractively before the invention of cosmetic filler. "Jeez, we'd already made the sex tape too. It's not like we didn't do all the homework."

"Put it over there," said Taneesha to the waiter, who set a crystal decanter and a set of glasses on the table next to Charlene.

"Pour us three big ones," said Charlene.

"I'll pass," said Taneesha, signing the receipt. "I've got to call New York and give them an update."

"The suits want to keep tabs on my alcohol intake," said Charlene with resignation. "How do they expect me to talk about *Beach Zombies III* all day without getting blasted? Cheers, honey." She handed me a tall, frosty glass. "Where were we?"

It probably wasn't smart to mix cocktails and work, but one cool, refreshing sip of rum-and-soda won me over. "Charles-Henri took a powder?"

Charlene took a deep swig and delicately removed a scrap of mint from her teeth. "If he wanted to dump me, there was a proper way to go about it. Like in front of the goddamn church with all the cameras. Me in a super-hot white dress slit up to here." She pointed to a place a few inches south of her crotch. "Like, Leo DiCaprio or Ryan Gosling as Best Man? My people can work with something like that. But Charlie leaves a *phone message* to say it's over? While I'm in *rehab* in the middle of nowhere? Total scumbag move, if you pardon my French."

"I agree." I wanted to get this on tape so much it hurt. "Would it be OK if I switched on the voice recorder now? Please?"

"Go nuts," said Charlene. Frankly, Charlene wasn't as bad an actress as the critics made out. For the next ten minutes, she gave me the same story, but this time with feeling. Two talented but troubled actors helping each other to help themselves. She described the Cha-Cha Challenge in sincere, self-help terms but left out the callous career advancement angle. When she got teary-eyed about broken hearts across the Atlantic, who could contradict her? Certainly not Charles-Henri.

To date, my ghost writing experience hadn't prepared me for an interview where the truth came in so many flavors. To top it off, I was getting decidedly rum rattled. They sure don't pour a wimpy mojito at the

Martinez.

"Who else are you talking to while you're here?" she asked.

"I've got an invitation to the screening of *Adieu Marseille* tomorrow morning. It's going to be bizarre to put on a fancy dress and watch movie stars walk down a red carpet at nine in the morning."

"Whaddya mean, tomorrow morning?" asked Charlene. "The gala screening of *Adieu, Marseille* is Saturday night. You got the invite with you?"

Of course. It was the cardboard amulet that made me part of the whole Festival elite. I fished it out of my bag proudly.

"Oh, sweetie," said Charlene, handing it back after a quick glance, "this invitation is crap. It lets you into a dumb-dumb theater on the rue d'Antibes, the same place we're previewing *Beach Zombies*. You're not gonna meet anyone but a couple of Lithuanian movie distributors there. The big Banville memorial bash is Saturday night at the Palace. Why aren't you going to that?"

"Because nobody knows that I'm writing this book," I said glumly, holding out my empty glass when Charlene held up the pitcher invitingly. "I've been hired by Charles-Henri's son, and nobody knows him either."

"Hold on," said Charlene, stopping in mid-pour. "Did you say 'son'? Charlie had a kid?"

Oops.

That's why I shouldn't drink on the job. Carlos never gave me explicit instructions to keep his Banville genes a secret, but he'd definitely made it clear that he preferred to live his life as Señor Ortega.

"Yep," I said, mentally kicking myself. "He had a

kid in Spain."

"You got a picture of this guy?" purred Charlene, filling my glass to the brim.

Of course, I had a picture. I'd been tempted to make it my screen saver. The handcuff photo of Carlos being escorted out of a Madrid bank was a huge part of my personal fantasy life. Did I want to share it with one of the internet's "Ten Sexiest Swimsuit Babes"?

Like hell I did.

Reluctantly, I called up the picture on my phone, and Charlene jumped on it, like any red-blooded woman would. "What's with the handcuffs?" she breathed. "He's into bondage?"

"He's not even in this country." I really didn't like the way this was going. "He's in Spain."

"Hell, that's the country next door," said Charlene. "You get that boy's gorgeous butt over to Cannes for Saturday night, and I'll get both of you into the Banville Tribute. That's a promise. Ta-NEE-sha," she howled. "We got us some red meat for the publicity department."

Within seconds, the press rep was at her side. "Get a load of Charlie's secret lovechild. He's gonna be my prom date tomorrow. Whatdya think? *'Liked the father, but loves the son?'* "

"Not quite sick enough, but I can work with it," said Taneesha, turning to me. "Give me more. I want all the details you've got on this guy."

Chapter Twenty-Eight

By the time I left the hotel, I felt like my mind had been vacuumed. The one detail that I absolutely refused to share with Charlene and Taneesha was Carlos Ortega's private phone number. They'd pushed for it, but I speed-dialed, shielding the screen as I did, and left a rather enigmatic message on his voicemail. It was Thursday afternoon, so he was probably teaching. I hoped it was a long, long, *long* class. He wasn't going to be thrilled with this new development. Not at all.

In fact, I couldn't think of a place that Carlos Ortega would rather *not* be seen than a gala tribute for the father he despised so fervently. Taneesha's game plan added insult to injury too. If she had their way, every flashbulb in the free world would be aimed at Charlene as she lip-locked with the secret son of her former fiancé. "The subtext is incest," Taneesha told me gleefully, "but trust me, it'll be subtle and tasteful."

Tasteful incest? That would go over *really* well with Carlos. I couldn't get Charlene or Taneesha to give me any clear answers about their plans for the sex tape the actress made with Charles-Henri either. Well, aside from the idea that it would be leaked "accidentally" when they thought it would get the most traction. If they decided to release on Saturday, right before the gala, nothing I could say would deter them. "*Major* simultaneous orgasms," Charlene told me proudly.

"We're talking Oscar-worthy performances from both of us."

Could this situation get any worse? I wasn't sure how. As soon as I got back to the hotel, I called my sister.

"Abby, I think I'm going nuts."

"*You're* going nuts? I'm driving to Bellevue with a crate of laxatives and ten platters of gourmet fish fingers."

"You got a minute?"

"In this traffic? I've got hours. What's up?"

I filled her in as quickly as I could. "Blame it on the mojitos," I concluded. "I shouldn't have mentioned Carlos, and once I did, I should have been smart enough to get him out of it."

"I doubt it. Once these sharks knew he existed, they'd have found a way to track him down."

"Probably," I agreed morosely. The minibar was looking mighty tempting right now, but Devil Rum got me into this predicament and it sure wasn't going to get me out of it. Besides, I'd have plenty of time to drink after Carlos fired me.

"If he hates the idea, he won't show up," added Abby. The transmission howled in protest as Abby shifted gears on the Long Island Expressway. She leaned on the horn. "The man's got free will. He can say no. End of story."

"But *I* want to go to the party, and the deal is, I don't get in without him. It's my best chance to get interviews for this book."

"Don't you ever think of anything besides work?" asked Abby. "Chill out already. No guy who breathes oxygen is gonna turn down a date with Charlene Trent.

She's Number Three on the internet's 'Ten Sexiest Swimsuit Babes,' isn't she?"

"Down to Number Five this year," I interrupted, unleashing my inner bitch. "Besides, I don't want him to 'like' going out with her."

"Why do you care? He's the creep who got you the slut dress, right?"

"Yes," I said, "but when he found out that I *didn't* sleep with his dad, he stopped hating me. When he finds out I told Charlene and her press agent about him, he's going to hate me all over again."

"Who needs him? You're in France, aren't you? Lose the Spaniard and go with the home team. That policeman with the English lessons? He sounds nice." She leaned on the horn again. "Honey, I'll rear-end that Kia on purpose pretty soon. Good luck, and we'll talk later, okay?"

Now I had nothing to do except wait for Carlos to call back and get mad at me again. I roused myself from misery long enough to transcribe my Charlene interview, but it felt like I was doing it for nothing. What was happening to my big breakthrough book? Unless I could convince Carlos to play Beach Zombie volleyball with Charlene, I'd be heading back to Paris tomorrow, tail between my legs, while everyone I needed to interview drank bubbly at the star-studded Banville Tribute Gala.

I was lost in gloom when the phone rang. "I didn't entirely understand your message," said Carlos. "What is so urgent? Did Charlene Trent have something nice to say about my father?"

"Not exactly." When I pressed her for positive feedback, she said that Charles-Henri was "a genius" in the oral sex department, but I suspected Carlos didn't care to know about that detail. "Guess what!" I said, using my perkiest Mary Poppins voice. "Charlene wants to invite you to a party."

"A party? What kind of party?"

"It's a tribute to your father's career."

"*¿Estàs loca?* I would rather spend a week with a sadistic dentist during an earthquake in World War III. You go to this party. That's what I'm paying you for."

"They won't let me in without you."

"Ah." There was a long pause. "Does Señorita Trent intend to use my presence for reasons of her own?"

"I think so." *For heaven's sake, what was the point of lying?* "I know so."

"Then convey my sincere regrets."

"It might be the fastest and easiest way to learn something good about your father," I ventured. "People are sure to praise him at the tribute."

The pause was so long that I feared we'd lost the connection. "I spent the last two hours in the emergency room," he said finally. "My mother tried to end her days again. Where and when does this horrible event take place?"

"Saturday night, at the convention center in the middle of town. There's a cocktail party, and afterward they'll screen his last film, *Adieu Marseille.*"

"Text me the details. I'll be there."

Charlene and Taneesha had won this round. I suppose I'd won too since the book project was still viable, but I felt worn out and ever-so-slightly weepy. I showered and climbed into my cozy double bed after setting the alarm for six a.m. I still planned to attend the

film preview in Cannes tomorrow morning. I didn't
want to be late.

Chapter Twenty-Nine

As breakfast buffets go, this one only rated a C+. The orange juice was bottled, not fresh-squeezed, and the *pains au chocolat* weren't half as good as the ones from my Paris bakery. Nevertheless, having skipped dinner last night, I was putting a sizeable dent into a basket of cardboard-flavored *croissants* next to the coffee urn. Charlene was right about this morning's event taking place in a VIP-free zone. Unless you wanted to meet a bunch of sweaty, anxious accountant-type guys tapping figures into their cellphones, there were thousands of more congenial joints to sip lukewarm coffee.

At 8:30, just as I was giving up hope on any interview action, the costars came out, namely Pierre Desportes and Amélie Prévert. Amélie was meticulously made up but very Casual Friday on the wardrobe front. I noted with envious leather lust that her skinny jeans were tucked into a pair of luscious, summer-weight red-soled boots with metallic heels. Pierre Desportes, the victim of Charles-Henri's upper-cut, wore denim too. His nose looked perfectly fine.

They chit-chatted with the distributors and looked just as disappointed by the buffet as I was. I sidled up to them after a few minutes and introduced myself.

"You're writing a book about that *connard*?" exclaimed Pierre. "Did you know that the bastard broke my nose? He attacked me for no reason at all."

"*Parano,*" agreed Amélie. "Charles-Henri, he was paranoid."

"He claimed I was upstaging him in the courtroom scenes. *Bon Dieu!* I was playing the *judge*, and he was playing the *prisoner!* Of course, I upstaged him." Pierre's voice was rising, and as it did his tone got screechier and thinner. "He kept telling to keep my voice down. *Non, non, non!* You will see in a few minutes, Mademoiselle Layne. I dominate those courtroom scenes! I *dominate* them!"

A bell chimed, and a young man in a bowtie gently but firmly herded people toward the theater. Before Pierre and Amélie escaped through the side door, I secured their contact numbers and cooperation for further interviews. I sank into an aisle seat just as the lights dimmed.

Ninety minutes later, I couldn't tell anyone what the movie was about. The leading man, Charles-Henri, was some kind of gangland boss with a heart of gold. His daughter, played by Amélie, was in love with a policeman, and Pierre portrayed a courageous, crimefighting judge. I noticed that Pierre's scenes were more convincing when he toned down his volume to a husky whisper although I couldn't understand very much of what he said. Like all of the actors, he delivered his dialogue in a thick Marseille accent.

Most of the action took place in dark alleys so I was blinking, my eyes watering, in the bright Riviera sunshine as I stood on the sidewalk and checked my messages. After the phone call from Madrid last night, I'd left a message with Taneesha that Carlos would attend tomorrow's gala. She'd called three times while I was at the screening.

"Don't worry about your gown, makeup, or hair," she said when we connected. "I've got all that covered. He needs dress shoes, and you bring your own high heels. Make sure those heels are *high* too. The officials threw a fit when some woman wore flats last year. Tried to keep her out."

"Are you kidding?"

"I wish. You and Charlie Junior have to be at the Martinez by four o'clock. No later. You'll come in the back door, by the kitchen, okay?"

"Is that necessary?" I asked. "Carlos and I aren't exactly superstars hiding out from the media."

"I already started the buzz that Charlene's date for tomorrow night is a major mystery man, and I don't want the tabloids horning in before we're ready for the reveal. Just make sure that Charlie Junior—"

"Carlos," I said for the one hundredth time. "His name is *Carlos*."

"Make sure that *Carlos* understands that he's all about Charlene tomorrow night. He doesn't even *look* at another woman. You'll be Jason Lord's plus-one, by the way."

"Jason Lord?"

"He plays the lifeguard on Zombie Beach. Totally sweet guy, but not the fastest surfboard on the waves, if you get my drift. We'll see you tomorrow. Don't be late."

"But…"

"Yes?"

"What have you decided to do about the sex tape?"

Taneesha laughed. "Why are you so hung up about that sex tape? You really don't think this Carlos dude can handle it?"

I imagined the reaction Carlos would have to a viral video of his dad showcasing his oral sex expertise on Charlene Trent.

Then I tried to un-imagine the whole thing.

"In a word?" I asked her. "No."

"In other words, I gotta deal with Mister Snowflake on top of everything else?" Taneesha sighed. "We're not releasing the sex tape until the "*Beach Zombie III*" launch in July, so he'll have eight weeks to talk it over with his shrink. You got any other bad news to muck up my day?"

"I don't think so," I said, matching her sigh and raising it with a second, even more extravagant sigh of my own. "I think we've covered just about everything."

Chapter Thirty

"We are *not* entering through the kitchen! No way! *De ninguna manera!*"

Carlos and I had agreed to meet in a quiet café near the Cannes train station, far, far from movie-mad crowds on the Croisette. The other café patrons, quietly sipping their Stella Artois beer, perusing the local papers, and placating their kiddies with ice cream, were simply enjoying the delightful Riviera weather on a sunny Saturday afternoon.

Not us.

"*¡De ninguna manera!*" he repeated, emphasizing every syllable.

I stared at him blankly.

"No way. *Este es bullshit!* This is…"

"I get it. Bullshit is a universal concept. Look at it this way. Going in through the kitchen gives you two more hours to enjoy *not* being known as Charles-Henri's son."

"How is that?" Carlos was packing an exceptionally rotten mood, and he wasn't giving it up without a fight. "*¡Es un secreto!* I am a man completely secret!" Up till now, his English and French had been almost word-perfect. Today, he was freefalling into stress-related Spanglish, and my meagre command of New York-style Puerto Rican was hard pressed to keep up.

"Do you honestly believe that you can hide out forever?" I asked. "I know that you've chosen to live your life as 'Carlos Ortega,' but your birth certificate, your passport, and your driving license all say 'Banville,' don't they?"

Carlos glared out the window at a pigtailed girl who was pushing a tiny pink baby carriage down the sidewalk and didn't reply.

"There are tabloid reporters who would kill for a scoop like this," I continued. "Lots of people would drop your name in a nanosecond for a small bribe. And then, there's Taneesha Roberts…"

"Yes, who is she?" said Carlos, zeroing in exactly where I didn't want him to go. "How did she find out about me?"

"She's capable of hacking into the Pentagon if she thought it would improve box office for the Beach Zombie franchise. As I was saying…"

"But that is not my question. Who told this Taneesha person about me?"

Well…that would be Miss Mojito Mouth.

"She has her methods," I said vaguely.

"*Madre de Dios,*" muttered Carlos.

"How is your mother doing?"

"I've engaged a private nurse to stay with her this weekend." Carlos ruffled his fingers through his jet-black hair. It had grown into a 1970s shag since our first meeting. It suited him well. "Thank you for asking about her."

Damn, this poor Spanish knight was walking into the lion's den in a couple of hours, and it was partly my fault.

Hell, it was mostly my fault.

No, it was *all* my fault.

Impulsively, I took his hand and had a puppy love thrill when he didn't pull away automatically. "I won't sugarcoat this for you, Carlos, because you're absolutely right. This party will feel like the dentist's office in an earthquake for you."

"During an atomic war?" He looked up at me. "Don't forget about nuclear bombs, monsoons, poison gas, and fallout."

"Look at the positive side," I said. "Think of tonight as…well…two whole *decades* before the first space alien attacks."

When Carlos smiled, I had a hard time believing that he'd ever had a bad session with a dentist. "Trust me, you'll like Charlene," I told him, "and think positive. Lots of people will be praising your father, so we'll be able to collect lots of happy anecdotes that will get your mother several steps closer to that clinic in Switzerland."

"Nevertheless, I have a very bad feeling about this evening. I feel…" Carlos stopped and searched for the right word. "I feel like I'm venturing into very hostile terrain."

"That's why we're sneaking in through the kitchen. And on our way out, we'll be surrounded by zombies."

"Zombies?" asked Carlos, standing up and stretching. "In a very strange way, I find that reassuring."

The kitchen of the Hôtel Martinez was controlled pandemonium. An army of white-clad Ninja chefs wielded sharp knives on hapless vegetables with samurai precision. "Seven course banquet for Steven Spielberg tonight," explained the desk clerk who'd been stationed in the pantry to greet us. "Your party's in Suite 407," he added as he hustled us into the freight elevator.

Suite 407 was at the end of a long, elegant 1930s-style corridor. The door was open a crack, so we walked right in to uncontrolled pandemonium. The TV was tuned to a tennis match, the sound system blasted Marvin Gaye, and the stench—a swampy miasma of nail polish fumes, hairspray, well-aged sausage pizza, and cigarette smoke—was almost overpowering. I stepped in first and discerned one of the occupants as Taneesha. She was sprawled on a recliner with cucumber slices over her eyes, and the lavender-haired boy from the photo shoot was painting her toenails fluorescent yellow.

"Hell-loo," he said looking up at me. "You must be Melody. I'm Joey Stahl, and I'll be doing your hair and makeup, so if you haven't shaved your legs or your pits, do it now. The bathroom's over there." Carlos rated a longer look and a wolf whistle. "Jason, baby," he called across the room. "You're not the cutest boy in Cannes anymore."

A brawny, suntanned arm made an obscene gesture from the depths of a striped divan. Taneesha lifted the veggies from her eyes. "Charlene! Jason!" she yelled before replacing them carefully. "Your designated dates are here."

A blond, prep school heartthrob untangled himself from a comforter on the divan and stood up. "Jason Lord. And you're…?"

"Melody Layne," I said. "And this is Carlos."

"Ya wanna coupla brewskis?" asked Jason, extracting two beers from the cooler in front of the supersize TV screen.

"No, thanks," I said.

"*Si, muchas gracias*," said Carlos gratefully, heading toward the TV. "What's the score?"

"Nadal is totally creaming this Danish dude."

"*Magnifico!*" said Carlos, popping the top of the beer and settling down to watch the match. I was delighted that he'd found an island of sanity before tonight's madness. For me, the sequined evening gowns on the rolling rack in the center of the room were much more enticing than the tennis action at the French Open.

"Charlene's got her top three picks in the bedroom, and the yellow chiffon has Taneesha's name on it." Joey flicked through the rack and chose a strapless, electric-blue sheath. "This one will suit your skin tone best."

How can you doubt the color sense of a guy with a lilac crewcut? Forty minutes later, I couldn't recognize myself. Joey told me he was going "Ultra Uma" with my hair, and the result was so elaborately waved that I was nearly seasick. Thanks to Joey's expertise, I was wearing more makeup than I'd normally put on my face in a month of Sundays. He'd slathered my face with some eerie green cream before dusting my cheeks with suntan foundation and layered several sets of false eyelashes over the silver he'd applied liberally to my lids.

The result was to die for.

And the dress? There's something very special about the first time you put on a designer evening gown. I made Joey take about sixty photos of me, which he did out in the hall since the suite, totally trashed, was more "*Animal House*" than Five-Star hotel. I now had the glam-iest picture on earth for my social media page, not to mention the backflap of the future Banville book.

Did Carlos, or my prom-date Jason, compliment me on my extraordinary duckling-to-swan transformation?

"No way," yelled Jason, crumpling a potato-chip bag and tossing it at the flat-screen. "That ball was *so* out."

"Wait for the replay," counseled Carlos. "It was on the line."

Taneesha sashayed out of the bedroom in a bright yellow gown that matched the sunflower-tinted polish on her nails. "Boys, turn off the TV and get into your tuxedos. The limo's here in twenty."

"Yes, ma'am," said Jason, standing up and dropping his trousers. Appropriately for a lifeguard, he was wearing a bright red Speedo. Carlos simply stood there, immobile, like he wasn't processing English all of a sudden.

"Why don't you change in the back bedroom, Carlos?" said Taneesha with more tact than I'd have expected. She handed him a garment bag, and Carlos disappeared, shutting the door just as Charlene emerged from the master bedroom.

"So whaddya think of my dress?" she asked.

Dress?

It took me a few seconds to process that the tiny patches of black lace adorning Charlene's legendary double D's were more than underwear. However, if you looked hard enough, there actually was a dress in play. The neckline plunged past her waist, and when she twirled it was evident that the slit on the see-through skirt went all the way to her equally legendary ass.

"It's very…" Even though I sling words for a living, I was at a loss for an appropriate adjective.

"Red's my best color, but since I'm in mourning for Charlie tonight, Taneesha thinks I ought to wear black."

"Black is dignified," I agreed, happy to have a word, any word, to offer. "Much more dignified."

The phone rang, and Charlene grabbed it on the first ring. "Send her up," she ordered. "The bling's here."

"About time," said Taneesha, clearing Joey's curling irons, hairspray cans, and rouge pots off the desk.

Sabine Rochas, a perky blonde with bright blue eyes, opened a crystal-studded briefcase lined with black velvet and extracted a gold clipboard. "Charlene, you're all tonal tonight, so I'll put you in the 'Moonlight Mist' collection." She handed Taneesha a double-strand necklace of sparkling white crystal, two thick crystal-studded wristbands, and a pair of enormous, beaded earrings. She checked off the items on her clipboard. "Taneesha, I'm giving you the full 'Jaipur' set in topaz. Earrings, bracelet, and pendant." She looked at me critically. "New Girl, I'm running low, so you'll get 'Jaipur' as well, but yours'll be sapphire. Is that it?"

"You got something for me?" asked Jason, sauntering over.

"You take your clothes off and lose them every chance you get. We're not wasting any more designer stuff on you. You get a nylon shirt with buttons this time," said Taneesha. "Where the hell is Carlos? *Car-*

los!"

Carlos walked in from the bedroom, his pleated dress shirt open to the waist. "I'm sorry, I couldn't find a way to fasten it."

"Ooh, do I have studs for the stud!" said Sabine with evident approval. She walked over to Carlos and let her manicured fingers pry around for the buttonholes. She took a lot longer than necessary in my opinion. "One, two, three, four, five, six little studs," she said at last. "Black onyx with platinum trim. Now for the cuffs."

"No," said Carlos, pulling away from her.

"Cufflinks," I whispered, moving in closer.

"Of course," he said. "Of course." Charlene stood in front of the full-length mirror by the door, shrugging to the left, then shrugging to the right. Sometimes the spaghetti straps flopped down, baring her breasts, and sometimes they stayed in place.

"Damn, it doesn't work every time," she said. "We'll just have to hope for high winds for the skirt."

"That woman was supposed to marry my father?" whispered Carlos as Sabine pushed the cufflinks through his French sleeves.

"Yep," I said. "You have to pretend that you're best friends."

"For how long?" asked Carlos.

"As long as it takes to walk down a red carpet."

"How long does that take?"

Frankly, I had no idea.

Chapter Thirty-One

"Carlos and Melody, you need to know that this red-carpet thing is gonna go *real* slow," warned Taneesha. "Especially if we're slotted behind a fashion icon like Nicole Kidman or Catherine Deneuve. They'll be stopped every thirty seconds to model their dresses."

Slow? It was hard to imagine anything slower than the progress of our limo which was crawling down the Croisette at a glacial pace.

"Red carpets are so much fun that you want them to last forever," interrupted Charlene. "Everyone's screaming your name and taking tons of pictures. It's a total high."

"It does sound delightful," said Carlos. He looked a little pale, but I gave him credit for putting up a good front. I truly hoped this evening wasn't going to be a nonstop horror show for him.

"We link arms as 'Team Beach Zombie' for the first three yards," repeated Taneesha for the hundredth time. "That's Charlene in the middle, flanked by the boys. Melody and I are the wings. When the photographers scream 'Charlene,' that's when Jason, Melody, and I fall back. Carlos, you just hang on to Charlene as tight as you can. Got it?"

Jason punched Carlos in the arm. "There'll be major booze when we get to the top of the steps, big guy."

"I will probably want some," said Carlos politely.

"Word to the wise, bro," said Jason, "fill up on the munchies because we're gonna have to sit through a real boring French movie after the speeches."

I was getting excited. Professional hair and make-up? Check. Gorgeous evening dress? Check. The only thing that was off? It wasn't evening. The Riviera sun was still so high in the sky that the whole production felt like an elaborate kindergarten dress-up party. And when we finally got to the red carpet, it turned out that we were behind Jennifer Lawrence.

Did Taneesha say that she'd be stopped to twirl her gown every thirty seconds?

Every ten seconds.

"Next year, I'm wearing red," hissed Charlene.

"Shut up and start smiling," said Taneesha. "We're up."

Charlene was right about the red carpet. It *was* fun, and I didn't mind slow. Who can walk that fast in high heels anyway? Nevertheless, when the photographers screamed "Charlene," I was happy to take a break out of the limelight.

"Who's her hunk?" asked a reporter who sidled up to us on the sidelines.

"Charles-Henri Banville Jr.," Taneesha shouted as loud as a carnival barker. That's when the crowd went nuts. I thought they'd been snapping a million photos a minute? Now the flashbulb action was off the charts.

"Mission accomplished," said Taneesha smugly as we made our way into the convention center a few minutes later, still blinking from the lights. "You zombies have earned yourselves a drink."

"About time," said Jason, snagging two flutes of

Champagne off a tray and handing one to me. "You and me, Melody, we're done posing."

It was just beginning for Carlos.

"Where have you been all these years?" yelled a reporter.

"He's been in Spain," answered Charlene coquettishly, pulling Carlos closer. "We've only just become acquainted."

"Did you know your father well?"

"*Solo lo vi una vez,* " said Carlos. "I only met him once."

"Once?" This caused a commotion. "When was that? Where was that?"

"It was…"

"You must be completely devastated by his death, right?"

"Maybe he doesn't speak English," someone shouted. "*Usted ama a su padre?*"

"Love him?" Carlos blinked at the flashbulbs. "Love him? If you want the truth…"

But Taneesha stepped in before Carlos could launch into the truth. "I'm sure that all of you understand that tonight's ceremony is an extremely emotional experience for both Charlene and Carlos. They will be available for interviews all day tomorrow."

Grumbling, the media posse pushed off toward Leonardo DiCaprio.

"That's not true," said Carlos. "I won't be here tomorrow."

"Do they need to know that?" asked Taneesha.

"No, they don't," said Carlos. "Thank you, Taneesha." He sipped some of the Champagne that the waiter handed him as he looked around the room. Giant screens suspended from the ceiling played clips from Charles-Henri's movies in a continuous loop. Charles-Henri as a Renaissance prince, a Resistance fighter, a gangster, a military officer. "Floods, plagues, alien invasions," muttered Carlos.

"Charlie did sci-fi?" asked Charlene.

Someone across the room was waving frantically in our direction. No, someone was waving at *me*. Who did I know here? Ah, it was Pierre Desportes. The actor pushed his way toward us purposefully, holding his cocktail glass high.

"What's with the shrimp waving a martini at two o'clock?" asked Charlene.

"The costar of *Adieu, Marseille*," I whispered.

"Mademoiselle Layne," said Pierre, kissing my hand formally. "I am so happy to see you again." In fact, he wasn't seeing me at all. His eyes were firmly planted on Charlene's wonder-bust. "Miss Trent, *je suis absolument enchanté*! This is for me a great honor."

"I saw the morning screening, Charlene," I said brightly since their conversation was hitting a wall. "Pierre simply dominates the courtroom scenes."

"Yeah?" Charlene chugged the rest of her Champagne. "Court scenes?"

"And it was Charles-Henri who coached that fabulous performance out of him."

"*Mais non, Mademoiselle*! Miss Trent, did you know that madman broke my..."

"Tough love," I interrupted. "Charles-Henri needed to get your attention in a forceful way so that you'd deliver your lines in that sexy little growl. And it works beautifully, Pierre. I was at the edge of my seat every time you called the courtroom to order."

"Well, yes, of course," said Pierre modestly.

"So...working with Charles-Henri made you a better actor."

"What? I would never..."

"Can I quote you on that for the book?"

"Well..." Pierre stared at Charlene dreamily as she slowly sucked an oyster out of its shell and licked her coral lips. "Yes, of course..."

A harried hostess tapped him on the shoulder. "Monsieur Desportes, they want the entire cast of *Adieu, Marseille* on the stage."

Pierre kissed Charlene's hand reverently. "I hope this is *au revoir* and not *adieu*."

"Oh, whatever to you too," said Charlene graciously, grabbing another drink from a passing tray. Pierre headed toward the gilded door, looking at least ten centimeters taller.

"I deliver," I told Carlos. "That's your first nice story for the night. And Charlene's going to tell you about how your father was helping her develop a healthier lifestyle."

"I was?" Charlene looked at me quizzically before picking up the cue. "Yeah, sure, he did. The Cha-Cha Challenge." She helped herself to a *foie gras* canapé. "Yeah, your dad was gonna help me lose the booze."

"You see, Carlos?" I said triumphantly. "Two good stories, and the night is young."

"I am not sure those were entirely voluntary statements, but I thank you nevertheless." When Carlos smiled at me, my heart flipflopped. "Did I say that you look very beautiful tonight?"

"Not like a nineteenth-century tart?"

"But not at all. In fact…"

"Tick, tock." Taneesha tapped her watch. "Speeches next, then the movie, so the time for bathroom breaks is now or forever hold your pee."

"I'm gonna snag us a bottle or two," said Jason, moving toward the bar. "We're gonna need it."

"Isn't that Ben Affleck over there?" asked Charlene. "He's so much fun. Let's go sit with him."

"Don't laugh too much at his jokes," warned Taneesha as they started to shimmy their way through the crowd. "Remember that you're playing the brave, bereaved bimbo tonight."

Carlos and I looked at each other. "I think we're supposed to follow them," I said.

"I suppose we could do worse," said Carlos gamely. "I quite liked *Argo.*"

But before we could make our move, a large wall of shimmering green sequins blocked the way.

"You stinking piece of Spanish shit," intoned the sweet, husky voice that launched thirty top-ten singles on the French charts. "How does it feel to have ruined my life?"

Chapter Thirty-Two

"*¿Quien es ella?*" breathed Carlos.

"Delphine Carroll," I whispered. I could understand his surprise. The recent photos on her website had been photoshopped till they dropped. The woman pointing her finger at Carlos bore no resemblance to the shy, slender waif who'd won French hearts singing "*L'Amour, l'amour*" in the 1979 Pan-Europe song contest. This was a brick wall loaded for bear.

"Madame Carroll," began Carlos. "I am…"

"You're a bloodsucking opportunist, that's what you are. Just like your scheming slut of a mother."

"My *mother*?" Carlos was on war-footing as well. "My mother was abused by your pig of a husband! She was a young, innocent girl and…"

"Innocent?" Delphine snorted. "Carmen Ortega knew exactly what she wanted, and she wanted my husband, pig that he was."

"*¡Mentiras!* You lie!"

"I found them in my bed! My baby died the next day. The fact that my baby's dead and you're alive is disgusting enough, but that you had the nerve to attend tonight's ceremony makes it even worse. You know what your scheming bitch of a mother did? She wore *my* nightgown while she seduced my husband!" Delphine spat at the ground, missing my left shoe by two inches. That was much too close for comfort. I stepped back, and Carlos put his arm in front of me protectively.

"You're screwing the Trent train wreck, and you're two-timing her with this whore, right? Your father would be proud of you." Delphine shook her head. "I'll give you some advice for free. Just don't spend all his money yet. Something tells me you won't have it for very long."

"We better go, my angel," said the nondescript middle-aged man at her side. "The ceremony is about to begin." Red-eyed, bad comb-over, in a tux that didn't fit quite right. While his face was oddly familiar, I couldn't place it. Taking his arm, Delphine turned on a dime and made tracks for the auditorium.

"I was only prepared for plagues, famine, and fallout," murmured Carlos when we were alone.

"You got a wicked witch as well."

"I don't know if I can stand much more of this," said Carlos. "Do you really want to go to this movie?"

"Once is enough for me."

"C'mon, you two!" shouted Taneesha from the auditorium entrance. "We're holding seats for you." When she got a better look at our faces, she grimaced and headed over. "What's the problem with you guys now?"

"Something came up," I said. "We're skipping the rest of the festivities."

"Are you nuts? It's a free movie, a fancy dinner, an A-List club in Monaco, all the Bollinger you can drink, and a chance to hang out with the stars."

I looked at Carlos. If he'd been auditioning for a role in *Beach Zombies IV*, he'd have nailed the part. "I don't think so."

"We got the red carpet pictures, so you fulfilled your side of the bargain." Taneesha pulled a plastic Ziploc bag out of her purse. "Before you cut out, render unto Swarovski what is legally theirs."

Reluctantly, I surrendered my crystal necklace, sparkly earrings, and glittery bracelet. Carlos fumbled a bit with his cufflinks and shirt studs but handed them over in short order. With his shirt undone and his black tie unknotted, he looked like one of those male model fantasies that only exist in designer cologne ads.

"There's a security door out the back that leads to the waterfront." Taneesha tucked the baggie in her purse. "I'll need the clothes back by tomorrow night."

And that's how I found myself on a Riviera beach at twilight, listening to the gentle Mediterranean waves caress the white sand, walking hand-in-hand with one of the handsomest men I'd ever seen.

Truth be told, the moment wasn't one-hundred percent perfume publicity. For one thing, I was so terrified of letting the ocean make contact with my borrowed ballgown that I'd quite unceremoniously hiked the skirt up to my knees, using the same hand that was clutching the straps of my sandals.

But even that couldn't kill the Champagne-fueled romantic possibilities of sea, sand, and—at least on my part—overwhelming sexual attraction. It wasn't just the good looks of the guy beside me. It was his grace under pressure. Throughout tonight's nuclear-powered stress test, Carlos had handled himself like a true gentleman. A romantic hero, in fact. Love, love, love. My heart was singing, *I'm falling in love, love, love…*

"Hate," said Carlos, stopping suddenly and staring

at the water. "Hatred is what has sustained me all these years. Hatred for my father, hatred for the way he treated my mother, hatred for the way he treated all women. My intense hatred has made me flee all relationships. I've loved no one since Paola. I've always been afraid that I might cause as much pain as he did." Letting go of my hand, he stooped to pick up a small rock that he flung toward the sea.

"And until tonight," he continued a moment later, "I never suspected that another human being could hate *me* that much. Perhaps it is some kind of karmic justice. Perhaps all this hate I've held within me has become a magnet for the hatred from others."

"Don't worry so much about Delphine. She's only one person."

"I certainly hope so," he said. "I can't handle anyone else hating me so much."

"I don't hate you." Going for broke, I stood on tiptoes, never easy in the sand, and let my lips brush his cheek.

"Melody?" He looked into my eyes, cupped my chin, and when his lips touched mine, there was an unspoken question in the air.

"Oh, yes," I answered.

My guidebook said there's an international fireworks festival on the Cannes beachfront every July.

I didn't have to wait that long.

Carlos brought his own fireworks to the party.

Chapter Thirty-Three

There was a plan. We dreamed it up in between frantic, ravenous, urgent kisses. Get back to Nice, get my things, and proceed to the mountain village of Vence where Carlos had scored a slightly bigger room than mine. Conveniently, Carlos had a rental Audi, so we climbed in and sped down the coastal highway.

We didn't get that far. Miraculously, there was a parking place next to my hotel. A free parking space? It had to be fate. We simply floated up to the fourth floor on the wings of destiny, draped our borrowed finery over the desk chair, and dissolved into the tiny double bed.

Thanks to Abby, I had an emergency envelope filled with condoms tucked into the side pocket of my suitcase, so that didn't hold us up either. A few hours later, it seemed like a six-pack wouldn't be nearly enough for one night.

"It's been much too long," said Carlos, kissing my fingers one by one. "I'd forgotten how nice it is not to be alone in bed."

"Me too," I sighed, "although there were always four of us on the mattress back home in New York."

"What?" asked Carlos. He was kissing my left breast now and looked up with concern. "Did you really have…?"

"Cats," I told him. "I have three cats."

"Ah." He resumed his kisses, this time favoring the right breast. "I am very allergic to those animals. They give me the rash and the sneezes."

Damn! Carlos wasn't perfect after all. Yet somehow this fatal flaw made him even more real. Stifling my traitorous feelings toward my faithful feline companions, I snuggled closer.

"Can you read my mind?" I asked him. "Do you know what I'm thinking about right now?"

"More sex?" he asked hopefully.

"Food," I said, "then more sex."

The shower was too small for mixed doubles, but towel-dried and dressed we were seated at a sidewalk trattoria less than thirty minutes later. I was wearing clean jeans and a lightweight hoodie. Carlos was still in his tuxedo pants but had appropriated an extra-large tee-shirt that I used as a pajama top: *Welcome to New York. Now Go Home.*

"It's not a very friendly attitude," he commented as the waiter poured the Chianti in our glasses.

"New York is all about attitude." I lifted my glass. "Do you know what I really, really like about you?"

"My amazing Iberian virility?"

"Anchovies," I told him. "I broke up with a guy in Brooklyn because he ordered one of those pizzas with pineapple slices on it."

"That is sacrilege." We clinked glasses in agreement. "And do you know what I like most about you?"

"Tell me."

"You are honest. All the way through this, you have been honest with me. And of course," he added, "you are also absolutely beautiful and incredibly kind and extremely clever and…"

"…unbelievably sexy?"

"That's been a disappointment," he said after a moment of reflection. He flinched as a chunk of bread smacked his gorgeous aquiline nose.

"You're not so hot either."

We'd both ordered tomato-less, Nice-style pizzas topped with onions, black olives, and those deal-making anchovies. They were terrific. Midway through dinner, we'd devised a new plan. We'd sleep at my hotel, although given our track record it was doubtful how much sleep we'd actually clock, and rise early enough to have brunch in the garden at the country inn where Carlos was staying.

Oddly enough, we did sleep. In fact, I slept better than I had in years. And the drive to Vence the next morning, through winding mountain roads scented with lavender, was all you could ask for on the romantic front.

Was this love?

It certainly felt like it.

We were sitting by the pool drinking mimosas and nibbling on delicious quiche and stuffed zucchini flowers. We had already tested the mattress in his bedroom. It was larger but just as wonderful as my hotel's.

"I can't help it. I'm from Madrid," said Carlos, sipping his drink and making a face. "I really prefer cheap Spanish Cava to this fancy French Champagne."

"When do you have to go back?" My own plane was at seven p.m., and I was already dreading the idea of saying goodbye.

"I should have been there this morning, but the

nurse was able to stay for a few extra hours. I have a four o'clock flight."

"I'm going to miss you." The idea of waking up tomorrow without him was heartrending. It was amazing how fast you can get used to bliss.

"We'll see a lot of each other. There are so many legal complications with my father's estate that I'm called to Paris almost every week."

"Legal complications linked to Delphine Carroll?"

"No, their divorce was final." Carlos stared at the tablecloth as if it held answers. "Why does that woman tell such awful lies about my mother?"

"Let's not spend our last hours on the French Riviera thinking about unpleasant people." I picked up our drinks. "Let's bring these bad boys back to the room."

Carlos had just enough time to whisk me back to Cannes before dashing off for the Nice airport. Our kisses were long and passionate, and he promised to be in Paris for the next weekend. With the party clothes in two plastic garment bags borrowed from the hotel clerk slung over my arm, I headed back to Cannes and I knocked on the door of Suite 407.

"Mercy buckets," said Taneesha, greeting me in a nylon leopard-skin bathrobe. "You missed some major fun last night."

"I'll say," boomed a voice from the couch. "Dinner, dancing, drinks, drinks, drinks."

"Jason? Is that you?"

"Yep." A disheveled blond head peered out from the couch and disappeared.

"Where the hell is George Clooney when you need him?" Lavender-haired Joey, wearing nothing but hot pink boxer shorts, slapped the espresso machine in frustration. "All I want from this thing is a goddam latte. Is that too much to ask?"

"Why are you all making so much noise?"

Charlene walked in from the master bedroom in a gauzy negligée. I couldn't swear I saw Pierre Desportes in the sheets before she closed the door, but I couldn't swear that I didn't see him either.

"You're glowing, girl. Did you screw baby Banville last night?" Charlene tried to tie the sheer bathrobe's pink satin belt twice before giving up. "What's happening with that coffee, Joey?"

"I'm trying," he said. "I'm *trying*."

"You're very trying," said Taneesha. "What else is new?"

"What was going on with *you* last night?" Charlene turned her attention away from the coffee machine. "Why were you fishing around for all that happy-crappy stuff about Charlie?"

"Well…" Should I tell her?

Why not?

I gave her the whole story.

"Shit," said Taneesha, who'd sidled over and taken a seat. "No one even said anything nice about him at the ceremony. That bastard was bad news."

"Sad but true," Charlene agreed. "Old Charlie wouldn't have drawn half as big a crowd if he'd been alive."

"Here you go, ladies," said Joey proudly. "Two homemade mocha lattes on the house."

"Yuck." Taneesha made a face after tasting hers. "Did you stir this thing with your mascara wand? Let's call room service."

They were all in pajamas and underwear. In fact, there were shoes, shirts, and socks strewn all over the place. Was this some kind of Hollywood orgy?

"Did you all stay in this suite last night?" I asked.

"We all stay in this suite every night," said Charlene. "Beach Zombies operate on a microbudget." She walked me to the door and paused. "Honestly, the only person who thought Charlie was a great guy was Charlie himself. If you want any nicey-nice stories about him, you better dig into those diaries of his."

"Diaries?" This was new. "What diaries?"

"Stupid little notebooks he wrote in every night. He was crazy possessive about them too. The only time he ever got angry with me was when I got behind him while he was writing. Slammed the book shut and called me a lousy bitch spy."

"You didn't happen to see what he was writing, did you?" I asked hopefully.

"Duh? It was all in French." Charlene scratched her head and yawned. "You find those notebooks, honey, you'll know if there was any good in him."

Chapter Thirty-Four

When the sweaty accountant with the thick gold wedding band tried to pick me up on the EasyJet flight back to Paris, I told him, feigning regret, that I already had a boyfriend. And for the first time in years that worn-out excuse was *true*!

Melody Layne had an actual *boyfriend*!

I'd forgotten how wonderful it felt to sleep with someone who didn't have cat food breath in the morning. Before the plane took off, I'd received two adorable text messages from Carlos saying he'd landed in Madrid and that he missed me. I texted him back with a lot of those hearts and kissy-lip emojis that I'd never used before.

I could barely believe it. Just like that, I'd traded in my "terminally single" ID papers for a fancy new passport with a "Sex" visa. I might even start reading the "Love and Relationship" stuff in the astrology websites again. Ever since Eric left, I stuck to the "Career and Business" sections. What did love have to do with me? Nothing at all. At least, not for the past two years.

And now I had a red-hot Latin lover…plus a red-hot book lead!

There was a whole goldmine of Charles-Henri's sinner-most feelings waiting for me somewhere. All I had to do was find these diaries, and since I had the keys to the man's apartment, what was stopping me? With a little luck, I'd find everything I needed, everything Carlos needed, and my life would dissolve into a glorious, Happy-Ever-After glow.

Of course, I video chatted with my sister about my romantic weekend as soon as I got to the apartment. Predictably, Abby went absolutely ape. "More, more, more!" she kept repeating, begging for details. I gave her all the dirt she could desire about Charlene, Jason, the dress, and the party, but I stayed (relatively) discreet about Carlos in bed. "He's wonderful," was all I told her. It was too new and too private. As soon as we hung up, the cellphone rang again.

"It has been ringing busy for more than an hour," said Carlos reproachfully. "It must be a problem on the line."

"You know what? I miss you already. You're still coming to Paris for the weekend?"

"That's why I'm calling. There's a meeting that I must attend, so I will arrive on Tuesday in the late afternoon. I'll book a hotel near..."

"Not if you value your life, you won't book a hotel. You'll stay here with me."

"If it won't be any trouble..."

"I love trouble like you."

"And I...ah, *maladicion!* I must answer this phone call. I'll let you know the time my plane arrives."

"And I'll text you my address! Ciao!"

Yes!

In just forty-eight hours, I'd be back in his arms again. I looked around the apartment. Marie-Christine's apartment was quite Frenchie-frilly already, but the balcony was overdue for a makeover. The fern needed a bigger pot and only a few of the geraniums, which were dried-out clusters of deadheads when I arrived, had all responded to my landscaper's daughter TLC. I uprooted the weediest ones, and I'd pick up replacements at the florist around the corner.

I'd wash the prettiest sheets, maybe even iron them, and make sure there were tons of yummy stuff in the fridge. I looked in the mirror, concentrating on my hair. Should I get blonde streaks? Joey told me it would add depth and volume to my dark-blonde hair. But could I get the highlights done before Tuesday? Today was Sunday, and most Paris salons were closed on Monday. I rummaged through the top drawer of the bedside dresser. Yes, the navy-blue lace lingerie set would be fine. Nightie? I'd rinse out the pretty pink silk one tonight.

Should I have some Champagne on ice when he got here? No. He said he preferred Cava, didn't he? Where could I find some of that sparkling Spanish wine? I took my little notebook to bed with me that night. Just in case I needed to make any lists...

I must have packed that nifty Riviera weather in my bags because Monday morning was warm, bright, and sunny just when I'd begun to believe that all those bright blue skies on the Paris postcards were digitally enhanced. I was at the Banville apartment by ten a.m., totally jazzed up on caffeine, and more than ready to initiate the "Diary Hunt" operation.

By lunchtime, my energy was flagging. I'd been through the kitchen cabinets, the sock drawers, the laundry bin. I'd looked behind the coffee machine, in the flower vases, the bedside tables, the medicine cabinet. I even checked the fridge because I'd watched those spy shows where jewelry and money were hidden in fake soda cans. There was nothing but energy drinks and tonic water in Charles-Henri's cans.

Maybe there weren't any diaries at all. A booze-fueled babe like Charlene isn't exactly the most reliable of sources. Her romance with Charles-Henri lasted a mere three months, and most of the time they were cruising on cognac. What if she just *imagined* that she'd seen him writing a diary?

I texted Ingrid to see if she had any notebook memories and, rather glumly, sat down in the gray granite kitchen to eat the chicken sandwich I'd picked up at the bakery. Ingrid texted back in twenty minutes. *Yes, I'd forgotten about the diaries. He wrote in them every night, but he never let me read them.*

Assuming he didn't torch them in a pagan ritual every full moon, those notebooks had to be somewhere. Maybe they were stashed in a safety deposit box at the bank? If so, wouldn't Carlos and the lawyers have opened it by now? But what about a safe somewhere in his apartment?

I raced back to the bedroom. In the dubbed CSI episode that I'd watched last night on Marie-Christine's teensy TV, the drug lord hid his cocaine behind the clothes in his closet. The bedroom still reeked of musky fumes. I tiptoed over the used condoms, avoided staring at the hard-core porn on the walls, and held my breath as I searched the closet. Nothing. There were lots and lots of shoe boxes, but all they contained were shoes. For good measure, I checked the coat closet in the hall too. Hats. Overcoats. Umbrellas. Nothing else.

People also hid safes behind paintings, right? Charles-Henri had tons of art. The sexy etchings in the bedroom were small, light, and easy to move, but none of them provided cover for a wall safe. Most of his other artwork was too big and too heavy to budge. However, shining my phone light in the cracks between the frames and the wall turned up nothing again. There were massive mirrors over the fireplaces, but I didn't intend to risk seven years of bad luck by fooling around with them.

I looked under the edges of the thick Persian carpets as well. Just as I was wondering if Charles-Henri had a panic room, I realized that I'd overlooked the obvious. He was a famous wine connoisseur, known for his interest in both quality and quantity. He'd be sure to have a wine cellar. I checked the key ring. I had the two apartment keys but nothing for a basement storage room that was *de rigueur* with Paris apartments. Even Marie-Christine had a storage room for her tiny flat. That was where she'd stashed most of her clothes after she cleared her closet space for me.

I'd just have to ask Carlos to get me the basement key.

By the time I'd got the apartment back into its pre-pillaged condition, it was nearly six. Tomorrow was another day, I told myself as I locked the door. And tomorrow night was going to be even better.

Chapter Thirty-Five

I decided not to return to the Banville apartment on Tuesday since I had tons of pre-Carlos prep work to do at my place. Early in the morning, I went to the Monoprix supermarket around the corner. I got loads of luscious foodie things, but nothing too perishable, just in case Carlos wanted to dine out. After checking the prices for salon dye jobs at a shop on the corner, I purchased a do-it-yourself blonde streaking kit as well. It was easy to use, and while the chemicals worked their stinky magic, I watched an online video of last Saturday's Banville bash in Cannes.

Predictably, it was slim pickings on the "jolly good fellow" front. The speakers generally confined themselves to noncommittal praise for Banville's award-winning performances. Breaking the mold, an Italian actress told a rather sweet story about how Charles-Henri had introduced her to a Norman specialty, *tripes à la mode de Caen*, which was now one her favorite foods. I wrote it up as "He expanded the cultural and culinary horizons of his coworkers" and looked up a recipe on a cooking site. If I really needed to pad the text, I'd include it.

Film critics at *Libération* and the London *Telegraph* praised Pierre Desportes for his compelling courtroom scenes in *Adieu, Marseille,* so I added those favorable reviews to the story about how Charles-

Henri's canny advice had optimized Pierre Desportes' performance. And I wrote in glowing terms about the brilliant "Cha-Cha Challenge," destined to restore health and happiness to a troubled but well-loved American starlet.

All of the above was more of a tribute to my embroidery skills than my writing ability. However, this manuscript was not for publication. It was just a preview of the private text that I'd deliver to Carlos for his mother's bedside reading.

Carlos texted that his "late afternoon" plane was due to land at eight p.m. For me, that's officially night, but by his Spanish standards, it was only a few minutes after lunch. When he re-texted me that the plane was delayed at least an hour, I decided to whip up a vegetarian lasagna just in case. It would keep for a few days if we didn't decide to eat it, and I needed something to do. I didn't want to sit around, biting my freshly painted nails to the quick as I waited for the doorbell to ring.

When the doorbell finally *did* ring, the lasagna was out of the oven, the red wine was "breathing" on the dining room table, and it was just dark enough for the candlelight to flatter my newly streaked hair. Carlos walked into the apartment at precisely five minutes before ten, dropped his bag on the floor, and wrapped me in his arms.

"Not here," I said, pushing him away as he started to kiss me. "Let's go outside."

"*Pero por qué…*"

I led him to the balcony and pointed to the Eiffel Tower in the distance.

"*¿Que pasa?*"

"Five, four, three, two, one." I kissed him just as the sparkling lights began glittering on their hourly cue.

"*Es bonito*," murmured Carlos between kisses. "*Muy bonito.*"

He was right. The Eiffel Tower is a beautiful chunk of architecture.

Of course, it's also an absolutely *humongous* phallic symbol. That symbolism was not lost on Carlos either. Which explains why we didn't get to the lasagna until shortly before midnight. "It is nice to be dining with you at a civilized hour," said Carlos approvingly when we sat down at the table.

The next morning, I liked waking up with Carlos just as much as I liked falling asleep in his arms. It was our first "at home" breakfast, and we already seemed to be slipping into a blissful domestic routine. He scoured last night's lasagna dish while I watered the plants. I made the coffee. He made the toast. We delayed talking about his departure as long as we could.

"The meeting is at eleven," he said finally. "Then I'll have to go directly to the airport."

"I wish you could stay."

"I don't want to leave either, but I will be back soon. I am teaching all day on Thursday and Friday, but I can take the first plane to Paris on Saturday morning. What shall we do Saturday night? Do you like to dance?"

"I love it. I took a salsa class last year. Would you…"

His phone rang. "Just one minute, Melody. *Buenos dias, mama.*"

There was flood of Spanish.

"*No estoy en Madrid, mama.* I told you that I was

going to Paris."

More Spanish.

I freshened our coffee cups.

"But you can ask Isabella to do that for you, *mamacita*. She is there to help you."

More Spanish, louder this time.

"Yes, mama, I will be home tonight. *Hasta luego.*"

He put down the phone and looked at me. "Where were we?"

"Dancing," I said.

"Could you find us a club with good music? And on Sunday, if you haven't been to see it already, I would like very much to go to the history museum. The Carnavalet, it's called."

"Sounds like a perfect weekend to me."

His phone rang.

"*Si, mama, recuerdo.* I will not forget."

"My mother," he told me when he hung up, "expects me to be in Spain at all times. The doctors in Madrid have not found anything to explain her condition, but I have high hopes for this Swiss clinic. Have you had any success on the stories about my father's good nature?"

"I almost forgot." I reached over to the desk and handed him the double-spaced pages I'd printed out last night.

"*Madre de dios*," he said a few minutes later. "He made that poor woman eat a cow stomach smothered in apple brandy and cream? That sounds very horrible indeed."

"It does," I said, "but since she liked it, it counts as a positive story."

"It's still a very slim manuscript." He handed me

back the folder. "My mother will need more than ten pages to convince her."

"I have a good lead on some positive stories. Both Charlene and Ingrid confirm that your father wrote a journal every night. I've looked in the apartment and can't find them. Did he have a safety deposit box?"

"He did, but there were no notebooks inside of it."

"I'm thinking that he might have stored them in the wine cellar, but I don't have a key."

"Wine cellar? I think not." Carlos retrieved a thick binder from his overnight bag and leafed through the pages. "No, he rented his storage space in the basement to another neighbor. For an amount that the lawyer described as scandalous. The lawyers have done a good job consolidating his tangled finances."

"Are his finances so complicated?" I asked as I poured him another glass of orange juice.

"The lawyers complain of many inconsistencies. For instance, he made regular payments to an agent who did not do any work for him."

"Are you sure of that? Tony Major sounded like he was doing the very best he could."

"Tony Major? The man in London? No, not him. It was someone else." Carlos ruffled through the pages and came to a name underlined in red ink. "Marius Dubrovski."

"That's him!" I cried, smacking my forehead. "That's who he was!"

"That's who?"

"The man who was with Delphine Carroll at the gala. I knew he looked familiar."

"You have seen him before?"

"He was at the funeral, sitting a few rows away

from me. Your father ditched him ages ago when he got his first Hollywood contract. They must have kissed and made up."

"So many questions, so many creditors, so many delays." Carlos sighed as he stuffed the papers back into the folder. "This Dubrovski must send a proper invoice as soon as possible if he thinks he has not been paid in full. *Estoy harto de esto.* Just to have my mother in a safe place, with good medical care, that's all I ask, but this legal paperwork is taking forever."

Chapter Thirty-Six

Jenna and I had a table by the window at a small but elegant Japanese restaurant in the Batignolles district. I'd planned to spend the evening in front of the TV moping about missing Carlos, but she'd talked me into accompanying her on a restaurant review. It didn't take too much to convince me, and very soon the combination of sake and sushi was working its magic. Every now and then, Jenna interrupted my Carlos-and-Cannes narrative to ask the waitress for more wasabi mustard, but for the better part of twenty minutes she hung on my every word.

"You see, Jenna," I concluded, "I've found the perfect man."

"No," said Jenna. "There is no such thing as a perfect man. I've already spotted a major, major, *major* problem with Carlos. Can't you see it?"

"Geography, right? He lives and works in Madrid, but we can…"

"Location is negotiable," interrupted Jenna. "That's not it."

I had to think. "Oh yeah, he's allergic to cats. That's always been a dealbreaker for me in the past."

Jenna sighed. "Where are these cats now?"

"With my sister in New York."

"And she is taking good care of them?"

"I'll say. They lived on dry food with me, but last

night Abby gave them beef carpaccio and shredded Chesapeake Bay crabmeat."

Jenna patted my hand sympathetically. "Trust me, your cats don't want you back. Concentrate on this man. There is something else that is very, very wrong with him, and it's worse than an allergy to cat hair."

I closed my eyes and remembered his hands caressing my body, the taste of his kisses, his incredible lovemaking. "I can't think of anything wrong with Carlos," I told her. "Nothing at all."

"Wake up, Melody!" Jenna rapped her fingers on the table. "How many times did his mama call him between eight a.m. and ten a.m. this morning?"

"Five times. I know, that seems like a lot, but she was very ill last week."

"What was wrong with her?"

"She overdosed and passed out. She's fine now."

Jenna leaned back against the red-velvet banquette and pressed her fingers to her temples like a psychic. "And now he's running to her bedside?"

"Well, of course he is. They live together."

"In the same house? *Mon dieu*, this is worse than I thought." Jenna leaned forward and refilled our cups with Japanese rice wine. "Have you never asked yourself why a very successful, very handsome, thirty-six-year-old man like Carlos has never married?"

No, I hadn't, but Abby had zeroed in on that right away. She followed up with, "You're absolutely *sure* he's not gay?"

"He hasn't met the right person until now," I said defensively.

The waitress brought a super-sized platter of mixed maki rolls to the table and set it between us. Dinners with Jenna were delightfully decision-free since she knew exactly what she wanted to taste and ordered for both of us.

"Besides, I like the fact that he's protective of his mother," I continued. "Poor Carmen has been unstable ever since Charles-Henri abused her."

"Poor Carmen may have been unstable long before that," pointed out Jenna. "Didn't Delphine Carroll say that Carmen seduced Charles-Henri, not the other way around?"

"I find that very hard to believe."

"Given the things that we both know about Charles-Henri's attitude toward women, I would tend to agree." Jenna speared a tuna/avocado roll with a chopstick and dipped it into the soy sauce. "However, it may be true. This mother in Madrid might be a very crazy woman."

"Carlos knows she has problems. He's been trying to send her to a specialized clinic in Switzerland for years, but until now he never had enough money."

"And now he does," said Jenna approvingly.

"Ah, but she won't accept the money unless she feels it came from a good man."

"Good luck with that." Jenna frowned. "Charles-Henri was a total scumbag. How is Carlos planning to get around that?"

"That's why he's funding this book project. He wants me to find stories about Charles-Henri's kindness and generosity."

Jenna burst into laughter. "That's going to be a very short book."

"If I ever find these damn diaries that Charles-Henri wrote every night, I have a chance of making it bigger."

"He kept a journal? What about? Comments on his conquests?"

"For all I know, they may be nothing but laundry lists." In fact, after Carlos left, I spent the afternoon going through the Avenue Foch apartment with no more luck than the last time. "The journals were important to him, and he was very secretive about them. I'm assuming he hid them. I've looked for a safe in the closets, behind the pictures, and I've found nothing. Can you think of anyplace else?"

"I have never owned anything so valuable that I had to hide it," confessed Jenna. "You need someone who's got experience with this kind of thing. What you need is a policeman or a burglar."

Burglar…I didn't have.

Policeman…I did.

"Jenna, you're a genius."

"I am, but I'm not so sure about this chef. Try the eel. It's a little tough, isn't it?"

Chapter Thirty-Seven

Bertrand had no problem with scheduling his next English lesson at Charles-Henri's apartment. When I got to the Avenue Foch address on Thursday morning, he was chatting with an attractive, forty-ish blonde in a pale blue suit and beige spectator pumps by the front door. She moved away and blew Bertrand an air-kiss as I approached.

"An old friend?" I asked as I fiddled with the key to the gate.

"A lady of the night. Working, *how do you say it?* Working the day shift."

"She's a prostitute?" I turned around and looked at her in amazement as she walked away. I'd have placed her as the chairwoman of a Fortune 500 company or the president of the local garden club.

"The ladies who work on the Avenue Foch are quite *distinguées* in appearance," said Bertrand. "The men see them, circle the block in their car, and if she hasn't moved from where she was standing, they stop the car to discuss the price. See, there is another." He pointed to an equally elegant brunette in a red designer suit on the other side of the street. She waved at him. "I worked in the internal affairs section of the police, so I was assigned to many departments. There was a case on this street for—again, how do you say it?—the morality detectives?"

"The vice squad."

"Ah yes, the vice's squad. There was a case for the vice's squad on the Avenue Foch, and I met many of the ladies and their protectors."

"This street is haven for high-class hookers?"

"*Absolument*, it is well-known for that."

"Then we know why Charles-Henri chose to live here." When we got into the apartment, Bertrand let out a slow whistle of appreciation and walked straight over to the handsome pastel sketch of two blond children hanging in the foyer.

"Maurice Denis," he said. "He always painted his children, very often at the beach like this."

"You're an art lover too?"

"I worked also with the squad of stolen art for two years. There was a drawing much like this one taken from a museum in Brittany. This one is much more beautiful," he added. "It is worth perhaps 150,000 euros at an auction."

I followed him into the living room where he stopped in front of a still life signed by Odile Redon. "Very beautiful," he said. "Are we here to discuss of the paintings?"

"I actually brought you here to help me find something. Charles-Henri kept some journals, and his son and I are hoping to find them. We think he kept them in a safe, but I've looked everywhere and can't find it. Not," I added, "that we could open it without the combination."

"Unfortunately," said Bertrand, "safes can be crackled quite easily. Where have you looked?"

He listened carefully as I gave him the report.

"But not the bookcase?" he asked when I finished.

"Well, I looked *inside* all the books."

"Ah, but the woodwork itself, it also makes excellent camouflage." Bertrand ran his fingers along the shelves. "Did you notice anything unusual behind the books?"

"No, I was just looking for things he used as bookmarks. Plane tickets, receipts, business cards. Oh, and that's where I found the threatening letter I asked you about."

"Did you really?" said Bertrand. "Let us get these books out and see what else we can find."

Bertrand and I began a game where he translated the French book titles into English with very creative results. However, an hour later we'd found no trace of a safe. We sat at the kitchen table, and I poured two tall glasses of orange-flavored Perrier, my new favorite soft drink.

"Charles-Henri Banville was a wealthy man," Bertrand remarked. "Did he have no other property where he might hide something of value?"

"No. He rented a furnished villa in Saint Tropez every summer, never the same one. He hasn't visited the Burgundy vineyard in years, and the farmhouse in Normandy where he grew up has been sold and torn down."

"He grew up in Normandy? On a farm?" Bertrand's eyes twinkled. "Then you must stop thinking where a Miami drug dealer on the television would hide his treasures. You should think like a Norman peasant. Let's inspect the bedroom."

"It's pretty disgusting," I protested as I followed him down the hall. "I've already been through all the dresser drawers. I looked in the closets, in the shoeboxes, everywhere."

"But not here?" He pointed to the bed.

No, I hadn't even touched the semen-streaked bed. Just the idea of what went on between those black satin sheets made me queasy.

Bertrand didn't have the same qualms. He shoved the mattress off to the side in one quick movement. "Voila!"

Heavens, there must have been at least twenty pocket-sized black notebooks! I felt like kissing Bertrand, but not in Charles-Henri's bedroom. Instead, I reached for one of the books and opened it reverently. Tiny, tiny writing. The dates were in roman numerals, an oddly classical gesture. I wondered if...

Bertrand's words interrupted my reverie. "The physical books, they belong to the legal heir, this son of which you speak. However, I am not so sure about the rights of the edition."

"You mean copyrights?"

"Yes. I am not so sure that his son can authorize them to be reprinted for your book. He must first consult to a lawyer."

"Carlos has a lawyer," I said, still lost in thought. These notebooks would be a gamechanger. Even if I couldn't quote from them, they'd be chockfull of clues that I could pursue. What if they contained his real thoughts about Ingrid? About Charlene? About Carmen?

"Now I wonder what this is?" said Bertrand, extracting a crushed shopping bag from under the books.

"More books?"

Bertrand shook the bag, and dozens of envelopes

fell out.

"Correspondence? Even better!" I reached for one eagerly and opened it up. I felt slightly seasick when I unfolded a printed note and recognized some all-too-familiar black type.

PREPARE-TOI POUR TA MISE A MORT

"Put that down immediately, please," said Bertrand, looking over my shoulder. He pulled a pair of latex gloves from his back pocket. "Once a *policier*, always I am a *policier*. Please put that paper down and do not touch the other ones."

"But…"

"This is only a precaution, Melody. Harassment letters could be a police business."

"Harassment? Charles-Henri isn't going to complain about harassment anymore. The poor man is dead."

"*Exactement*," said Bertrand, gathering the letters and putting them back into the bag. "Charles-Henri Banville is dead. And that is what makes the letters most interesting."

"His death was accidental."

"And the coroner was most likely correct in that judgment. Nevertheless, my colleagues in Bordeaux will want to examine these letters. It may be the business of the police now."

Police business?

Carlos was already complaining about the delays in the legal process. If the police got involved, it would only get worse. Did Bertrand have the authority to appropriate the letters? He was a cop, but he was retired. He didn't even have a badge anymore. Did French cops need warrants? Maybe not. I'd watched a

French police drama on TV a few nights ago, and the Parisian police inspector just tossed people behind bars without charging them or reading rights. It was clearly a different system.

I followed Bertrand into the kitchen where he carefully scotch-taped the shopping bag closed and deposited it into a clean garbage bag that he found in the pantry. What could I say? What was I, an American tourist with no legal expertise, entitled to do in this peculiar situation?

It was out of my hands since Bertrand was already on the phone with the receptionist at police headquarters in Bordeaux. *"Oui, j'ai besoin de parler avec le brigadier qui s'occupait de l'investigation du déces de Charles-Henri Banville. Oui, j'attends."*

Apparently, even ex-police officers have the privilege of cooling their heels on hold, even when they claim to have new evidence about the death of a world-famous celebrity. I heard the recorded voice ask countless times if he wanted to call back, consult the internet, or wait for an officer to respond.

Bertrand waited.

"Mise à mort," I said because there wasn't much for me to do except make polite, language-oriented small talk. "That's a new French expression for me. I don't think I've heard it before."

"It is originally a Spanish term," said Bertrand. "It refers to the moment when the matador makes the kill at the bullfight. *Ah oui, Commissaire Lacroix? J'ai quelque chose…"*

Chapter Thirty-Eight

I breathed a *huge* sigh of relief that night after I reported the day's activities to Carlos. I was so afraid he'd be upset with me for inviting a third party to the avenue Foch apartment and prompting a police investigation into those harassment letters. In fact, he didn't seem to care about that at all.

On the other hand, he cared about Bertrand. He kept asking if Bertrand was attractive to me, if Bertrand was attracted to me, if Bertrand was handsome, if he was married—I had no idea—and if he had tried to make any advances toward me.

But was Carlos troubled by the existence of letters that threatened his father's life? Or by the fact that Bertrand was shipping all of that hate mail off to the police in Bordeaux? "I'm glad that he knew he was hated," said Carlos. "He deserved to be fearful." On the other hand, he was just as happy as I was about the discovery of the diaries. "Now perhaps you can find some of these good stories. Do you think you will have a longer manuscript to show me on Saturday?"

Only if I could spin straw into gold. These notebooks were not easy reading. In fact, they just about defied the whole reading process. First of all, Charles-Henri had scribbled his comments in miniscule ant-print. Luckily, Marie-Christine had left a magnifying glass in the desk drawer. That helped a little, but not much. Charles-Henri referred to his movies and contacts only by initials and used a curious form of shorthand, often letting single letters designate whole words.

His skinflint attitude toward paper and ink permitted him to cram entire weeks onto each page. I set myself the task of putting the sixteen books into chronological order. Tomorrow, with bright sunlight streaming in the windows, I'd start decrypting them. By concentrating on dates that coincided with events I knew about, I could get my bearings.

I half-wondered if Charles-Henri had immortalized my meeting with him in New York. However, by the time I'd attached little sticky notes with calendar dates on each of the covers, I was too tired to care. I fell into bed and slept like a rock until dawn, confident that Friday would be a busy and productive day.

Friday morning, however, was a letdown. The first diary began in XI.XII. MCMXCVIII (December 11, 1998) so the Carlos-oriented events that interested me most, his birth and their disastrous meeting at his high-school graduation, weren't covered. The last entry was penned four months before his death, so I wasn't going to find out what he thought about me either.

His Academy Award in 2005 was succinctly summed up as *"Enfin!"* (about time!) No mention of great Los Angeles weather, his party date, or his state of mind. It was about the same for the Tony Award (2001) and both of the French César awards (2007, 2014) he'd won. The César he'd lost to Maurice Gallois in 2008 was commemorated with a string of obscenities underlined three times.

Because of the rich pickings—restaurant bills,

traffic tickets, etc.—that I'd harvested from the arctic explorer books, the 2000-2001 period he'd spent with Ingrid Svenson constituted my best-documented time zone. "Childish" and "demanding" were the adjectives that turned up next to "IS." His other comments about the fateful weekend in that freezing Alpine shack? "IS knows shit about snow," "IS can't cook," "IS is a frigid bitch."

There were little stars next to "AM" interspersed with the "IS" references. I wondered if that was "Anne-Marie" of the lipstick-smudged napkin. Magnifying glass in hand, I made slow but steady progress through the pages devoted to the filming of "NM" (*Les Neiges du Matin*) in Grenoble which largely consisted of "AJ idiot" and "TP uncooperative" which were probably references to director Alain Jouval and co-star Thérèse Perrin.

By the time there were stars next to "TP," I'd figured out that part of the code. It was quickly followed by "IS Grenoble—what a bore." That had to be when Ingrid found Charles-Henri and Thérèse in bed in his trailer. I didn't find any more references to Ingrid until two weeks later. "IS fixed. HK 2000 euros."

HK? Something he bought? Or someone?

I checked the cast and crew listings for *Neiges du Matin.* The only name that clicked with those initials was the set designer, Hans Kauffmann. Wait a second...I shuffled through my Ingrid notes. Yes, the night after Charles-Henri had refused to listen to her about the babies, she'd slept with...here it was...an Austrian set designer named Hans. She'd described it as a chance meeting, but...

I leaned back in my chair, pushing the diary away

from me in disgust. Had Charles-Henri *paid* Hans Kauffmann to seduce Ingrid? It made a horrible kind of sense since he'd spread that story in order to destroy her credibility when the paternity suit came up. Good grief, when I found the diaries, I'd been hoping to find some evidence that Charles-Henri Banville was a better man than everyone thought he was.

Nope.

He was worse.

Chapter Thirty-Nine

I woke up Saturday morning feeling bluesy and subdued. True, Carlos would be here in time for a late lunch and thanks to Alberto, the waiter at the café downstairs, I had the address of a great salsa club near the Place de la République. I'd doublechecked the bus and subway routes to the Carnavalet Museum and consulted the weather app on my phone which predicted sunshine and blue skies for the next three days. It was going to be a perfect weekend.

Why was I so down?

In a word? Work.

I wasn't getting what Carlos wanted, and I wasn't getting what I wanted either. All I'd discovered about Charles-Henri was non-stop nastiness, and that would make a very one-dimensional book. Moreover, whatever I wrote would probably make the people who'd been hurt by him in the past hurt even more when they saw those stories in print.

Since I had Jenna's account of her close encounter with Charles-Henri Banville, I searched for the dates that that corresponded to her near-rape. "Uncooperative" and "probably lesbian" were the comments next to JB on the day he'd ambushed her in his hotel room. "Bitch complained" was underlined a few days later. "Deal VH, two exclusives, *merde!*"

VH had to be Valentin Hulot, the station head

who'd fired Jenna a few days after the incident. The reason that a major celebrity like Charles-Henri granted two half-hour interviews to the producer at a minor cable station was no longer a mystery. Jenna had been sold down the river for sixty minutes of airtime. I wonder if she wanted to know that. Probably not.

One thing was sure: Hell hath no fury like a womanizer scorned. Charles-Henri exacted serious revenge when he didn't get what he wanted from a woman. With all that money, all that fame, and all those women who *did* want him, why did he need to prey on unwilling ones? Females were literally handing themselves to him on a plate, if that woman who threw her panties on the table in that New York restaurant was typical. Did he need the challenge that badly?

Did the women who got paid for their time fare better? It was unlikely that Charles-Henri left the delicacies on the Avenue Foch untasted. I'd have to ask Bertrand if any of his elegant acquaintances would consent to speak with me. Their stories would probably be protected by some sacred French form of hooker/horndog privilege but there was no harm in asking.

I put the notebooks away and took a long, hot, soapy shower. Thinking about Charles-Henri always made me feel soiled, and touching his hand-written notebooks intensified that unpleasant sensation. However, by one o'clock I was fresh, clean, and ready for love. I plugged some cheerful ABBA music into the CD player, and by the time Carlos walked in the door and took me in his arms, my world was almost perfect.

Almost perfect…and Carlos sensed it right away.

"What is wrong, *mi corazon*?"

"It's this book, it's your father, it's…"

"No," said Carlos, putting his finger to my lips. "Let's have a vacation from all that. Today we will think only of beautiful things."

"It's just…"

"…hunger?" he asked. "Do you like Thai food? I noticed a restaurant around the corner."

"Love it," I said, grabbing my jacket.

Two orders of pad thai later, we were sipping jasmine tea and talking about everything and anything except He-Who-Shall-Not-Be-Named. We spent the next part of the afternoon discovering the riches of Paris Past in the Carnavalet Museum but decided against tackling the block-long lines at the nearby Musée Picasso. Hand-in-hand, we walked through the picturesque Marais district, crowded with shoppers and tourists, peeking into boutiques, stopping once for ice cream and a little later for coffee.

Since the dance club didn't open until eleven p.m., we had more than enough time back at the apartment to catch up on sexual healing before piling into a taxi. When we arrived at the club, Alberto and a bunch of his friends invited us over to their table so neither of us had any shortage of dance partners. But when it comes to dancing with a stranger and dancing with a lover, there's no contest. Every minute that Carlos twirled me across the floor, it was a miracle of emotion in motion. With the other men, it was just dancing.

We didn't get back to the apartment until three in the morning, so our Sunday got off to a very, very late start. It was nearly noon when I opened my eyes. Carlos wasn't beside me, but his jacket was still draped reassuringly over the chair. I brushed my teeth, combed my hair, and pulled on my pink robe. I found him, lusciously unshaven, with a pot of coffee, two mugs, and a pile of papers that he was neatly correcting in red pen.

"Vacation's over already?" I asked, kissing the top of his head.

"The academic year ends in June." He patted the thick stack of paper. "So many essays to grade, so little time."

"Any good ones?" I sat down and poured myself some coffee.

"Some of them are very promising." He rose and brought a breadbasket to the table. "I went out earlier for some pastries."

"You *are* the perfect man!"

"No," he said, echoing Jenna, "there is no such thing as a perfect man."

"You'll do until one comes around," I said, biting into a *pain au chocolat*. "These are my favorite. How did you know?"

"This is not our first breakfast." He smiled as he selected a croissant. "Tell me, what was troubling you yesterday?"

"I'm not finding much of anything that will convince your mother, or anyone else, that your father was anything but a monster."

"Are you surprised?"

"Not really, but I'm finding things out that I don't really want to publish. Remember Ingrid Svenson?"

"A very nice lady. I liked her."

"I like her too, and your father treated her worse than she thinks he did. Publishing that information would be very painful for her."

"Then don't publish it."

"But I want to tell the truth."

"Truth is often overestimated," said Carlos. "The truth is not always convenient."

"I know." I stirred my coffee once, twice, three times.

"Does this mean that you wish to stop working on the book?"

"No, not at all. I'm just a little lost and depressed about these notebooks. I hardly know where to start."

"Start at the beginning and see where they lead."

I cleared the plates. "Make some room for me at the table so we can work together." Carlos transferred the corrected papers to the extra chair, and I got out notebook number one from 1998. "How long do we have?"

Carlos looked at his watch. "Not enough time. My plane leaves in four hours."

We worked in silence, stopping only now and then for kiss, a hug, and more hot coffee. The 1998 notebook was no easier than the others I'd spot-checked. I spent a lot of time going through the lists and casts and crews of old movies, trying to match initials.

"Perhaps there's another way of going about this. It's a rather impersonal approach, but it might work," I said as we walked hand-in-hand to the taxi-stand in front of the café.

"Anything is better than nothing. What is your idea?"

"He's played scientists, athletes, detectives, and all kinds of heroes. Maybe there are people out there who got inspired in their careers by him. I'm going to start looking at his fan sites."

"That might work," said Carlos. "If there's a fan club in Outer Mongolia that you need to investigate, don't hesitate to book a plane ticket."

"That's nuts. I wouldn't need to go in person. I can check out fan clubs by telephone or email."

"I'm telling you to spare no expense." He dropped his bag in the trunk of the taxi and gave me another last kiss for good measure. "I mean that, Melody. No sacrifice is too great for my mother. There is nothing, absolutely *nothing*, that I wouldn't do for her."

Chapter Forty

I had a new work routine: one hour spent combing through happy-face Banville fan-sites followed by forty-five depressing minutes of notebook slog. I gave myself a fifteen-minute break after the notebooks, which were mostly composed of lewd sexual references and rants against coworkers.

The fan sites were much more fun. A woman from Montreal recounted that she'd designed her daughter's wedding reception around the theme of *L'Amour d'été,* one of Charles-Henri's most romantic films, while a winemaker from the Loire Valley provided a glowing report about the actor's visit to his vineyard—"An excellent palate! He certainly knew his Sancerre."

Admirers from around the world reported on their close encounters in airport lounges and film festivals. Whenever they left their addresses on the site, I fired off a query asking them to expand on their experiences. I'd already received gushing stories about how sweetly he signed autographs and posed for pictures. The less time people spent with Charles-Henri, the more they liked him.

I spent my breaks drooling over photos of sun-soaked Seville. Carlos was using his frequent flier miles to bring me to Spain for an entire week! Since he had end-of-term faculty meetings and exams to grade, he'd booked me on a fight to Madrid next Tuesday. He'd pick me up at the airport, and we'd drive to Seville where he'd give a speech on Wednesday. After that, it was just sightseeing and fun. "We have a very romantic hotel not far from the Alcazar Palace," he'd told me. "We'll take our time driving back to Madrid."

Madrid was the only part of the trip that made me nervous, mainly because my support group was being uncharacteristically unsupportive.

"You're finally going to meet Momzilla?" asked Abby when I told her about the trip. "Stuff garlic cloves in your pockets and pack a wooden stake."

Jenna was as wary as my sister. "That guy's been dancing to her music all his life," she warned. "Believe me, she's not going to want to share him."

He hadn't mentioned where we would be staying in Madrid. At his house? In a hotel? Would Mama welcome me, or would she despise me because Carlos and I were sleeping together out of holy wedlock?

Of course, she had an affair with a married man, didn't she? Though it felt awfully disloyal to Carlos, I couldn't quite dismiss Delphine Carroll's spin on the situation. A rich, glamorous, and sophisticated man like Charles-Henri would be a prize for a starstruck teenager.

I was torn as well. The writer in me was dying to pose some tough questions to Carmen; the part of me that was in love with Carlos was terrified of taking off my kid gloves in her presence. I never had much experience in family issues like this. My mother disappeared long before I'd suspected there were problems in their marriage. My father was always kind and concerned about his daughters, but when you came to it, he was much more intuitive about petunias than people. A jealous, possessive parent like Carmen was way off my radar.

I was getting faster and faster with the notebooks, cross-checking the initials in the diaries against the names of his movies, television shows, and costars. Around 2007, he'd started giving more than one star to some of the actresses, which I assumed was a sexual rating system.

The notebooks tended to confirm that hunch. Charlene described sex with Charles-Henri as fabulous, and it looked like Charles-Henri felt the same. The night they met at the Golden Globes ("GG—boring") was followed by "CT" with an unprecedented five stars. A few days later, "Cha-cha" was followed by exclamation points and more stars. Seemed like Charlene's story about the mercenary marriage scam checked out as well.

Charlene's string of sky-high ratings continued right up to his return to France to film "*Adeline des Alpes*" on location in Chamonix, a high-altitude ski resort. "Stupid script," "pervert director," and "MD pretty" were the major themes for the first week on the set.

The only MD connected to "*Adeline des Alpes*" was Manon Dupont, an actress whose name meant nothing to me. She had the title role, and the most surprising thing about her was the total absence of stars next to her name by the end of the third week. Charles-Henri's costars usually tumbled into his bed within a few days. Was he actually being faithful to Charlene and the Cha-Cha Challenge?

Maybe yes, maybe no. The next comment about Manon Dupont was "MD childish" and after plowing through years and years of Banville diaries, I knew what that meant. All women who resisted Charles-Henri's advances were invariably labelled "immature," "uncooperative," or "lesbian." What did puzzle me was the February 10th entry: "MD birthday 1,500 euros." What was so special about this Manon Dupont that she rated such an expensive present? Especially when there were no stars next to her name. The internet was uncharacteristically mum on her, just an ancient Wikipedia entry, so I looked up "*Adeline des Alpes.*"

It was Franco-Swiss telefilm that retold the Heidi story in a WWII setting. Manon portrayed Adeline, a waifish refugee, and Charles-Henri was the crusty grandfather who ran a ski shop. The bio of Manon Dupont revealed that she turned fourteen years old on February 10th on the set. No wonder nothing happened between her and Charles-Henri. I closed the diaries for the night and decided to take a nice, long shower.

Chapter Forty-One

The fan club ploy exceeded my expectations. People who knew Charles-Henri well may have hated him, but he had a worldwide network of admirers who were overjoyed to share their fleeting impressions of the star. They sent pictures of Charles-Henri blowing his nose at a tennis match ("He caught a cold, poor sweet thing, watching Federer!"), chugging down wine in sidewalk cafés, and even patting the occasional poodle.

None of this stuff would be useful for a serious biography, but it was perfect for the little propaganda project that Carlos wanted. Since making Carlos happy also made me happy, I stopped mucking my way through the diaries. If I worked hard, I'd be able to give Carlos a decent-sized manuscript when I got to Spain. With luck and a good designer, he'd have a nice-looking paperback, selling for $11.99 on an internet bookstore, by the end of the month.

"He said my little Jojo was the most adorable beagle he'd ever seen," wrote a woman from Boston. "He even gave Jojo a piece of his steak." So far, Charles-Henri's affinity for small domestic animals was his most consistently winning trait. I gave the puppy-dog stories as many paragraphs as I could.

In between transcribing terrier tales, my mind wandered back to that birthday present. What did 1,500 euros buy an adolescent in 2015? A fancy bicycle? A piece of jewelry? If so, I had my first genuinely heartwarming story about Charles-Henri. All I had to do was track down Manon for the details. That, however, was proving surprisingly difficult. "*Adeline des Alpes*" seemed to be her only acting job and "Dupont," I found out after a frustrating social media search, was one of the most common last names in France.

Bertrand called just as I was running my feel-good manuscript through the English-language spellcheck.

"May I see you very soon?" he asked.

"For an English lesson?" I retyped *Lyon*, the French city, which my English language spellcheck had transformed into *Lion*.

"Not exactly," he said, "but I very much wish to see you in person."

"Can it wait a few days? I'm heading to Spain tomorrow and…"

"Spain?" he interrupted. "Did you say Spain?"

"Yes, I'm going to Madrid to see Carlos."

"Carlos?"

"The son of Charles-Henri Banville. I thought I told you about him. He's the man I'm writing the book for."

"I can meet you at the café downstairs," he said. "It will only take a few minutes of your time."

I looked at my watch. I was already packed, and the spellcheck was almost done. "In an hour?"

"That will be perfect." He rang off without another word.

Bertrand wasn't there when I arrived. Alberto escorted me to one of the romantic corner booths. "Are you meeting that sexy Spaniard?" he asked.

"I'm seeing him tomorrow," I told him. "There's another man tonight."

"How Parisian of you," said Alberto approvingly. He winked at me as Bertrand made his way to the table. Bertrand did not look particularly happy to see me as he shed his black leather vest. In fact, he didn't look happy at all.

"Is something wrong?" I asked.

"Hopefully not," he said, "but I am glad we can see each other." He caught Alberto's eye. "Some coffee, black, *s'il vous plaît,*" he said. "And for you?"

Not a cocktail? It was seven pm, and Happy Hour was in full swing at every table except ours. Bertrand said nothing until Alberto delivered our order.

"You must understand," he said at last, "that I cannot speak entirely freely. However, those letters we found in the home of Monsieur Banville have proved very interesting to the police. They revealed many specific threats to Monsieur Banville's life, and, as a result, there will be a new investigation."

Good lord, had the coffee gone cold all of a sudden or was it me?

"They must consider the possibility of homicide."

Murder? Thanks to Agatha Christie, Sue Grafton, and James Patterson, I'd read about thousands of murders. I must have seen a zillion more of them on television. But that was just make-believe. This was someone I knew. Well, someone I hardly knew. But Charles-Henri ...*murdered*?

"The police, they must be very careful in a case like this."

"Of course," I murmured. How would Carlos react

to this news? He hated his father, but the idea that someone actually killed him was something else altogether. What would he...?

"For the moment," continued Bertrand, "all the assets of the estate must be secured on the ice."

"*Frozen*. In English, we say that the *assets are frozen*," I said absentmindedly. What would Carlos...?

"About Carlos Ortega," said Bertrand.

I looked up from my coffee. Had I said his name aloud?

"Do you know him well?

"He's my...we're...we're together."

"I see." Bertrand sighed and patted my hand. "It is the big romance with him, *non*?"

"Yes."

Bertrand withdrew his hand and looked at the ceiling. "Then this is the part that is delicate. Many of the letters that threaten Monsieur Banville with death, they have their postmarks from Madrid. Do you understand, Mademoiselle? Someone in Spain hated him very much."

"Are all of the letters from Spain?" I asked.

"Unfortunately, Monsieur Banville did not always save the envelopes. However, there is a definite connection to Spain..."

"You're not suggesting that Carlos wrote those letters, are you? Because Charles-Henri Banville made enemies all over the world, including most of his directors, producers, costars, and ex-girlfriends."

"I suspect that is true," agreed Bertrand. "But the police will, as you Americans say, follow the money. Monsieur Banville was an extremely wealthy man. He possessed a remarkable art collection, a valuable

Parisian apartment, a vineyard, and seventeen rare antique automobiles." He paused. "*Cui bono*."

I'd heard that Latin term somewhere. "Who profits?" I asked.

"*Exactement*," said Bertrand. "Who gets his money?"

Chapter Forty-Two

I couldn't sleep. As much as I tried to blame it on the caffeine, it was all about Carlos and my conversation with Bertrand. I tossed, I turned, and every time I switched on the lights to see what time it was, my carry-on suitcase stared at me across the room. The only good thing about being six time zones away from my sister was being able to call her at three in the morning.

"Just getting dressed for the clubs," said Abby when she picked up. "Whassup?"

"It's about this trip to Spain tomorrow."

"You're not still bugged about the mom thing, are you? I was just kidding about the garlic. I don't really think she's a vampire."

"It's not that." I recounted everything Bertrand told me.

"Hold on," said Abby when I was finished. "Let me text the gang to say I'll be late. Okay," she said a few minutes later, "fill me in. You've called off the trip, right?"

"Why would I do that? Just because a retired policeman thinks that Carlos wrote a few lousy letters?"

"Not just *letters*, honey. They were *death threats*."

"Carlos would never do anything like that."

"What makes you so sure? You've only known him for fifteen minutes."

"Carlos isn't like that."

"Prisons are full of people who aren't 'like that,' honey." Abby sighed. "This guy's swimming in the dark side of the gene pool too."

"What gives you that idea?"

"Just what you've told me. His dad was a sexual predator, and his mom's a suicidal whacko."

"That's not his fault."

"No, it's not his fault, but are you sure you want to deal with it?"

"I have to deal with it, Abby. I'm in love with him."

There was silence on the other end.

"Besides, he's innocent until proven guilty, right?"

"Right." There was a pause. "But I want you to send me at least ten texts a day if you go on this crazy trip. And if Mystery Man even gets anywhere near a post office, promise me you'll clear out."

"I promise. Does that make you feel better?"

"Sorta. Get some sleep."

Funny, after that I did sleep. Honestly, I wasn't worried about Carlos, but for some reason it was reassuring to know someone else, somewhere in the world, was a little bit worried. I'd set the alarm for 8:30 so I'd have no problem getting to the airport by noon, but it was Carlos who woke me up at eight.

"It's off."

"What's off?"

"Our trip. I am so sorry, *mi corazon*, but there are complications. We'll go to Seville another time, I promise."

"Complications?" I sat up and rubbed my eyes. "What sort of complications?"

"Just tiresome formalities with the estate."

"You're coming to Paris? That's good too."

"No, I have to go to Bordeaux. The police have some questions about my father. I can't afford any delays in the settlement, so I'm going right away. In fact, I'm on the way to the airport now. We'll make plans for next week, okay?"

"Carlos, about Bordeaux…"

"I've canceled our plane tickets. I'll call you later."

The manuscript, all seventy pages of it, was tucked neatly into the side pocket of my carryon bag, already packed with my prettiest summer clothes. Carlos was walking into something bad, and I was damned if I was going to let him walk into it alone. After he hung up, I looked up the Paris-Bordeaux train schedules. The city was only three hours away.

I punched Carlos on speed dial, and he answered on the second ring.

"I'm already packed, and I'm coming to Bordeaux," I told him. "Just tell me where to meet you."

"But darling…"

"What's wrong with a romantic weekend in Bordeaux?"

"There's nothing romantic about Bordeaux," protested Carlos. "It's a snobbish, conservative town filled with people who worship nothing but grapes."

"What's wrong with that? Merlot and Cabernet are two of my favorite food groups."

Carlos laughed. "All right, *mi corazon*, we'll meet in Bordeaux and make a tour of the city's best winebars. I have a reservation at the Hotel de la Presse. I'll text you the address."

Corinne LaBalme

"Hotel de la Presse?" I said. "I can find it."

Chapter Forty-Three

The high-speed train sped southward so quickly that fields, forests, factories, and feudal chateaux blended into one long blur. I wasn't concentrating on the scenery anyway. I was wondering what to say to Carlos. He already knew about the hate mail. He just didn't know about the Spanish postmarks. That was certainly what the police wanted to talk with him about. Did I tip him off or not?

On one hand, knowledge is power, and I certainly wanted Carlos to be as well-prepared as possible for this interview. On the other hand, wouldn't it be better for him to act honestly surprised about this development? If I clued him in ahead of time, would he look suspiciously defensive?

By the time the train arrived, I'd decided not to decide on anything, at least not until I saw him. The Iberia flight had landed on time, and Carlos had made a lunch reservation at a place near the waterfront called Chez Christophe. "It's very famous bistro," he told me. "Any cab driver will know it." His appointment at the commissariat was at four, he added, so we'd have enough time to try the restaurant's famous crème brûlée dessert. I didn't have time to drop my bag at the hotel and change first, so I hoped my travel clothes would be acceptable

My fears about showing up at a fancy restaurant in

jeans and sneakers dissolved as soon as I walked in the door. Chez Christophe was delightfully dark and dive-ish with a gleaming ham on the front counter and strings of dried peppers hanging from the rafters. I spotted Carlos before he saw me, at a table in the rear, in animated conversation with a man whose air of proprietary confidence gave him away as Christophe even before I saw the name embroidered on his apron.

Carlos rose, kissed me, and introduced me to him as the "Señorita of his Dreams." "Christophe was just telling me about the specialty of the day. It's a local fish that is stewed with wine and mushrooms. Does that sound good to you?"

"Delicious."

The chef kissed my hand. "An excellent choice. And what will you have to drink, Don Carlos?"

"A fine Spanish Rioja, if you please."

"We don't serve that poison here," said Christophe. "You'll have the same Médoc that you had the last time."

"If there's nothing better than the local stuff," said Carlos.

"Barbarian!" said Christophe over his shoulder as he headed for the kitchen.

"You two know each other well?" I said when we were alone.

"I've been working on that book about Empress Eugénie with one of the professors on the Bordeaux history faculty for the last two years. We usually have dinner here when I'm in town."

The waiter slipped a large wooden platter of cold cuts on the table along with a jar of pickles and a basket of coarse-cut brown bread.

"Are you hungry?" asked Carlos as I reached for an enormous chunk of bread.

"Always." I snagged a slice of ham with my fork. "And you?"

"I think I'll wait for the wine."

Christophe was at our side a minute later with two glasses and a bottle. "Fine Bordeaux is wasted on this man," he said as he poured a quarter inch in my glass, "so you will do the tasting, Mademoiselle."

"It's heavenly," I said after I sipped the ruby-red liquid.

"This wine and this woman, they are both far better than you deserve, Señor Ortega," said Christophe. He filled both our glasses carefully and lumbered off to the kitchen.

"I take neither for granted," said Carlos, "but I prefer you to the wine. I brought you something from Spain." He slid a small velvet box from under the napkin and slid it across the table.

I wasn't used to this fairytale stuff. But Carlos was Prince Charming, wasn't he, and I was beginning to feel very Cinderella-ish around the edges.

"It's a very small token, but I wanted you to have something to remind you that I'm always thinking of you, even when we're apart. I had planned," he added, "to present it to you over a dinner in a restaurant near the Alhambra palace, but since we're here…"

I opened the box carefully. A dark blue stone set in an engraved, Art Nouveau style bangle. "Do you like it?" he asked while I searched for the words to tell him how much I liked it. "I don't have much experience with jewelry."

"I don't just like it, I love it!" I leaned across the

table and kissed him. "It's absolutely beautiful."

"It will look even more beautiful when you wear it. May I?" When I nodded, he reached over and fastened it to my left wrist. "Did you know that there is historical and heraldic signification to gemstones, Melody? Sapphires are considered to be the symbol of trust, honesty, and loyalty. For that reason, the sapphire is the true expression of my regard for you." He lifted his glass. "To the most marvelous woman in Bordeaux."

The moment was damn near perfect. I'd have to be an idiot to wreck it, but here I went...

"About this meeting this afternoon with the police..." I began.

"Tiresome French bureaucracy," said Carlos. "Let's not ruin Christophe's wonderful food and wine with boring things like that."

Carlos left me at the entrance of the Fine Arts Museum at three-thirty and told me that the Titians were wonderful. They were, and I thoroughly enjoyed the peace and quiet, quite unlike the Louvre, which had been crowded as a rush hour metro when I'd queued up to see the Mona Lisa. The Bordeaux museum closed at six, and there was still no word from Carlos. I bought a few postcards in the boutique on the way out and settled down at a window table in a nearby café. "*At the Café des Arts*," I texted him adding a few heart emojis.

By seven, I'd consumed two Perriers with lemon, written all the postcards, and was gearing up for a panic attack. "R U OK?" got no response either.

Finally, at seven-fifteen, I got a message. "Be there soon, love."

When Carlos arrived ten minutes later, he was not the same man who'd left me at the museum four hours earlier. Still gorgeous, mind, but rumpled, crumpled, and seriously down at the mouth. He looked around at the dingy café with distaste as he slumped onto the chair across from me. "This is not what I planned."

"We're here, there's wine, it'll do," I said. I held up the card advertising the wine-of-the-day and gestured to the waiter to bring two glasses of it. Carlos was lost in thought until the waiter deposited our wine on the table.

"*Santé*," he said, lifting his glass. "Here's to a perfectly horrible afternoon." He sipped the wine and made a face. "This wine is terrible."

"What's wrong?"

"What isn't wrong? Do you remember those damn letters? The ones that threatened that *hijo de puta* with a hideous death? At least half of them were postmarked from Spain. Not just from Spain, from *Madrid*! And not just from Madrid!" Carlos put his head in his hands. "They were mailed from the local post office at the end of my street!"

"Carlos…"

"They asked me over and over and over if I wrote them. But that's not all they think." He drained his glass and raised it to catch the attention of the waiter. "They also think I may have killed the bastard!"

"But how could they think that? You were in Madrid."

"No, I wasn't! Not that weekend! I was here to work on that damn Eugénie book with Professor Fourget." Carlos nodded as the waiter refilled his glass. I'd barely touched mine.

"They wanted to know if I timed my visit in order to murder my father. How would I even know he was in

Bordeaux? I didn't! They asked me what I would usually do on Saturday night in Bordeaux. I said I would probably have dinner with Professor Fourget, usually at Christophe's restaurant. That's what we often did after a day of work. But no! Not that night!"

Carlos stared at the ceiling. "We had been working on the book for two years. That's a lot of dinners. They checked to see if there had been a reservation at Chez Christophe, and yes, we had canceled it. How was I to remember, on that particular night Professor Fourget had some emergency at his apartment and left the library early?"

Carlos sighed. "The police took my phone. That's why I could not call you. They did not want me to invent an alibi with anyone I know. Then they spent a long time to find out if indeed I was indeed working on a book. Professor Fourget, of course, is on vacation, but they finally, *finally* located his assistant who was able to confirm that."

Carlos drained his second glass. Luckily, they pour rather stingy drinks at the Café des Arts. If he continued at this rate, I'd have to carry him back to the hotel.

"Of course, they asked what I did that night without a dinner with my colleague," he continued. "I ate my dinner alone, I don't remember where, and then I went back to the hotel. I must have paid for my dinner with cash because there is nothing, *nada*, on my credit card. Does anyone remember what time I returned to the hotel? Of course not. I don't remember, so how does anyone else?"

"Carlos…"

"Listen to me, Melody. This situation is very serious. For the police, I am a suspect of homicide."

"But you didn't do anything wrong."

"No," said Carlos, "but I don't think it matters. My father cursed me at birth, and he continues to curse me from beyond the grave. We should see if there is still a late-night train to Paris for you. I don't think you should stay here with me, my dear."

I leaned over the table and kissed him long and hard. "You're not getting rid of me that easily."

Chapter Forty-Four

We settled for cheese omelets at a neon-lit diner on the way back to the hotel. Carlos reverted into teacher mode. He provided a nonstop patter about regional history, everything from Queen Eleanor of Aquitaine's dowry to the finances of the Black Prince's army throughout dinner. However, he made it clear that anything happening in twenty-first century Bordeaux was out of conversational bounds. When we got back to the hotel, he collapsed into a deep, fitful sleep while I was in the bathroom changing into my sexiest nightie.

The next day we woke up to gloomy skies and claps of thunder. Huddled under the red umbrella I'd been prescient enough to pack, we dodged Venice-style puddles as we raced from one indoor tourist site to the next. Clearly, Carlos never met a museum he didn't like, and today they served his purpose of avoiding any discussions about his current situation. I thought we'd have a chance to talk over a relaxed dinner, but as we passed Bordeaux's gorgeous eighteenth-century theater, a scalper waved some tickets at him. "Verdi," said Carlos as he handed the man a wad of cash after a few minutes of negotiation. "Can you believe our luck?" After a hurried *croque monsieur* in the café across the street, we sank into our seats just as the curtain rose on *La Traviata*.

It wasn't until Sunday lunch back at Christophe's

that I slid the manuscript onto the table. "It's only seventy pages, but when it's padded out with a lot of pictures, it will make a respectable-sized book."

"This is very impressive," said Carlos, flipping through the pages. "What's does this mean?" He pointed to a passage. "He drew a picture on a cast? What does that mean? The cast of a movie?"

"The plaster cast that was on a little boy's arm. A little boy in Boston who'd broken his arm. It was one of the fan club stories."

"I broke my arm when I was ten. No one drew pictures on the plaster for me," said Carlos. "You've done a remarkable job, Melody, with little to work from. Unfortunately, it may be too late for my purposes. However, since the original book project was set into motion by my father before I was involved in it, there will not be any conflict about your payment."

"Why would there be a conflict? You're the only heir."

"No one is inheriting anything until the police are satisfied." He pushed some of Christophe's excellent risotto around on his plate. "Professors don't earn much, but that was never a problem for me. I got by perfectly fine. Then my mother's condition deteriorated, and just when it looked like a private clinic was the only answer, all of this crazy money drops into our laps."

He shook his head. "There's been so much red tape to battle that I haven't had a chance to think about what any of this means to me. Why did this man, who ignored me all his life, make me his heir and executor? Thanks to him, I'm a member of the one percent that I've fought against all my life." He lifted his glass, but this time he put it down before taking a sip. "What would I have done with these tainted funds? I suppose I would have established some kind of foundation after making sure my mother was cared for. But now I'm in the middle of a criminal investigation, suspected of murder."

"But the coroner said it was an accident, didn't he? Your father was drunk, and he fell off the boat, right?"

Carlos shrugged. "If he was drunk and unsteady on his feet, it would be relatively simple to push him off the deck."

"But how could the police prove that?"

"Normally they would dig up the body for an autopsy. But they can't do that, can they? Because the body was cremated."

"Whose idea was that?" I asked.

"Mine." Carlos lifted his glass. "Since the miserable bastard left no instructions for his funeral, the lawyers asked me what to do. I told them to burn the bastard to Hell and that I would be honored to light the first match."

He clinked his glass against mine. "If the police haven't already confirmed that fact, they will soon. You see how this is going, Melody? I hated him, I needed money, and I inherited all of his. Death threats were mailed from my post office. I was alone in Bordeaux with no alibi on the night that he died. And there is no longer any forensic evidence to investigate because I had it destroyed."

"Carlos…" I began.

"Melody, I really meant what I said the other night. We should not see each other anymore. Not until this is settled. I have nothing to offer you except problems."

"No one is going to convict an innocent man, and I'm not leaving you just because times are tough." I grabbed his hand and squeezed it. "You hated your father, but that doesn't mean you killed him. You were in Bordeaux that night? Well, so what? Lots of people were in Bordeaux that night. As far as I can see, the only solid links to Madrid are the letters, and anyone could have posted them."

"Do you really believe that?" He stared at the red checked tablecloth.

"Anyone in Madrid," I repeated confidently. "It's a public post office, and anyone can buy a stamp."

"That's true." When he finally looked up, his eyes were grim. "That's why the police also suspect my mother."

Chapter Forty-Five

I held his hand as tightly as I could in the taxi. When he dropped me off at the train station on his way to the airport, I plastered on my biggest phony grin and told him that everything would be all right. He lobbed an equally radiant smile right back at me and said he was sure of it.

We were both lousy liars. I was worried about Carlos, and he was worried about his mother. She already telephoned five times since last night, and each phone call plunged my lover into a deeper, darker Iberian gloom. Carlos hadn't told me much about her medical condition except that the doctors in Madrid were mystified by it. Would the police be equally mystified? Or would they interpret her post-funeral overdose as a sign of guilt?

I did an internet search of death threats while Carlos was shaving this morning. French law didn't play lightly with *menaces de mort*—six months in prison was mandatory. And if Charles-Henri's death wasn't an accident, someone was guilty of his murder as well. I stared out the window at a blur of greenery as the train raced north toward Paris.

Death threats…prison…murder…

I wasn't lying when I told Carlos I believed in his innocence. I could practically hear my sister screaming at me, *That's just because you're sleeping with him!*

And yes, that was right. Carlos was so kind and gentle in bed it was impossible for me to picture him throwing someone off a boat. But what could I do to prove that to someone who hadn't been kissed by Carlos? Carlos had no alibi for the night in question, he was getting the money, and he'd never made a secret about hating his father. Except...

I thought back to all the happy faces at his funeral. There was no shortage of people who despised Charles-Henri Banville. If I could make a list of all the people who held grudges against the actor, it might take some of the heat off Carlos and Carmen. *Faster,* I whispered to the train. All I had in my arsenal were those little black books. Bertrand knew about the diaries, so it was only a matter of time before he requisitioned them.

I started photocopying the diaries on Marie-Christine's printer as soon as I got back to the Paris apartment. I didn't even stop for lunch, refusing to pause until the last stack of paper was collated. I breathed a huge sigh of relief and resumed reading where I'd left off. In February 2015 Charles-Henri was filming *Adeline* with Manon Dupont in Grenoble while carrying on a steamy long-distance affair with Charlene Trent in California. *AF 66* was scribbled in red. I checked the Air France site...yes, that was the direct Paris-Los Angeles flight. I penciled the info in the margin.

Dr E—botox. It figured. He was playing second fiddle to a fourteen-year-old kid in a TV movie and romancing a twenty-two-year-old starlet. The flattering English-language memoir he'd hired me to write was merely the final flourish on a well-planned career reboot. Thanks to his dermatologist, he'd already made the first down payments on a fresh, unwrinkled face.

I flipped ahead a few years to the final entries which were penned two weeks before we met. I might never know what he'd thought of me that night, but now that I'd cracked his code of stars and underlines, I might be able to pinpoint some situations that upset him.

Like this one: *MD has gone too far!* What was that about? Hold on...MD again three days later, but this time he'd scratched the sum of 5,000 euros next to the initials. The number was underlined five times, an indication of extreme displeasure. Words like "idiot," "ugly," "stupid," and "frigid" were invariably underlined but usually only once or twice.

MD.

Manon Dupont?

It had to be her. I sat back in my chair and tried to get my mind around the story that suddenly looked all too clear. Blackmail. Hush money. Charles-Henri couldn't keep his hands off any woman he met. But this time the female in question was barely fourteen years old. He hadn't even dared to put any stars next to her name in his diary.

I pulled up the *"Adeline des Alpes"* poster on Wikipedia. Manon, her reddish hair tied in tight braids, looked achingly innocent and as pure as the white snow in the background. Charles-Henri had been charmed enough by her to buy her a fancy birthday present. Undoubtedly, he'd been grooming her for an assault.

But he didn't get away with it, did he?

Someone was blackmailing him. Manon herself? Her parents? Somebody on the set? I did another internet search. There was no shortage of Manon

Duponts online, "Dupont" being the French equivalent of "Smith," but none matched the bright-eyed, auburn-haired girl who costarred with Charles-Henri Banville on the telefilm. No social media accounts. That didn't make sense. She couldn't have vanished.

Unless something had happened to her?

I picked up the phone and speed dialed Bertrand. "You've got to find Manon Dupont," I told him. "She'll be the answer to everything."

Chapter Forty-Six

Bertrand made an appointment for me at five o'clock that afternoon at a police station in the 8th arrondissement, a few blocks north of the Champs-Elysées. As I'd expected, he asked that I bring the diaries with me, and after passing through security, an officer at the reception desk directed me to a small courtyard office cluttered with stacks of file folders, piles of Xerox paper, and a plethora of used Styrofoam coffee cups.

"Thank you for your call, Melody," said Bertrand, rising from his desk and closing the file he'd been reading. "You have become quite the expert on Charles-Henri Banville, haven't you?"

"I'm just doing research like I would on any project." I looked around the office. Bertrand's English-language grammar books were lined up on the shelf, and the wallet-size picture he'd shown me of his children was framed in an 8x10 chunk of plexiglass on the desk. "I thought you'd retired?"

"Ah, shall we say, I have been recalled to service on this particular case. Please take a seat. Would you like some coffee?"

I nodded, and he pressed a button on his desk. A uniformed officer materialized in an instant and took our order. Bertrand chit-chatted about the Paris weather until the coffee arrived.

"Now, Mademoiselle, tell me about this Manon Dupont. Why does she interest you so greatly?"

"She was making a television movie with Charles-Henri in the Alps—"

"When was this?" Bertrand interrupted.

"In 2015, from February until late March. And he gave her a birthday present, an expensive one, and that's very strange in itself."

"It wasn't her birthday?"

"Yes, it was her birthday, but he spent 1,500 euros on it."

"Gifts for leading ladies can be costly," said Bertrand. "Furs, jewels…"

"She was only fourteen, and he never bought gifts for his other lovers. According to all other accounts, he was remarkably cheap."

"May I see this entry?"

I spread the notebooks on the desk and opened the relevant one triumphantly. I'd marked the page with a blue sticky note. "Here it is."

"*Merci*," said Bertrand. His smile faded as he scanned the page. "How on earth do you read these things without a magnifying glass?" He pulled his desk lamp closer as he flipped through the pages. "I only see three references to money."

"Exactly. He didn't make notes about what he spent for restaurants, transportation, or clothes. He only did it when there was something fishy about the payment."

"Fishy?" prompted Bertrand. "What does that mean?"

"Unusual. Like when he paid someone to sleep with Ingrid Svenson."

"Ingrid Svenson? The fashion mannequin?" asked Bertrand in disbelief. "Why would he do something like that?"

"She was pregnant, and he didn't want her children. It was an attempt to discredit her claim for child support."

"I see." Bertrand frowned. "If I am following your line of thought, you also think that there is something— what was the word?—'fishy' about this relationship with Manon Dupont?"

"Charles-Henri preyed on women, all women. It was a compulsion for him," I said. "The relationship with Manon Dupont didn't work out well because there aren't any stars next to her initials. You see, he rated them after he seduced them."

"Like restaurants?" asked Bertrand, making a tsk-tsk noise with his teeth. "Perhaps there was simply no relationship with Manon Dupont."

"But the payments start after they worked together. The figures next to MD, they're not regular, but they get bigger and bigger. It had to be some kind of extortion."

"These notations may *possibly* relate to extortion, but there is not yet any proof. What did Mademoiselle Dupont say when you asked her about this?"

"That's the problem. I can't find her. It's like she dropped off the planet. She'd be twenty years old now. What twenty-year-old doesn't have any social media?"

"The police have better resources than you do. We will find her, do not fear. In fact," he continued, "I am more worried about you, Mademoiselle. You appear to be very tired and overcome of stress. You must relax and let the police work. There will be plenty of time for

you to write your book after the investigation is finished."

"It's true that I haven't been sleeping very well," I admitted, "but it's hard to relax when Carlos is suspected of any of this."

"Carlos?" Bertrand looked blank for a moment. "Ah, yes, the young Charles-Henri Banville calls himself Carlos Ortega, doesn't he?" His fingers strayed to a thick file on the table, but he slid it under another before I could see what was written on the cover. "In many ways, he is a most appealing young man."

"You've met him?" This was a surprise. "You went to Spain?"

"Why should I go to Spain? He's in Paris."

"In Paris?" I sank back into the chair.

"I took his fingerprints a few hours ago."

"But…" I couldn't process this. Carlos was in Paris? No way. He had a ticket on the ten o'clock flight from Bordeaux to Madrid this morning.

Carlos had no reason to lie to me.

But neither did Bertrand.

I twisted the bracelet around my wrist and looked at the policeman. His face was perfectly impassive. Had his colleagues been waiting for Carlos at the airport? Was that why Carlos hadn't answered any of my texts today? And they'd taken his fingerprints? My heart went completely cold. "Any evidence you have is purely circumstantial. You've no right to arrest him."

"Arrest him? *Quelle idée,* Miss Melody! Carlos Ortega has not been arrested. Nobody is arrested. In fact, I will need your fingerprints as well. We must account for everyone who was present in the apartment on the Avenue Foch, including myself, the concierge, and the cleaning lady. I asked for the set of keys that you used. Did you remember to bring them?"

I rustled through my purse on autopilot. "Where is Carlos staying?" I asked as casually as I could while Bertrand zipped the gaudy Gucci keychain into a plastic evidence bag.

"If he has not told you, that is not my information to divulge. However, as a man, I respect his decision to protect you from involvement. While he is not under the arrest at this time, he is, he is…" Bertrand thought for a minute. "He is, as they say on your American detective shows, a perp of interest."

"He's not a *perp*," I said with a little more edginess than necessary. "Perps are criminals. I think you mean he's a *person* of interest."

"*Oui, c'est bien cela*," said Bertrand, tranquilly jotting the English words down on a notepad. "Person of interest," he repeated. "Indeed, Carlos Ortega is a person of extremely great interest to the police. If you permit, I will speak to you as I would speak to my daughter. Keep a safe distance from him while we proceed."

Chapter Forty-Seven

Like so many totally run-of-the-mill interactions in France, there was a faint whiff of sexuality in the air when the handsome young police officer pressed my fingertips into an inkpad fifteen minutes later. I couldn't compare the process to American methods because after ten years in Manhattan I'd never been inside a New York police station.

What had happened to my quiet little life? A few months ago, I defined "crisis" in terms of printer jams and kitty barf on the rug. An "exotic" evening was frozen lasagna and a foreign movie on PBS. Now I was halfway around the world dealing with a murder investigation, a dead movie star, and a mysterious, drop-dead gorgeous boyfriend.

Of course, the drop-dead boyfriend was more like a deadbeat boyfriend right now. Had he checked into one of the city's seven zillion hotels? Was he staying with friends? Aside from the restaurant guy in Bordeaux, I didn't know any of his friends. What did I really know about Carlos anyway? He liked museums, he liked pizza with anchovies, he liked Spanish wine and Italian opera. Up to now, I thought he liked me too, but apparently, he could forego the pleasure of my company quite easily.

I, on the other hand, ached for his touch, his voice, his arms wrapped around me, shutting out the world in a cocoon of bliss. I stood in front of the police station with no idea where to go next. Normally, I'd go home and work, but that wasn't very appealing right now. Instead, I made my way to the nearest café. That's one of the great things about Paris. There's always a café around when you need one.

But once I sat down, I had no idea what I wanted. It was five o'clock. Too early for a cocktail and too late for lunch...unless you were Carlos. Coffee would keep me up all night, and I never cared for herbal tea very much. The late afternoon sun played on the facets of the sapphire in my bracelet as I studied the menu. Sapphire for honesty. Sapphire for trust. Sapphire for loyalty. When the waiter came by for the second time, I ordered a Perrier and checked my email.

There was a message from the Banville lawyers asking for my bank details so they could make a wire transfer for the sum of 20,000 euros. You couldn't fault Carlos for follow-through on his financial commitments. I thought about sending him a thank you note for expediting the payment but refrained. It would just be another message for him to ignore.

I keyed the euros into the calculator on my phone. That was over 22,000 dollars! I'd been playing footsie with overdrafts for years, so this windfall represented a major change in my life. I wished I could celebrate with someone.

I wished I could celebrate with Carlos.

My telephone pinged. "Are you up for a really early dinner tonight?" Jenna asked. "There's a hot Italian place in Montparnasse, and the editor wants the info for tonight's podcast."

I thanked her and got the address, madly grateful

not to be going home to an empty apartment. It would take me just about an hour to walk to the restaurant, and the exercise would help counteract some of the heavenly tiramisu, pasta primavera, panna cotta, and whatever else that Jenna was bound to order for us. Now that I was not officially poor anymore, I might even pop into a few shoe stores on the way.

The one thing I wouldn't do tonight, I told myself, was be a total bore about any Banville business.

Easier said than done. I must have passed fifty double-wide posters for "*POP 1980: Le Concert Cool*" along the way. That meant I was running into giant-sized images of Delphine Carroll and a bunch of other aging French rock stars on almost every block. The four-night Paris gig opened tomorrow night at the Olympia concert hall, and the posters were all slapped with bright yellow "sold out" stickers.

I wasn't looking forward to interviewing Delphine. Unlike Ingrid and Charlene, who were good girls at heart, Delphine was pure poison. As far as I was concerned, she was evil enough to deserve her relationship with Charles-Henri. Although I'd have to speak with the wicked witch sooner or later, later would be better. I justified this by telling myself she'd be less distracted and more accessible for an interview after the concert tour was over.

Jenna waved from a corner table as soon as I entered Mamma Lola. The table was already overloaded with food. "Tomato-mozzarella salad, fried calamari, and roasted eggplant," she said after we greeted each other with traditional French kisses. "We've got pizza and red-pepper risotto coming next. Do you like peppers?"

"Love them." As I slid into the seat, a waiter filled my glass with bubbly pink wine.

"So how are things with Carlos?" she asked.

"Not so good," I said after sipping my wine. "We're taking a break from each other."

"What a bummer," said Jenna. "I'm really sorry it didn't work out."

I stared at her in disbelief. "What do you mean? You never liked Carlos. You told me he was a spoiled mama's boy."

"Yeah, but if he killed his daddy, he can't be all bad."

"What do you mean?"

"Don't you ever read the papers?" Jenna rustled in her purse and pulled out a copy of *Le Parisien*. The cover of the color tabloid showed Carlos exiting the same police station where I'd just met Bertrand. At least he wasn't sporting handcuffs.

At least not yet.

"Does it say he killed Charles-Henri?" I scanned the headlines for a clue.

"No, they're just questioning him. You never said he was so hot. I can see why the editor used his picture on the front page. That's a face that will move a thousand papers."

"Carlos is a lot more than a pretty face." I tried the eggplant parmesan. "This is over-salted."

"Don't change the subject. This book of yours is getting more interesting by the minute. When are you seeing Delphine Carroll? You said she nearly punched Carlos out in Cannes?"

"I thought I'd wait until after her concert tour wraps up."

Jenna put down her fork in dismay. "It's now you have to see her. *Now!*"

"If I wait until after the concert tour…"

"After the concert tour, it'll be long-distance." Jenna took the paper from me, inadvertently dragging my lover's picture into the salad dressing as she turned to the arts section. "See that? Delphine's got solo concerts scheduled in Germany, Belgium, and Switzerland, and she's hinting about Las Vegas."

I studied a picture taken of Delphine right after she won the Pan-Europe Trophy. Despite shoulder pads worthy of a Dallas Cowboys linebacker and the shaggy, super-gelled hairstyle popular in the day, she projected a delicate, waifish charm. That was long, long ago.

"She should write a thank you note to whoever whacked Banville," continued Jenna. "It's given her sorry old career a mega-boost."

"Yeah, I know. Her concerts are all sold out."

"Not when you know the right people." Jenna picked up her phone and pressed speed dial. "Michel? Yes, I'll hold." She held her hand over the mouthpiece. "This is the benefit of having a big family. I've got masses of relatives in useful places. My cousin is covering the opening for *Libé* even though he hates that granny music. *Oui, Michel*, remember the American writer I told you about? The one who's dating the Banville boy? Can you get her in to the Olympia tomorrow night?"

I started to protest.

"*Oui, Michel, c'est parfait.*" She rang off. "It's all set. Concert ticket and backstage pass." Jenna took a bite of the eggplant and made a face. "Damn, you're right about the salt. This stuff tastes like it was marinated for three weeks in the Atlantic Ocean. Now…do you think Delphine will attack you backstage?"

"I hope not," I said. "She outweighs me by fifty pounds."

"Michel will be hoping for a real catfight. That way, he can report on something other than the music."

Chapter Forty-Eight

When you write a memoir for a living person, you never know the "end" of the story. People can change jobs, get divorced, switch political parties, or move to Argentina and open a ranch two days after the book is printed.

Charles-Henri's story, on the contrary, had a beginning, middle, and a very definite end. I just didn't know what kind of end it was. A tragic accident? Cold-blooded murder? Crime of passion? The outcome of the police investigation would have a definite impact on the tone of the biography I intended to write.

As promised, his old schoolmates from Rouen mailed me a thick packet of their personal childhood memorabilia. While I doubted that the local PTA had taken out a contract on the actor after his refusal to make a public appearance to raise money for the village school, it was clear from my initial interview with Véronique and Jacques that Charles-Henri haters had been around since kindergarten. Could the poison pen letters stem from some silly playground grudge decades ago but not forgotten?

While I was sorting a stack of old school photos, Jenna's cousin Michel texted with the address of the café where we'd meet before the concert. It was near the Garnier Opera, but thankfully it was not the Café de la Paix. That place would always mean Carlos to me.

Last night, after leaving Jenna, I did send a brief text to say the wire transfer was in progress, but there was no reply. Even a one-word answer would have encouraged me, but I guess Carlos knew that. He gave me no encouragement at all.

I dressed carefully for my rendezvous with Michel. Skinny jeans, my favorite green tee shirt, my trusty denim jacket because the nights were still cool, and a pair of beige platform sandals. I took extra time with my makeup and tied my hair back into a ponytail with a silk scarf. I wasn't doing this strictly for Michel. It was mostly about holding my own with Mean Delphine.

Of course, I might also walk extra slowly around the Café de la Paix, just in case anyone I knew was sitting at a sidewalk table. Carlos had chosen that mythic restaurant for both of our first two meetings. Was it a sentimental choice? Or simply convenient? I had to add that to the many things I didn't know about him.

A good-looking, thirty-something man with sandy-blond hair and flashy designer glasses waved at me as soon as I entered the café. "Jenna sent me the selfie you two took last night," he said. "I'm delighted to meet you." We ordered two glasses of the rosé of the day, and Michel added a plate of tapas "just to tide us over."

His English was nowhere near as perfect as Jenna's, so we chattered away happily in French. Michel was primarily a music critic, but like most journalists he had an eye for a story, and right now the fresh investigation into Charles-Henri's demise was the talk of Paris. He quizzed me on all the people I'd met so far and gave me a few useful contacts, notably the singing coach that Charles-Henri hired while preparing for the Broadway musical he did in 2012.

Carlos was the red meat that all French journalists wanted to sink their teeth into right now, and Michel was no exception. I stopped short of giving him Carlos's private phone contact, but I did furnish his office number at the University of Madrid, which Michel could have easily found out on his own.

We had so much fun that we had to race-walk to make it to the concert in time. Michel was exactly the kind of good-looking, well-dressed French guy that Abby wanted me to meet. Yes, he had a family but no, he didn't hate his family or call his mom twenty times a day. He visited them in Chartres, one hour from Paris, once a month for a cheerful Sunday lunch and helped out with their garden in the summer. Apparently, we both had landscaping in our blood.

When we sank into our red-velvet orchestra seats, he told me to wake him up if he started to snore. "Everything they'll sing, I've heard a million times." Since the songs were new to me, I quite enjoyed the show. It was clear that Delphine, dressed in fringed black leather, was the star among the stars tonight. She had more solos than the others and got bigger applause.

She'd had very long, sharp-looking, rhinestone-studded false nails applied to her fingertips since I'd seen her in Cannes. They glinted under the spotlights like tiny crystal machetes. Now I had an additional reason to keep her at least three inches farther away than arm's length.

Michel roused himself after the last encore and pulled two backstage passes from his pocket and handed one of them to me. "I've got to check in with at least five of these guys for my story, but I want to hear

Delphine's spin on the Banville case too. If we get separated, let's meet at the entrance at"—he looked at his watch—"eleven, and we can get a nightcap?"

Backstage, corks were popping, and little plates of shrimp toast and mini-pizzas were handed around. Michel was quickly dragged into a corner by a stringy-haired rock singer in faded blue jeans, and I was on my own. The singers were there to meet the press, and since I had no assignment, I held back. The crowd around Delphine was three deep. I edged a little closer, hoping against hope that she might not remember me.

She did. When I was four feet away, she shot me the kind of look that would make a saber-tooth tiger cringe. She held up a silver-tipped finger, pointed to me, and then at her watch. For some reason, she wanted to talk. I slunk back toward the buffet table and pretended to get a phone call. Of course, I had a huge mouthful of shrimp toast when she made her way over to me. She stared at me contemptuously while I chewed, sending a clear message that the act of swallowing was obscene.

"Where's that Spanish piece of shit?" she asked.

The fact that Carlos and I weren't in contact anymore could only do me good in her eyes, so I used it. "No idea. Haven't heard from him."

"He's dropped you for someone hotter?" Delphine lifted a steel-gray electronic cigarette to her lips and inhaled deeply. "Like father, like son." When she exhaled, I thought I caught a whiff of brimstone. "You're better off. Who needs a jailbird for a boyfriend anyway?"

"He's not in jail."

"Not yet," advised Delphine. "Are you still writing

that book on my ex-husband?"

"Actually—"

"Can I have your autograph, Miss Carroll?" interrupted the barman, holding a pen and paper to Delphine.

"Of course." She smiled, signed her name, and drew a big heart around it. She kept the pen and scribbled a phone number on my wrist. "Call my agent, and he'll set up a time. I've got dirt you wouldn't believe."

Michel was at my side within minutes. "I'm so disappointed. She didn't even lay a hand on you."

"She sure did." I pushed up my sleeve and showed him the number. "She wants me to call her agent to set up an interview."

"Good on you," he said. "Dinner? Drinks?"

"I think I've OD'd on shrimp toast," I told him. "Raincheck?"

"No problem." He gave me four of those kisses that don't mean anything in France when we parted at the metro station, and we made tentative plans to catch a movie next week. It had been a pleasant night on the whole and a boon on the professional front. No bio of Charles-Henri would be complete without quotes from Delphine, and it looked like those were in the bag.

As the metro wound its way through underground Paris, I texted Jenna my heartfelt thanks for setting up the concert date. Before she could reply, my email alert pinged. "We found Manon," Bertrand wrote. "Shall we meet at your café tomorrow? At noon?"

"Absolutely," I wrote back.

Manon's story was bound to be sordid, even by Charles-Henri standards, but right now I welcomed anything that would get Carlos out of police scrutiny. As soon as Carlos was safely off the hook, we could hook up again. I fell asleep as soon as my head hit the pillow. Carlos and I would be together again very soon.

Chapter Forty-Nine

Bertrand had his nose buried in the menu, but he looked up and smiled broadly when I arrived. "May the French police invite you to lunch?" he asked.

"To what does the American teaching establishment owe the honor?"

"You are much more than an English teacher to me, Melody. You are my very valuable confidential source. Therefore, I must maintain your health and welfare with food and wine."

Alberto wandered over and told us that the day's special was salmon cooked with creamed sorrel. I'd tried sorrel, an edgier French version of spinach, last week, and liked it.

"Sounds perfect," I said.

"Make that two," said Bertrand.

"A carafe of Chablis?" asked Alberto.

Bertrand nodded. "And a bottle of mineral water, please."

"Well?" I asked when Alberto left to place the order. "Where is Manon? Why did it take so much time to find her?"

"Ah! That is because we couldn't find out 'where' she was until we knew 'who' she was."

"I'm not following."

"Manon calls herself 'Mandeepa' now. She lives on an ashram in a remote region of northern India."

I sank back in my chair. This was worse than I thought. If she was hiding in a monastery halfway across the world, Charles-Henri must have totally traumatized her. "Were you able to talk with her?"

"Oh yes," said Bertrand. "When Mandeepa Dupont begins to speak, it is almost impossible to stop her. Especially when the subject is Charles-Henri Banville."

Alberto put the carafe of wine on the table and opened the mineral water with a flourish. Bertrand filled our water tumblers and poured a half inch of wine into his glass.

"Well?" I asked impatiently even though I'd learned by now that nothing could rush a Frenchman when the rituals of food and wine were in play. "What did that sex-crazed maniac do to the poor girl?"

Bertrand tasted the wine and pursed his lips in approval before filling both our glasses. "She claims that Charles-Henri Banville saved her life."

"Then she's telling you a pack of lies." I picked up my glass and drained half of it in one gulp.

"I don't think so." Bertrand refilled my glass. "Mandeepa says the whole purpose of her present incarnation is a search for truth and purity."

"Purity and Charles-Henri? That doesn't sound like the truth to me."

"She says there were a lot of drugs on the set of *Adelaide des Alpes* and that when Charles-Henri discovered that the man who did *le maquillage...*" Bertrand looked at me for help. "What is that word? The person who puts on the lipstick and the powder?"

"Makeup," I said. "The makeup artist."

"When Charles-Henri discovered that the makeup artist gave her cocaine to make her stay alert, he was furious. Charles-Henri took the girl under his wing and warned her of all the dangers of show business. She says that Charles-Henri was like a father for her."

"So why did she extort all that money from him?"

"Mandeepa does not believe in material possessions and has relinquished all of her bank accounts. *Bon appétit*," he added as Alberto brought two plates of grilled salmon to the table. He tasted the fish and smiled in satisfaction. "If indeed those numbers in the diaries refer to payments, they were not made to Mademoiselle Mandeepa Dupont."

"But she accepted expensive gifts from him, didn't she?"

"Ah, yes. He bought two ridiculously expensive Shih-Tzu puppies for her birthday. Those dogs are now living with her on the ashram. It appears they have developed a fondness for curried lamb."

Unfortunately, Manon's pretty little story rang true to me. Child abuse was just about the only sin for which Charles-Henri didn't stand accused. The Shih-Tzu anecdote clinched it. A fondness for small domestic animals figured in many accounts of the actor's life. I finally had an authentically "nice guy" story about Charles-Henri, and it was too late to help Carlos very much.

"How is the work proceeding with the book?" asked Bertrand.

"I met Delphine Carroll last night. She'll be my next interview."

"*L'Amour, l'amour.*" Bertrand hummed a few bars, and I recognized the tune immediately because Delphine got a standing ovation when she sang it last night. "We danced to *L'Amour, l'amour* at my wedding," he added. "Did she say anything of interest?"

"She just told me to contact her agent to arrange an interview." I'd tried calling twice this morning, but there was no answer. Given Delphine's delightfully winning personality, she might have steered me to a nonworking number on purpose. "We haven't managed to connect yet."

"The divorce of Charles-Henri and Delphine was extremely ugly," said Bertrand. "There was no love lost between Miss Carroll and the victim."

"That's an understatement." I filled him in on the vile accusations Delphine flung at Carlos in Cannes.

"An interesting but illogical chain of thought," said Bertrand as he mopped up some of the sorrel sauce with a chunk of bread. "The young man named Carlos was not yet born when her marriage fell apart."

"She still holds him responsible for the death of her baby. She thinks Carlos and his mother, both of them, ruined her life."

"You must be careful when you are with Delphine Carroll," said Bertrand. "People with such a loose grasp of facts can be dangerous."

"You think that she might have written the letters?" If Manon was off the hook, I'd be happy to substitute Delphine as criminal-in-chief.

"The police are considering many possibilities," said Bertrand. "It is unfortunate that the last diary entry we have from Charles-Henri was written so long before his death."

"The diary wasn't on the boat?"

"It was in his pocket when he fell overboard. Unfortunately, the ink dissolved away in the water. We have sent it to a specialized forensic laboratory in

Lille." Bertrand shrugged. "We must wait to see if these experts can salvage anything."

"In the meantime, I'll keep looking through the diaries we have. I'm sure that I can turn up something that can help."

"If there is a killer at the loose, it is better for the police to deal with that person than a... what are you again?...a spirit author."

"Ghost writer." The relief I felt made the fresh salmon taste even better. The police were spreading a wider net which meant that Carlos was no longer the one and only suspect. "Can I ask you a question? Now that we know that this wasn't about blackmail..."

"Do not jump on that conclusion so quickly," said Bertrand. "We do not believe that Mademoiselle Mandeepa was involved in extortion, but our experts are still troubled by strange bank withdrawals in the account of the deceased. We must look carefully into anything unpleasant or unusual in the life of the victim at that time the withdrawals begin. You have studied the diaries of Charles-Henri Banville. Does anything come to your mind?"

Unpleasant? Unusual? By screwed-up Banville standards, early 2015 was an oasis of calm. No nasty libel suits. No harassment charges. Steady work. Although *Adelaide des Alpes* certainly wasn't the highpoint in his career arc, Banville was finally racking up some good karma by unselfishly mentoring a struggling child actress.

"Not really," I said. "For once, he seemed happy. According to the director of *Adelaide,* he never held up production with tantrums and fights. In fact, he was looking forward to getting married to Charlene Trent."

"He was planning to marry Charlene Trent?" asked Bertrand. "*Mais non*, that's impossible."

"I think he really cared for her."

"He may have cared for her," said Bertrand, "but he couldn't marry her."

"Why not?" I asked.

"Because he was still married to Carmen Ortega."

Chapter Fifty

How had I forgotten about Carmen? More to the point, how had Charles-Henri forgotten about her? And, even more to the point, how had I forgotten to check out whether there was a divorce or annulment on the record? I was losing my edge. Was it because I'd fallen in love with my major source for that data? It was downright embarrassing that Bertrand had to fill me on a vital piece of information that I should have fact-checked weeks ago.

As soon as I got back to the flat, I dug into my notes. The word "wedding" came up in virtually all my conversations with Charlene about Charles-Henri. Naturally, I assumed that the circled capital "M" in Charles-Henri's notes about his phone calls to Los Angeles meant "marriage."

Press clippings from early 2015 backed that up. Editors of celebrity magazines definitely took the wedding rumors seriously. I found a two-page story on the Cha-Cha Challenge in early 2015, and there was an inset picture of Charles-Henri and Charlene in a round-up entitled "For Whom the Wedding Bells Toll."

I made myself another cup of coffee. Did "bigamy" have any meaning for a big-time sinner like Charles-Henri? If he saw his relationship with Charlene simply as a means to enhance his US image, he didn't need to marry her either. Their love affair was enough to generate oceans of ink by itself.

Except…I couldn't quite believe that it boiled down to a coldhearted PR ploy. As I'd just told Bertrand, Charles-Henri lived an unusually scandal-free existence while he courted Charlene. In his sex-rated diaries, no stars appeared next to any female names except hers during their courtship. On the *Adelaide* set, he behaved kindly to a troubled kid instead of throwing his own tantrums right and left.

Charlene gave me the impression that she protested a bit too much when she claimed that she'd never loved Charles-Henri. After the breakup, she went on an epic bender, crashing two cars in a week, a record even for her. Call me a hopeless romantic, but I think that when those boozy train wrecks crossed paths, they honestly fell in love.

They could have found some kind of colorful cult figure who could preside over a "pretend" ceremony if they really needed the white-dress-and-tux photos. But even a rent-a-priest from the Church of Eternal Isley Brothers would be bound to ask if there was anyone present who knew that Charlene and Charles-Henri could not be joined in holy matrimony.

I tried to imagine the chaos if Carlos showed up. Or worse…? What if frail, black-veiled Carmen did her Iberian Gothic number, clutching a bouquet of faded roses in her wasted fingers? Charles-Henri couldn't take a chance like that, not if he was hoping to rebuild his career in Hollywood with a feel-good photo-op. He'd unleash a PR nightmare. The honeymoon with the press would have been over before it began.

Not that there were any honeymoons on my horizon either. I'd nourished more than one fantasy about marrying Carlos, and look how well that turned out for me. Yesterday's mail brought me a thick envelope from the Beach Zombies production office, a thank you note from Taneesha for my help in Cannes, plus an 8x10 color photo of me and Carlos on the red carpet in Cannes. A photo that was taken only a few hours before we fell into bed together.

Every time the phone rang, I hoped it was Carlos. I had to stop setting myself up for disappointment, right? The phone rang, and I grabbed it, once again expecting to hear his voice. Expecting some kind of explanation for the radio silence he'd enforced. No such luck. Unfamiliar number and an unfamiliar male voice.

"Mademoiselle Layne? Delphine Carroll will be able to see you for thirty minutes tomorrow at four in the afternoon." He rattled off an address in Montparnasse and rang off without bothering to enquire if the time and place was convenient for me.

It was. All I had going for me right now was this book, and Delphine was a key interview. I'd been through all the recent press about her, and most of it was soft soap. Her parents were from Mantua, and she loved Italian food. She dreamed about playing Las Vegas. She enjoyed long walks on the beach. If you ask me, that was probably because she liked hanging around with sand sharks and moray eels. Her favorite color was blue. Her favorite movie was *The Sound of Music*.

In short, there was nothing in print that painted her as the high-octane viper I'd met in Cannes. As I pulled out my Delphine Carroll files for a night of pop princess prep, I wondered what kind of Italian food she liked. If I brought some take-out ravioli from the Italian place down the street, she might be persuaded to nosh on that instead of my entrails.

Chapter Fifty-One

Thirty minutes go by pretty quickly in an interview situation. I was so scared of missing one second of my allotted time that I parked myself in a café across from Delphine's lair fifteen minutes ahead of time. From the outside at least the apartment building, housing a greasy-looking burger joint on the ground floor, was a far cry from the splendor of Charles-Henri's lodgings. Delphine was the bigger star when they broke up, so she wouldn't have cashed in on alimony. Charles-Henri didn't finalize the big movie contract that made his career until right after the divorce.

The inside lobby wasn't any more upmarket than the façade. The avocado vinyl padding in the elevator was slashed in many places, its cheesecloth backing peeking through, and the metallic accents had been keyed with tags and rude graffiti. There were three apartments on the fifth-floor landing, but the door on the right was ajar, so I headed there.

"Miss Carroll," I called. No one answered, so I pushed the door open and entered. One of Delphine's songs was blasting from the CD player, so she probably hadn't heard me. The apartment reeked of cigarette smoke. Stacks of sheet music were piled on an upright piano. I profited from the solitude by taking a panorama picture of the surroundings. Cell phones make décor notes obsolete.

A Niagara-ish toilet flush drowned out the chorus of *L'Amour, l'amour,* and Delphine emerged from a door marked with a porcelain "WC," rubbing her hands on her yoga pants. "Stupid cleaning lady," she muttered. "She always forgets the towels." Side-stepping an open suitcase half-filled with rumpled clothes, she slumped onto a black leather couch. "At least you're on time."

I pulled up a chair and set my voice recorder on the coffee table. "It's very kind of you to see me."

"Someone has to tell the truth about the bastard. Let's not waste time by pretending that he had any redeeming qualities, okay?"

"But there had to be some good times," I said coaxingly as I pressed the record button. The story depended on a few pre-divorce anecdotes about marital bliss. "When you first met, you must have been in madly in love with each other."

"Madly in love?" The fat Yorkshire terrier I'd seen at the funeral waddled over to the sofa, and Delphine leaned over and scratched its head. "Charles-Henri wanted to feed on my fame. And I wanted children. That's all I've ever wanted. I wanted my perfect blond children." Delphine rummaged between the sofa cushions. "He was so beautiful. He promised me those children." She unearthed a crumpled packet of cigarettes and lit up. "No children for me. But with the Spanish slut? With that Swedish bitch? Children."

"I'm sorry…"

"He wasn't sorry, and that's what sent me over the edge. They were sleeping in my bed. Did you know that? That Carmen bitch, who was paid to wash and iron my clothes, was wearing my fanciest pink satin nightgown when I found them. Did you know that?"

Actually, I did. Delphine flung that story, minus the fabric specifics, at Carlos in Cannes. "Carmen is twisted, you know what I mean?" Delphine had switched to present tense somewhere along the line. "She's not just mean and sly, she's not right in the head. She was crazy for Charles-Henri. And Charles-Henri, well, we weren't having sex. Not with my history of miscarriages. Carmen figures she's got a clear field, and while I'm at the hospital for my pre-natal tests, she—" Delphine stubbed out her cigarette in an already overcrowded ashtray and stood up. "You know, I can't talk about this anymore. We're done. Goodbye."

She'd barely given me five minutes!

I learned nothing new, and if she was planning to sing in Berlin tomorrow night, she'd be leaving Paris in a matter of hours. "I know this is painful to talk about, but it's very helpful to have your side of that story," I said in my most soothing, pseudo-psychiatrist voice. "Otherwise, you see, I'll be depending too much on Charles-Henri's impressions of that time."

"What impressions?" Delphine peered out at me from behind the rumpled tissue that she was using to dab at her seemingly dry mascara. "That bastard never told you a single thing. You said it yourself. He was dead before you even got to France."

"I've been digging through his diaries, and they provide a very clear idea of what went on in his head." The diaries didn't start until long after the divorce, and I hadn't run across any entries with DC initials. Delphine, however, didn't know that. "His diaries have been enormously helpful, a virtual window into his soul," I added as I wriggled into my jacket. I slipped the recorder into my pocket but didn't switch it off.

"You're making that up," said Delphine. "He never kept a diary. I lived with that monster for three years. I'd know."

"He didn't start writing them until the 1990s," I said. "After that, he made notes about everything and everyone. Rehearsals, restaurants, parties, even dental appointments." I was at the door, but Delphine was right beside me, her steak knife fingernails digging into my sleeve.

"You actually have them?" she asked in the sultry whisper voice that had driven countless love ballads to the top of the charts. "These diaries, you have them?"

"Not anymore," I said, resisting the impulse to pull away in case her claws snagged the fabric. "I'm working with photocopies. The police have the originals."

"The police?" Delphine edged even closer. I could smell stale tobacco on her breath and in her hair. "They're getting ready to arrest that Spanish bastard of his, aren't they?"

"I have no idea." Sadly, that was the truth. "Thank you for seeing me," I said as I gripped the door handle.

"But we must see each other again. I have so much more to tell you." A few minutes ago, she'd blown me off, but now she was all come hither. "I'll be flying back to Paris between the Berlin and Brussels concerts. Do you have a card? That way, I can contact you directly."

Happily, I did have cards with my French contact info. I'd ordered them from an internet site a few weeks ago, and I was quite pleased with the design accent, a stack of books and quill pen, next to my name, address, phone, and email. I proudly handed her one, and she stuffed it in her pocket.

"Wait for my call," she said, returning to her go-to nasty persona as she slammed the door in my face.

Chapter Fifty-Two

I love French food. I just don't mess with cooking it. It's no fun when there isn't anyone to share it, and it's even less fun to eat in a restaurant when there's nobody across the table. I was counting the days until Jenna got back from her vacation in London. I discovered a French chain store that specialized in gourmet frozen meals, so on most nights I repressed my Julia Child fantasies and tossed a pack of readymade *jambon aux endives* or *poulet aux amandes* into the microwave.

I was choosing between frozen chicken and frozen scampi when I got a text from Michel. He was having lunch tomorrow in the Bastille district with Lisette Lacoste, the vocal coach who'd prepped Charles-Henri for his first singing role in 1998. Did I want to join them? Of course, I did. He sent me the name of the restaurant, the time, and we made a date. Since there wasn't much to transcribe from my ten-minute Delphine interview, I watched television and made it an early night.

I spent the next morning researching Lisette Lacoste. She'd been a very successful soprano before taking up fulltime tutoring, so I watched several of her performances on the internet. While no opera aficionado, I had to admit that she made a bang-up job of dying on canopy beds while belting her heart out to the balcony.

After an hour of Puccini and Rossini, I got out the "2010-2012" diary file and turned to the weeks before the opening of the *Père Goriot* musical. With great satisfaction, I penciled Lisette Lacoste next to the numerous "LL" entries that had puzzled me before. Another mystery solved. I was pleased to see that there were no stars scribbled next to her initials either. Apparently, Charles-Henri hadn't put the moves on his teacher. It would be a relief to get a Banville interview from someone without a sexual axe to grind.

It was with a happy heart that I entered the Grandes Marches, a brasserie nestled into the white-tiled façade of the modernist Bastille Opera building on the east side of Paris. Michel waved me over to a corner table as soon as I entered. After he introduced me to Lisette and ordered a platter of shellfish, the three of us chattered away like old friends. "Lisette's teaching a master class today," Michel told me. "People come from all over the world to work with her."

"Chinese mezzo-sopranos," said Lisette, wheedling the flesh out of a crab claw with diamond-laden fingers. "Mostly accents and enunciation."

I was in awe. I'd never seen anyone lick their fingers with such panache. If you dialed Rent-a-Diva, Lisette would be the five-star premium option. Her silver-gray hair fell nearly to her waist in luxuriant waves, and the fringed velvet shawl draped over her shoulders wouldn't have been out of place on the set of *La Traviata*.

She was also a fountain of gossip about the latest opera management reshuffle, Michel's subject for his paper's weekend edition. It was a pleasure to watch him sweet talk Lisette into confiding all she knew about the cut-throat, behind-the-scene dramas that rivaled anything on stage.

It wasn't until we'd nearly finished our main courses that Michel introduced the subject of my Banville book. Lisette was off and running with very little prodding. "Not much range and no previous training, but Charles-Henri worked hard." She gave me more than I needed about the technical aspects of the *Père Goriot* score but provided excellent insights into the actor's work ethic. When she dashed off after scarfing down a *baba au rhum* dessert in double time, Michel and I ordered coffee and spent a few minutes silently organizing our notes.

One coffee followed another. It was clear that Michel saw me as something more than a colleague, but why wasn't I more excited by that prospect? On paper, Michel was perfect for me. He was a charming journalist with a completely normal outlook on family relations and no criminal charges hanging over his head. Michel also came with Jenna's AAA seal of approval. Was I *that* hung up on some moody Spaniard who didn't give me the time of day? Yeah, I guess I was. Nevertheless, I made a movie date with Michel for Saturday night. If Carlos decided to contact me at the last minute for a wild weekend of sex and salsa, it was too bad for him. I'd be busy.

I loaded up on groceries on my way home, so it was nearly dark when I pushed the elevator button at my apartment, looking forward to a nice long shower and a quiet dinner. But my door swung open even before I turned the key in the lock. I never leave home without checking the lock at least three times, so I was prepared for the worst before I peeked inside. The worst, however, was far worse than I imagined. It looked like a traveling tornado decided to rearrange the furniture. Before even crossing the threshold, I fished out my phone and speed-dialed my favorite man with a badge.

Chapter Fifty-Three

"Don't go in the apartment," he instructed. "Wait for an officer to arrive." Bertrand didn't sound nearly as shocked and sympathetic as I'd have liked, but I guess career cops are used to break-ins. For me, it was a first. I moved to the far end of the hallway wondering exactly what Bertrand expected me to do if the intruder made an exit? Whack him in the face with a sack of frozen broccoli quiche? It turned out that I didn't have much more than five minutes to worry about that. Two strapping young officers bounded up the stairs with guns out. Happily, the local precinct was only two blocks away.

They entered the apartment cautiously, guns pointed to the floor just like in the TV shows, and gave each other an all-clear after checking the bathroom and bedroom. However, that apparently wasn't an invitation for me to join them, so I cooled my heels in the corridor along with my rapidly defrosting dinner. One of the officers snapped photos of the door lock while the other checked the windows and the balcony. It wasn't until Bertrand arrived that I was allowed to enter my girl cave. It wasn't until then that I started to tremble.

Bertrand sent the officers to interview the neighbors. I could have told him that the two other tenants on my floor left at dawn and rarely came home before midnight, but I felt too blitzed to tell him that. I wandered around the apartment. It was mess. Drawers overturned, papers everywhere. Bertrand sat me down at the kitchen/dining room table, found a glass in the cabinet, and poured me a tall glass of chardonnay from the open bottle in the fridge.

"Is there anything missing?" he asked, opening a small notebook. "Cash? Electronics. Jewelry?"

"What money I have is in my wallet. And I don't have any jewelry. Not real jewelry... well...except for this." I looked down at Carlos's sapphire bracelet. "Everything else I have is just plastic junk from the mall."

"I observe that the television set is still here. Your computer?"

"I had my laptop with me."

"And you left the apartment at...?"

"A little after noon. I had a lunch date down at the Bastille. I just don't...all this mess..."

"Quite obviously, they were looking for something. Are you absolutely sure there's nothing missing? Try and remember. What was the exact state of the apartment when you left it this morning?"

I stared at the tabletop, bare except for the wineglass, the jam jar with my colored pencils, and Bertrand's notebook. "I was working here at this table." I closed my eyes and tried to reimagine the scene. "Wait a second. Where's the file?"

"The file? What file?"

"The folder with my photocopies of the 2012 Banville diaries. It was open on the table when I left." I swiveled the chair around to the bookcase. The manila folders for the other years had been neatly stacked on top of it this morning. There was nothing there.

"They're gone! All my photocopies! All my notes!" Tears were tickling my eyes. "Weeks and weeks of research notes. All gone."

"*Du calme*, Mademoiselle. We have the originals at the prefecture. We shall of course permit you to make new copies." I took the paper napkin that Bertrand handed me, and when I finished wiping my eyes, I noticed that his were gleaming. In fact, he was smiling much too broadly given the situation. "Mademoiselle," he said, opening his notebook, "who knew that you possessed these diaries?"

Chapter Fifty-Four

I took a long, cold swig of white wine while I contemplated those nasty implications. Random theft was creepy enough, and I was already mentally wiping every surface the intruder might have touched with bleach and scouring pads. But if someone took the diaries? That meant that this crime had been committed by someone I knew or, at any rate, someone who knew of me.

"Who did you tell about these diaries?" asked Bertrand again. "Think back from the beginning when you arrived in France."

"I didn't even know he kept diaries until Charlene Trent mentioned them. That was during the Film Festival in May. But I didn't tell her that I found them."

"That would seem to eliminate Mademoiselle Trent, but we will check on her whereabouts," said Bertrand. "Who else?"

"I asked Ingrid Svenson about them."

"The model?" Bertrand wrote down her name. "What did you tell her about them?"

"I just asked her if she knew about them. I haven't spoken with her since I found them. The revelations about her are really painful."

"What sort of revelations?" asked Bertrand.

I could keep the story out of the book, but I couldn't keep it from the police. After all, they had the diaries. "Charles-Henri paid someone to seduce her when she thought she might be pregnant. He did it so he could claim she'd been unfaithful and muddy the child support waters. Ingrid is obsessed with the idea that her children are the result of this one-night stand rather than Charles Henri's. It's why she's always resisted paternity tests."

"Ah yes, I think you mentioned that before," said Bertrand. "Who else?"

"You. My sister Abby in New York. Jenna Bardet, the food blogger, but she's been really encouraging about the book. Besides, she's in London," I added, pointing to the postcard of Big Ben that I'd pinned on the bulletin board.

"Do you have her contact number?"

I punched her name on my phone and handed it to him. "I mentioned the diaries to Delphine Carroll yesterday, but she knew nothing about them since he didn't start writing them until years after their divorce. And I told Michel Bardet, the music critic. I think that's it."

"No one else?"

"It's not something I'd broadcast. Those diaries are my personal scoop. I'm basing most of my research on them."

"Are they so valuable that another writer would want to steal them?"

Oh Lord, why was every new possibility worse than the last? I went to the fridge for the Chardonnay and got another glass from the dish rack. "Join me?"

Bertrand shook his head. "I'm on duty."

I refilled my glass to the brim. "It's not just what Banville wrote down in his agenda. It's all the notes I wrote in the margins. Anyone who's got those photocopies has my all of my research."

"I doubt that you have anything to worry about that, Mademoiselle. I have—what is the word? A hunch. This has been an insider's job, but this insider does not intend to write a book."

I thought it over. "The problem with that is that I told you about everyone, and they all have alibis. My sister's in New York, Jenna's in London, Delphine's got a concert in Berlin, and I was having lunch with Michel this afternoon while this happened."

"That's not exactly everyone, is it?" said Bertrand. "Are you not forgetting Carlos Ortega?"

Damn.

He was right.

It was the very first time I'd forgotten about Carlos Ortega in weeks.

Chapter Fifty-Five

Bertrand left shortly after the officers came back to report that none of the neighbors had heard or seen anything. The officers stayed until nine, filled out the paperwork that they said I would need for the insurance, and stayed until the locksmith arrived. I was on the phone for an hour with Marie-Christine, who was very matter-of-fact about the break-in. I faxed her the police report and the locksmith's bill since she said she'd handle the insurance claim from New York.

After getting the official police blessing to clean up, I scrubbed the counters and sorted what paperwork I still had until I was too weary to keep my eyes open. It was just the living room that had been trashed. Thankfully, nothing appeared to be out of order in the bedroom or bath, but I changed the sheets and towels on principle. In fact, I even burned a sprig of rosemary in the sink since I'd read somewhere that the herbal smoke can banish evil spirits. I checked the new chain-lock at least five times while I was brushing my teeth and fell asleep before I'd finished my chamomile tea.

Having dined on half a bottle of white wine and a pot of tea, I woke hungry as a horse the next morning. The broccoli quiche I'd intended to eat for dinner last night had partially thawed while the detectives did their work, so I popped it in the microwave and wolfed it down. Not exactly breakfast material, but it was good. I read the New York Times on my laptop and listened to old Beatles songs while I ate. I didn't want to think about last night right away because I really didn't want to go where those thoughts were leading.

It wasn't outside the realm of possibility that someone else overheard me talking about the diaries. I'd discussed them with Jenna and Michel over drinks and dinners in restaurants. Lots of people eat in restaurants, right? But it was a big "if" to think that we'd been sitting near enough to someone whose interest in Banville's scribbles would push them toward crime. I didn't think that Jenna or Michel would have mentioned anything to anyone intentionally either. As journalists, both of them understood the precious nature of private sources. I truly didn't think they'd betray that trust.

Delphine was my personal pick for an orange jumpsuit modeling career, but she'd never made a secret of her contempt for Charles-Henri. It was hard to imagine her getting any satisfaction from anonymous death threats. Public shit fits, like the one she staged at Cannes, were more her style. And what was her motive? Bertrand kept harping on about the money. As an ex-wife, Delphine didn't stand to see a red cent from the Banville estate. The big winners, the only winners, on the cash front were Carlos and Carmen.

As usual, Carlos didn't have a convenient alibi, or any kind of alibi at all, for yesterday's break-in. I'd shamelessly checked out his teaching schedule on the university website last week and discovered that he didn't have any classes at all this summer. He could be anywhere. "*Carlos, Carlos, Carlos,*" I muttered to myself. "If you wanted the damn diaries, all you had to do was ask me for them. But that would involve talking to me, wouldn't it?" I raised my finger and pointed to the framed portrait of us taken in Cannes, all I had left of Carlos. "Seeing me is not what you…"

I broke off because our Kodak moment wasn't on the kitchen counter anymore. C'mon…now his *photograph* was hiding from me? Impossible. The cops must have moved it while they were looking around. After a few minutes of TSA-worthy searching, I realized the picture just plain wasn't there. Everything else on the kitchen counter was in its proper place— napkins, paper towels, coffee machine, sugar bowl, candle. Only the picture was AWOL.

l made another cup of coffee but let it cool while I collected my thoughts. Who would want a picture of me and Carlos…except Carlos? He'd break into my apartment like a coldblooded thief and then get warm- and-fuzzy enough to steal a souvenir of our relationship? That made no sense at all, but when you came down to it, what made sense about Carlos? The guy was a puzzle wrapped in an enigma with a hundred crazy strings attached. And what *really* made no sense? I felt the teensiest bit thrilled that he still cared enough about us to steal our picture.

The police, however, would be delighted for another reason to implicate Carlos Ortega. It was another handy hunk of hemp for the noose they were already knotting around his neck. Did I want to present this evidence to them on a silver platter? No…but I couldn't lie to the police either. I cased the apartment again, hoping against hope that a less Carlos-oriented object was missing as well. No dice. It wasn't like I could put off contact with the police either. I really needed to make those photocopies if I was going to continue working on the book.

I didn't have much time to second-guess my motives or my emotions because the phone rang a few seconds later. After inquiring whether I had slept well, Bertrand asked if I'd like to come to the prefecture in the afternoon. I said yes but didn't add anything about the missing photo. Somehow, before our two o'clock appointment rolled around I hoped to come up with an explanation that didn't involve Carlos Ortega or kleptomaniac space aliens.

"Carlos, did you take our picture?" I texted. "It's important."

I didn't expect an immediate reply, but I got one.

MESSAGE BANK FULL.

It was getting harder and harder to love that man.

Chapter Fifty-Six

Bertrand wasn't back from lunch when I showed up promptly at two o'clock, but one of his assistants gave me a plastic box with the diaries, still with my colored post-its attached, and showed me to a small room with a high-tech copy machine. It had fancy options that allowed me to enlarge the journal pages with Charles-Henri's ant-size scribbles significantly while still leaving plenty of room for margin notes. Research would be easier on the eyes from now on. However, I didn't feel like planting a kiss on the thief's cheek for that little bonus. Even if the thief was a maddeningly gorgeous Spanish hunk.

Copying took the best part of an hour, but I hadn't come up with a theory that exonerated Carlos when I'd tell Bertrand about the missing picture. On the positive side for Carlos, cops dealt with motives. I honestly didn't see any criminal motive for Carlos to take the diaries or the picture. I hoped they didn't either.

When I was showed into Bertrand's office, he didn't give me an opening to speak my piece right away. "We have confirmed all of the alibis," he said. "Mademoiselle Jenna Bardet is indeed in London, and Delphine Carroll was in rehearsals in Berlin all day yesterday. Ingrid Svenson is vacationing on the yacht of her fiancé in Bermuda, and Miss Charlene Trent is currently filming 'Beach Zombies IV' in South

Dakota." Bertrand paused and looked at his notes. "Are there any beaches in South Dakota?"

"I don't think it really matters. All those people are off the hook?"

"Not necessarily," said Bertrand. "It is always possible to hire another person to perform disagreeable little chores."

There was no time like the present, so I told him about the photo. "Interesting," said Bertrand when I finished. "A picture of you and Carlos Ortega?"

"Yes, but I don't think that means Carlos is the criminal who broke into my apartment."

"I never suggested that. I merely stated that this is an interesting development." He shuffled through a pile of folders and extracted one. "By any chance, did Mr. Ortega ever speak to you of his mother?"

"He's very devoted to her."

Bertrand opened the file. "Yes, they live at the same address."

"Her health is very fragile," I volunteered. "Carlos wants to send her to a specialized clinic in Switzerland because the doctors in Madrid haven't been able to figure out what she has."

"The doctors know perfectly well what she has." Bertrand extracted a legal-size page from the dossier. "The poor woman suffers from *esquizofrenia*. She was diagnosed with it twenty years ago."

"Schizophrenia?" What else had Carlos been less-that-truthful about?

"Delusions, suicide attempts, minor acts of aggression. Her doctors have recommended a secure mental institution, but that has been opposed by her son. He has kept her in her own home, with private nurses, at considerable personal expense. He appears to be a very loyal and courageous young man."

Loyal. Courageous. For now, I'd leave all the Carlos-oriented compliments to Bertrand since my own adjective list was topping off with *conniving, lying,* and *duplicitous.* Why would he hide the facts about his mother's health to me? And why, under the circumstances, did I still feel some shred of loyalty to him?

"I didn't have the details about Carmen Ortega's health issues until this morning," Bertrand continued. "Obviously, this information changes many of the legal aspects."

"Legal aspects?"

Bertrand looked at me in surprise. "The diagnosis of severe mental illness, combined with no communal life for decades, would allow Monsieur Banville to obtain a divorce without his wife's consent."

"He could have married Charlene Trent after all?"

"And if he had, the bulk of his estate would have passed to her instead of his son. We must, obviously, always keep our eyes on the money."

Once again, the money led straight to Carlos. "I still don't think he did it," I said to myself as much as to Bertrand.

"Did what?"

"Anything. Everything. Broke into my apartment. Wrote letters. Killed anyone. Besides the fact that I'd have given the diaries to him right away if he asked, he knew where I kept them. Right on top of the bookcase. He wouldn't have needed to toss my place."

"Only someone who was looking for something else would have reason for such a search."

"But what else could they want? They took all the diaries I have."

"Yes, but the diaries you have, the last entry is many weeks before the death of Charles-Henri, *n'est-ce pas*?"

"But that's because the one he was writing fell in the water and got ruined."

"*Exactement*," said Bertrand, once again flashing the cat-with-a-canary grin that I found so disconcerting. "Somebody doesn't know that."

Chapter Fifty-Seven

Did Carlos know that? That's what Bertrand kept asking, over and over again, and I honestly had no idea.

"One time, when I said I didn't know where to start reading, he told me to begin at the beginning. He never even wanted to look at them. He hated everything his father had touched."

"You did inform him of where and when you found the diaries?"

"Under the mattress in Paris? Yes."

"Then he would certainly be aware that you didn't possess the latest diary. The current diary would have been with his father in Bordeaux. Did Carlos ever ask you if it had been traced?"

I shook my head. "As I said, he never showed any interest in what his father wrote. That's good, isn't it? I mean, about not being guilty."

Bertrand shrugged. "What is perhaps more in his favor is that he made no attempt to visit the marina while he was in Bordeaux. It would have been logical to search the boat where his father died."

"While he was in Bordeaux? The weekend we were in Bordeaux? You were following him?" Bertrand studiously avoided eye contact. "You were following us?"

"The police in Bordeaux may have made that decision. I was not yet officially involved."

Even though I was sitting down, with my feet firmly planted on the floor, I felt dizzy. I'd been tailed by the police as I wandered through southern France with my handsome Spanish lover? A Spanish history professor who might moonlight as a cat burglar, a poison pen, and a murderer? That sort of thing happened to people in books, but not in the sort of books I write. I'd occasionally been puzzled by the frequency with which shipments of Scandinavian area rugs fell off trucks when I worked on the bio for the CEO of the carpet warehouse, but I'd never come close to anything like this.

Back in New York, I saw a mugger crouching behind every trash can, a rapist lurking in every alley. Far from my Manhattan discomfort zone, had I allowed the scenic charms of Paris to erode my edge? Had I been so bedazzled by contact with celebrities that I'd lost all my natural inhibitions? Back home, the "normal" Melody Layne erred on the side of caution in personal relationships. In France, for the first time in my life, I'd fallen into bed with a man I hardly knew. And I'd fallen for him so hard that, despite the fact that he'd lied about too many things to count, I still cared for him.

"This situation is indeed very complicated, Mademoiselle," said Bertrand, echoing my thoughts. "It would be wise not to schedule any more interviews about this book of yours until I have a better idea about the way in which this case is proceeding."

"No more interviews?" Even though I longed to whack the first draft into publishable form quickly, a timeout from all these angst-ridden Banville anecdotes would be welcome. "That's no problem," I told him. "I have enough to work on for the moment."

"This matter should resolve itself soon, but until then please let me know if anyone contacts you about Charles-Henri Banville. In fact," he added, "why not check in with me every day?"

I was surprised by just how relieved that made me feel. As a crime victim debutante, I appreciated having someone, especially a well-armed someone, watching my back. All I wanted to do right now, however, was head back to my lair. If I passed an animal shelter on the way, I'd probably adopt a big dog with giant teeth.

I stopped at an office supply store on the way home to buy a holepunch and a four-ring notebook. On my return to my apartment, I fastened the shiny new chain-lock and got to work. Twenty minutes later, I had a tabletop covered with holepunch confetti and a lime-green notebook filled with Banville's diary pages.

I certainly wasn't going to write "Top Secret Banville Diaries" on the label. I needed something that would bore people. No, I needed something that would convince them that the notebook was nothing but bullshit. Bingo! I scribbled "Bovine Diarrhea: Causes and Cures" and pasted it to the spine of the notebook before sliding it into the bookcase.

I hadn't checked in with my sister for a few days, and that was weighing on me. Abby was not going to like the burglary story at all. Since it was cocktail hour in France, I poured myself a glass of Chardonnay first. Abby launched into a rant about alternate-side-of-the-street parking near Saint Luke's hospital as soon as she picked up, so I let her vent for a good five minutes before telling her about yesterday's events.

Surprisingly, she took the robbery story pretty well.

She was happy that I had a friend in the police and didn't seem too troubled about the loss of the Banville files. "You've got the copies, right? You'll be fine." On the other hand, she became seriously unglued when I filled her in on Carlos and his mother. "Let me get this straight. He told you that she'd never been diagnosed?"

"Several times," I said sadly, "although I don't know why he didn't tell me. It's not her fault if she's ill."

"Look, I don't just deliver these drugs. I have to know when and why they're prescribed, and let me tell you, schizophrenia can be a big bouquet of bad if it's not treated correctly. If this woman goes off her meds, she might do anything."

"There was an attempted suicide a few weeks ago. She was hospitalized."

Abby sighed. "Some research suggests that there's a genetic component. If Carlos is worried about his own health and sanity, he'd have an additional reason not to confide in you. Try and draw him out on that the next time you see him."

"The next time I see him probably rhymes with never. He's not even answering my calls anymore."

"That," said Abby, flashing me a thumbs-up from a parking garage in uptown Manhattan, "is the most encouraging thing I've heard about the guy so far."

Chapter Fifty-Eight

Restoring my margin notes in my new Banville photocopies was less difficult than I'd feared. All those previously inscrutable initials now represented real people. "IS" signified the beautiful-but-betrayed Swedish model Ingrid Svenson; "CT" corresponded to his Hollywood heartthrob Charlene Trent; and "MD" was Manon Dupont, the troubled child-star he'd mentored. What was once a series of question marks had fleshed out into a three-dimensional story.

The problem?

I didn't like the storyline one little bit. I still wanted Carlos Ortega to be the hero, and it's pretty hard to cheerlead for a guy who chases you off the playing field. "Secretive" and "uncommunicative" don't necessarily imply "guilty," but they don't inspire confidence either. Both Bertrand and Abby had warned me against him. Jenna actively promoted her cousin Michel as better boyfriend material. If I started a Carlos fan club right now, Carmen and I would be the only members.

I looked down at the notebook page I was working on. I tried to forget about the warm Parisian sunlight that poured through the windowpanes and imagined myself in a remote Alpine cabin, on a freezing winter night, in the early days of the actor's relationship with Ingrid. I'd tracked down the location of the tiny chalet he'd rented, and thanks to receipts that he'd tucked into his books, I knew three of the mountaintop restaurants where he'd indulged in cheese fondue and white wine, presumably with Ingrid Svenson, when he wasn't two-timing her with the (still unidentified) Anne-Marie who'd left her number on the lipstick-smudged napkin I'd found tucked in one of Charles-Henri's countless reference books about Arctic snow.

Ingrid...yes. She was another person who liked Carlos. In fact, she'd called him "generous and honorable" after their discussion at the Vichy gala. She rejected the financial provision Carlos proposed for her sons, but the very fact he'd made any offer at all threw a wrench in Bertrand's "follow the money" investigation. If Carlos had been willing to make a settlement on Lars and Erik when Ingrid hadn't even asked for anything, it was proof that he wasn't entirely motivated by greed, wasn't it? I needed to fill Bertrand in on that detail as soon as possible.

I flipped forward to the Manon/Mandeepa era when Charles-Henri started to make mysterious payments that were linked to the initials "MD". Bertrand was satisfied that Manon Dupont hadn't blackmailed the actor. Had he looked into the possibility that Charles-Henri might be making these payments "for" Manon? That someone was threatening her, and he was protecting her?

Try as I might, I couldn't make that theory fly. When Charles-Henri spent money, it was on himself. He liked fancy art, fancy cars, and fancy designer suits. He'd been quite cheap with girlfriends, and if Manon had been threatened, he'd probably contact the police and keep his own cash safely tucked in his pocket.

Besides, this was the period when he was hot and heavy with Charlene. He called her several times a day. If there was anything he was worried about, wouldn't he have shared it with her?

Unless this was all about Charlene?

I ruffled through the pages and highlighted the numbers that looked like payments with a yellow marker. The last time that "5,000 euros" showed up in the notebook, with characteristic angry underlining, was one week before his very public breakup with the Hollywood actress. Coincidence? Was someone that anxious to get the wedding canceled?

Unfortunately, that brought me right back to Carlos. Under French inheritance laws, Charlene would inherit the bulk of the actor's estate if they'd been legally married. As his son, Carlos would still receive something, but there was always the possibility that Charlene would have children of her own. As far as I could see, Carlos and Carmen were the only people who stood to gain by preventing Charles-Henri's marriage.

I needed some fresh air. Not only that, I needed to get away from this damn book and all of its unsettling implications. Since it was already noon, lunch at the café downstairs sounded like a perfect solution. I accessorized my faded jeans with a vintage Velvet Underground tee shirt and the pale pink ballet slippers I'd bought on sale last week. I knotted a gauzy, totally superfluous scarf around my neck as I headed down the stairs. I had never worn scarves in the summer before. Slowly but surely my wardrobe choices were getting Frenchier and Frenchier.

Alberto showed me to a window table and

convinced me to try the quiche of the day, tomato and goat cheese. Minutes later, he brought me a glass of Sauvignon and a slightly crumpled copy of *Le Parisien*, open to the sports pages. It was tennis season, and while I couldn't care less about serve-and-volley, I found myself checking out Rafael Nadal's rankings just because he was Carlos's favorite player. No…I had to stop doing things like that. I had to stop thinking about Carlos altogether. Surely there was something of interest happening somewhere in the world that had nothing to do with Carlos. I turned to the front page…and there was Carlos.

Tall, dark, handsome as usual, but sporting a very jaunty set of handcuffs on his wrists. He was sandwiched between a pair of burly Spanish policemen. Now was this the same bondage picture I knew and loved? No. This picture was taken last night. Carlos was wearing the same blue-and-white striped shirt I'd helped him pick out in a Bordeaux boutique a few weeks ago.

It looked very good on him.

"Is that your friend who dances so well?" asked Alberto peering at the headlines as he slid the plate of quiche on the table. "The cops think that he's a *corbeau*?"

For some reason, the French used the word for crow, *corbeau,* to designate people who send poison pen letters. I scanned the first paragraph in disbelief. "It looks like he's confessed to writing threatening letters to his father."

"So few people write letters anymore," said Alberto. "*Bon appétit!*"

In fact, I had no appetite at all. In addition to the

charges related to the threat letters, Carlos, my previously precious, adorable Carlos, was also under investigation for murder. The authorities in Madrid would hold him in custody until his extradition to France could be arranged.

My quiche cooled, untouched, as I read and reread the article. He confessed to those letters that he claimed to know nothing about? Did this man ever tell the truth about *anything*? The blue sapphire in my bracelet glinted in the sunlight. Trust. Honesty. Loyalty. Right. I didn't even bother to unfasten it. I yanked it off so hard that the catch broke as it scraped my skin. I'd throw the damn thing in the trash. No, I'd throw it into the Seine. Not good enough. Not final enough. What I wanted was a live volcano so I could toss it over the rim into a boiling, hellfire abyss of molten lava.

No, even *that* wasn't good enough. I knew exactly what to do with it. I'd stuff the broken bracelet in an envelope and mail it right back to Spain. Carlos couldn't have made it any clearer that he was over our affair. I wanted him to know that it was over on my end too. No more texting. No more phone calls. He could rot in a Spanish dungeon for all I cared.

The phone chimed "*I will survive.*" I had to change that thing. *Hit the Road, Jack*?

It was Jenna. "Honey, I just saw it on the television news. The guy actually *confessed*?"

"To the letters," I said stubbornly since defending Carlos was still my automatic default. "Not to murder."

"He'll do time for the letters. You're over him, right?"

I looked down at the broken bracelet. "Loving him isn't a very smart idea, is it?"

"His loss," said Jenna. "You need a change of scene and a change of mindset. I'm going to review the five hottest restaurants in Dijon this weekend. Why don't you come with me?"

"Dijon? Is that where the mustard comes from?"

"It's one of the food capitals of France, and we can drink lots of Burgundy wine to celebrate your success."

"What success?" As far as I was concerned, "success" and "Melody Layne" weren't on the same side of the street right now. We weren't even in the same area code.

"Just think!" exclaimed Jenna. "You've been dating the daddy-killer son of an international sex offender! Anything you write about those disgusting Banville bastards will zoom right to the top of the bestseller list!"

Chapter Fifty-Nine

The French countryside is beautiful, even when you're racing through it at a mindboggling rate on the highspeed TGV train. Tidy farms, romantic manor houses decorated with stone turrets, and herds of marshmallow-white cattle chomping away to their heart's content in emerald-green pastures.

Jenna and I were in the first-class car. It was nearly empty, so we appropriated a club car configuration, four seats around a central table, for the two of us. Jenna, already in work mode, covered the table with glossy food magazines, tapping copious notes about the articles into her tablet.

She'd spent all Friday afternoon preparing for this weekend. She'd had discussions with her editor about the restaurants to be reviewed and made arrangements for the neighbors to feed and walk her ten-year-old spaniel. She'd canceled Sunday lunch with her parents, booked a hotel room with twin beds for two nights, and lined up the restaurant reservations.

All I did was pack a bag. My closest friends and family were so far away from France that the 300-kilometer distance between Paris and Dijon was meaningless to them. The only Parisian that I'd told about my weekend in the provinces was Bertrand, who was extremely positive about the idea. "A little vacation is just exactly what you need," he'd said. "Dijon is a magnificent city. You will love it." Even though he had my cellphone and email, he also wanted the name and address of the hotel Jenna had chosen. "When will you be coming back to Paris?" he asked.

"We've got a bistro lunch on Monday, and then we're taking the train at four o'clock," I replied.

"Excellent," he said, "that's excellent. Enjoy yourself very much."

It should have been easier to enjoy myself. The scenery just got better and better as the TGV train rolled through the fabled Burgundy vineyards. I had a juicy novel in my handbag, Jenna's great company, and the prospect of five free gourmet dinners in an exciting new town.

Instead, I felt like I was nine years old again, laid low by a horrible Monday homework assignment that drained all the fun from the weekend. I'd set myself a simple task. It was one simple gesture—sticking a piece of jewelry in an envelope—but that gesture would finalize my breakup with the first man I'd ever really, really loved. It was the only sensible, intelligent thing to do, but I just couldn't make myself do it.

"He's already broken up with you," Jenna pointed out. "Get it done before lunch. That gloomy face of yours will put me off my food, and I need to concentrate on what we're eating."

The five-star hotel where Jenna booked our room was only a short walk from the train station. She pushed me into the first stationary shop we passed, blocking the door with our rolling bags while I chose a blank greeting card with a drawing of a single rose for Carlos. She was notably less enthusiastic about my postcard selection, a trio of tabby-cats snoozing next to a big jar of Dijon mustard, but I couldn't resist. I bought five of them.

Since the room wasn't ready, we left our bags at the front desk and headed across town to the first restaurant, a gracious Michelin-starred dining room where giant picture windows opened onto a lush, well-tended courtyard garden. "I've got work to do," said Jenna, handing me a pen as soon as we sat down at a corner table. "You start writing."

She buried her nose in the menu, and I stared at the flowerbeds, hoping that Mother Nature would provide some inspiration. I had a good fifteen minutes ahead of me since Jenna would take her time deciding what to order for the two of us. Unfortunately, my mind was just as blank as the greeting card. The complimentary wine-and-currant-syrup cocktails that the waiter whisked in front of us didn't help either. I managed to address the envelope, but I dried up right after that.

Hoping to grease the wheels, I turned to the kitty-cat postcards. I had no trouble composing a message to Abby. No problem figuring out what to say to Sharon and Marty, my old East Village neighbors, either. But Carlos…Carlos…

"Give it to me," commanded Jenna. "No words at all is the most effective message." She slipped the bracelet and the blank card into the envelope, licked the flap, and produced a book of stamps from her wallet. She pasted five of them on the envelope, "for good measure," and when the sommelier showed up for our wine order, she handed him the envelope. "Can you ask someone at the front desk to post this?"

"*Bien sur*, Madame," he said, appropriating my darling bracelet as matter-of-factly as he took Jenna's order of white wine.

"Don't you feel better now?" asked Jenna when he left.

Not really. I felt empty. I reached for one of the pastries that the waiter had brought with the aperitifs, but cheese puffs, however satisfying, couldn't fill the void where my heart used to be.

"It's Michel's birthday next week," said Jenna. "We're getting a DJ and taking over the whole second floor of a cool organic pizza parlor near République. Michel really wants you to be there. You like him too, right?"

"Michel's nice," I agreed absently. How long would it take a letter to get from the Dijon post office to Madrid? Two days? Three days?

"My cousin's a whole lot more than *nice*. I'd go for Michel myself if it didn't seem incestuous." Jenna speared a chunk of parslied ham with a toothpick. "If I were you, I'd have kept the bracelet. After all the heartache that guy put you through, you deserve a little bonus."

My eyes were still on the envelope. The sommelier handed it to a busboy who scurried out the door with it. It was gone. My Spanish romance was a thing of the past.

"Carlos needs a bonus more than I do," I answered. "He can pawn it to cover his legal fees."

"That's generous of you," said Jenna. Her eyes gleamed as the waiter approached with a large silver tray. "You're having the scallops with cream and caviar, and I've got the salmon *millefeuille* with watercress and pearl onions. *Bon appétit!*"

Chapter Sixty

I did feel slightly better. Without that pretty little sapphire glinting at me every time I looked at my wrist, I was able to forget about Carlos for whole minutes at a time. After lunch, we went shopping for Michel's birthday present and, rather than buy two small presents, we pooled our resources on a fabulous pearl gray cotton sweater. We also popped into a few casual boutiques and bought ourselves new tee shirts. Mine was violet with white stripes; Jenna's was lavender with a navy fringe.

Paying for anything beyond bare necessities reminded me a little bit of Carlos. If he hadn't recommissioned the book on his father, I'd be living on day-old bread and store brand mineral water. Instead, I was in Dijon buying fancy designer gifts for a man I hardly knew. Of course, I hardly knew Carlos either.

After several hours of retail therapy, I treated us both to manicures in a teen-oriented boutique with a cartoon princess theme and a Lady Gaga soundtrack. I chose bubblegum pink with silver sparkles; Jenna opted for a black-and-gray polish combo that made her fingertips look like tiny granite gravestones. Back at the hotel, we slipped into our swimsuits and hit the in-house spa.

It was such a warm summer night that we walked to our dinner restaurant with our hair still wet. Unlike

Jenna, I hadn't gone the shampoo route after getting out of the pool. The faint scent of chlorine brought me right back to my suburban childhood days, and I wanted to keep that memory going as long as I could. After a dinner of *boeuf bourguignon* washed down with copious glasses of ruby-red, full-bodied Nuits-Saint-Georges wine, we stumbled back to the hotel and fell asleep so quickly that neither of us had time to find out if the other snored.

We split up after breakfast the next morning. Jenna, all business, intended to stay in the room until lunch so she could write up our first two restaurants "while everything we tasted is still in short-term memory." I picked up a bunch of tourist brochures at the front desk and decided to join a walking tour of the old city. We made plans to meet at our next restaurant at one o'clock.

I felt guilty about how much I enjoyed the tour. Carlos was always ready with his polished patter about French monuments...but the whole point of the story always reverted to something Spanish in a matter of minutes. It was quite refreshing to be in France and have the historical focus on France for a change. By the time I found the dingy little side street where our basement bistro was hidden away, I realized that I hadn't felt so relaxed and confident in weeks.

That, of course, was the cue for the fun to stop. Jenna was halfway through her first glass of Chablis by the time the waiter showed me to our table. "It's a pre-set menu for lunch, so we're both having the same thing," she told me. A few minutes later, the waiter returned with an enormous platter of gray shells that he ceremoniously placed in the middle of the table.

"*Escargots* with garlic and butter sauce are the big specialty of Burgundy," said Jenna. She picked up one the shells with a pair of metal tongs and dug into it with a tiny, pronged fork. She extracted a slippery black blob and sighed with content. "How did your mother serve snails in America?"

I looked at the platter with dismay. As a landscaper's daughter, I knew everything about snails except why anyone would actually eat the repulsive little pests. "We put pans filled with beer on the ground, and when the snails belly up to the bar, they get drunk and drown. Sometimes my dad grinds them up for compost."

"What a ridiculous waste of delicious protein." Jenna sniffed. "But at least the poor creatures die happy with the beer in their bellies." She excavated another hot mess from its shell and handed me the fork. "You should eat them before they get cold."

Close up, the shriveled-up snail looked and smelled about as appetizing as garlic-flavored ABC gum. "I know," I said, sneaking the repulsive glob into my napkin when she looked away. "The butter sauce is a bit too rich for me. You can have mine."

By the time the snails were gone and we'd polished off our double order of *coq au vin,* apple pie *à la mode,* and coffee, the morning's bright blue skies had faded to an ominous black. Neither of us had an umbrella, so we ducked into a movie theater and bought tickets for the newest Marion Cotillard release just as the first raindrops splashed down on the sidewalk.

I enjoyed the movie and was pretty proud of the fact that, except for several essential details, I'd followed almost all of the action. "I still don't understand how her boyfriend knew about the first husband…" My voice trailed off when the lights flickered on. Jenna was slumped down in her seat, her face as gray as her granite-colored fingernails.

"Let's get out of here," she muttered. "I need some fresh air." I held her arm since she wobbled slightly on the way out of the cinema. Fortunately, the rain had stopped. "What's wrong?" I asked, taking her arm.

Breaking away from me, she rushed toward the trashcan on the corner. I caught up with her just in time to hold her long copper curls out of the way as she retched into the plastic bin liner. "*Mon dieu, mon dieu, mon dieu*," she whispered before the cascades began again.

I had a handkerchief ready when she stood up again. Her skin tone had gone from gray to green, which was not in my limited medical knowledge an improvement. "Do you want a doctor?"

"Just want to get back to the hotel." She leaned against the trashcan and wiped her lips. I looked around downtown Dijon, not at all sure where we were. "Can you handle a taxi ride?"

"I think so."

Luckily, Jenna held it together through the taxi ride and the elevator to the fourth floor. However, she dashed into the bathroom and slammed the door as soon as we got to our room. I turned the television on as loud as possible to give her the sonic illusion of privacy.

When she staggered out of the bathroom toward the bed, she murmured, "Food poisoning."

I was already there since I'd spent the last ten minutes checking out internet health sites. "The main thing is to stay hydrated," I told her. "When you feel up to it, you can have some plain rice or dry toast."

"It doesn't make sense." Jenna crawled under the covers, still in her jeans and tee shirt, and shut her eyes. "Everything we ate was the same."

"Except the snails," I confessed. "I hid mine in my napkin when you weren't looking. The food websites say that snails can be quite bad for you if cooked improperly."

"As God is my witness, I'll have my revenge," mumbled Jenna. "That place is going to get a review that will send it back to the stone age. We've got a reservation at a bistro near the Darcy Gardens tonight, so if you want to go by yourself…"

"I'm not leaving you. There's always room service if we feel up to it."

Jenna spent most of the night in and out of the bathroom, and I didn't get to sleep until about three a.m. When I awoke four hours later, Jenna, still looking green around the gills, was studying the train timetable.

"Feeling any better?" I asked.

"Only about losing ten pounds in ten hours," she said. "I'm so sorry, Melody, but all I want is to sleep in my own bed in Paris and forget that food exists. Would you mind terribly if we went home early? We can come back and finish the story another day."

"That suits me fine," I told her. "It was great to get away from work, but I'm starting to miss it."

"Perfect. The ten-thirty train will get us to Paris by noon. I'll call the front desk and tell them we'll be checking out today instead of tomorrow."

Both Jenna and I slept through most of the train trip. She still was unsteady on her feet, so I insisted on going back to her apartment with her. I picked up her dog from the neighbor while she took a hot shower and got into bed. Having skipped both dinner and breakfast, I bought a cheese sandwich at a bakery on the way home. It was nearly three o'clock when I slid the key to my apartment into my brand-new lock. While the first part of the weekend had been loads of fun, I found myself quite pleased by the prospect of being alone again.

Except I wasn't alone. If the balding man who was rifling through the files in my bookcase hadn't turned around and looked at me with exactly the same horrified panic that I felt, I wouldn't have been so bold.

"Don't move," I said, pulling my phone out of my pocket. The man looked like someone I'd met before, but I wasn't in the mood for introductions. "Don't move," I repeated. "I'm calling the police."

"There won't be any need for that," said a familiar voice behind me. "The police, we are already here."

Chapter Sixty-One

Under other circumstances, it would have been distressing to have a high-ranked member of the police force puttering around my apartment, making himself totally at home. As it was, I simply sat in the kitchen like a zombie while Bertrand cut and plated my sandwich, retrieved a jar of mustard from the fridge, and made a pot of tea. Two uniformed men had already handcuffed Marius Dubrovski and accompanied him downstairs with the barest minimum of professional courtesy.

"Marius Dubrovski?" I asked through a mouthful of bread and camembert cheese. "What was he doing here?"

"He was the first talent agent that Charles-Henri Banville pushed aside when he received his first big contract," said Bertrand, reaching over to the counter for the sugar bowl. "At present, Monsieur Dubrovski is the close friend and business associate of Delphine Carroll."

"I saw them together in Cannes. Wait…could he be 'MD'?" I smacked myself on the forehead and then wondered why on earth people do that. It really hurts. "Was Marius Dubrovski the 'MD' with the money?"

"I must say, the police considered that possibility long before you did." He refilled my teacup. "He had many reasons to hate Monsieur Banville."

"But what did he have against me? And how did he get in here anyway?"

"How did he get in? Much too easily, since his brother is a locksmith. My men are having a very interesting conversation with Raoul Dubrovski right now. As to why Marius Dubrovski was here...?" Bertrand dropped a sugar cube in his tea. "It was a trap. I informed selected people of interest that you had recently obtained the last three weeks of Monsieur Banville's diaries."

"But I don't have them. They were destroyed, weren't they?" Bertrand stirred his tea and made no comment. "Or do they exist? Bertrand, do you have the diaries?"

"At present, that is not relevant." He dropped another sugar in his tea. "I planned to have this situation resolved before your return. May I ask what brought you back to Paris so early?"

"Bad snails. But about the diaries, do you...?"

"You must take care with *les escargots.* They can be very sneaky and slippery," said Bertrand, sounding suspiciously snail-like himself. "I apologize for this afternoon's inconvenience, but we considered all of the ramifications very carefully. This seemed like the best plan, and neither of us thought you would object."

"Neither of you?"

Bertrand's phone vibrated, and he lifted a finger to indicate that he'd been expecting this call. He nodded as he listened. *"Oui, très bien, très bien. J'arrive. A tout de suite."* He rose and reached for his jacket. "I must go now, Mademoiselle, although we have much to discuss. Perhaps you will come to my office tomorrow morning. Ten o'clock?"

"It's a date." As of the last thirty minutes, I knew less about Banville-gate than I did before and that, I realized, was not much at all. "I assure you," said Bertrand as he shook my hand at the door, "that everything is falling into place quite nicely. Have patience. You will soon be able to proceed on your future ghostbuster projects with confidence."

As soon as Bertrand left, I secured the locks on my door and proceeded to finish my camembert sandwich. I had no idea what to do next, so I binge watched French television until I was too tired to keep my eyes open. Jenna called around dinnertime to say she was on the road to recovery, but I didn't share the afternoon's events with her. Nothing made sense anyway. I just hoped that Bertrand would channel some serious Sherlock Holmes vibes tomorrow. If the butler did it, I needed to know. I mean, I *really* needed to know.

I showed up ten minutes early the next morning and was ushered into Bertrand's office immediately. He'd clearly put down roots since our last visit. There was, for instance, no need to send an assistant out for coffee given the shiny new espresso machine perched atop the file cabinet. Three pots of prickly cactus caught the rays next to the window, and a framed photo of a buff young couple in front of the Sydney opera house adorned the back wall. "My son, Jean-Yves, who will be married in Australia next year," explained Bertrand. "That is the reason that I am learning my English with you, for the voyage to Sydney."

Bertrand insisted on showing me all the features of the coffee machine, waxing eloquent on the virtues of the vanilla, chocolate, and hazelnut flavors. I was impatient for news but knew enough not to rush him whenever there were food and drink issues to be resolved. When, at last, I had a cup of mocha-scented decaf and Bertrand had a plain espresso—"I don't see the point of these flavors"—he produced a small paper bag filled with sugary neon-pink and emerald-green cookies and arranged them on a plate.

"I stopped at a North African bakery this morning. I have been thinking about the movie '*Casablanca*' this morning."

"Because you've rounded up the usual suspects?"

He smiled. "In truth, I was thinking of the song from the film. " 'Hearts filled with passion, jealousy, and hate,' those are the words, *n'est-ce pas*? There is very much passion, jealousy, and hate in this case. Even more than usual."

At last we were getting down to business. "You told me that this was all according to a plan. What was that plan? Did you expect Marius Dubrovski to show up at my place?"

"We were expecting someone," said Bertrand vaguely. "We had examined the bank records of Mr. Dubrovski. His cash deposits mirrored the withdrawals made by Charles-Henri Banville. This suggested blackmail to us, and we were also interested by the fact that Delphine Carroll was seen in Bordeaux at the time of Monsieur Banville's death."

"She told you that?"

"*Mais non*," said Bertrand, "but famous people, they cannot remain invisible in the age of social media, even if they choose to wear the big hat, the wig, and the sunglasses. We found pictures taken by her fans both on the streets of Bordeaux and at her hotel."

"You laid a trap for her too?"

"She was singing in Brussels last Friday night, so I arranged for a Belgian colleague to ask her some insignificant questions about her divorce. He also mentioned, in passing, that the last diaries had been found. She became quite agitated, he reported."

"If Charles-Henri intended to see her in Bordeaux, he'd certainly have written that down." I sank back in my seat as I reflected on what this meant. "Did she kill Charles-Henri? Did she push him off the boat?"

Bertrand's expression reminded me of the way my cats bared their fangs before they pounced on a catnip mouse. "Murder may be difficult to prove at this time. However," he added, with a cheerier grin, "she was not so careful about the death threats. We have found the detective whom she engaged to post the letters from Madrid. He was also paid to make regular reports on Carlos and Carmen."

"Are you saying that Delphine Carroll wrote all the death threats?"

"Not all of them," Bertrand answered. "Many people disliked him, but she is most certainly involved in the letters that implicated Carlos and Carmen Ortega."

"Then why did Carlos confess?"

"Ah," said Bertrand, "it did look like someone wanted very much to convince the police that Carlos murdered his father for monetary gain. But there was, how shall I say it, there was too much evidence pointed toward him. With Mr. Ortega under arrest, other people might relax and make errors. And of course," added Bertrand judiciously, "if Carlos Ortega was indeed guilty, he was in jail where he belonged."

"But that's terrible! You accused someone publicly

of a crime and locked him up when you had no evidence? I don't know how things work in Europe, but in America I think Carlos could sue you for false arrest."

"But why on earth would he do that?" asked Bertrand. "It was all his idea."

Chapter Sixty-Two

I spent a lot of time at police headquarters over the next few weeks. Bertrand set up a little table in his office so I could be on hand as the resident Banville diary expert, during which I developed a liking for, and nearly depleted, Bertrand's supply of vanilla coffee. I also made a deposition, and when my notebooks (and the Cannes red carpet photo of me and Carlos) turned up during a search of Delphine Carroll's Montparnasse apartment, I was summoned to a basement in order to identify them as my property.

"I don't see why they wanted my picture," I told Bertrand during one of the rare moments he shared a coffee break with me. He was spending much of his time in Bordeaux these days.

"You apparently convinced Delphine Carroll that you and Carlos Ortega were no longer together. Monsieur Dubrovski retrieved the picture in order to prove that you were not to be trusted on that account. For the moment," Bertrand added, "your notebooks and the photograph must be retained as evidence."

"When will I get them back?"

"It may not be very long because the two of them are singing like little birds in the springtime," said Bertrand, making a flapping motion with his hands. "We can already charge Marius Dubrovski with breaking and entering and Delphine Carroll for reception of stolen property. Then there is the issue of blackmail. It was his operation, but as he told her of it, Mademoiselle Carroll is an accessory after the fact. I fear," he said, "that she will not make her Las Vegas debut as planned."

"What were they blackmailing him with?"

"It turns out that, before he was summarily fired by Charles-Henri Banville, Monsieur Dubrovski handled all the notably ungenerous details of the actor's clandestine marriage settlement with Carmen Ortega. Monsieur Banville had taken no steps to begin divorce proceedings, and Monsieur Dubrovski correctly assessed that the luster of the actor's impending marriage to Charlene Trent would be dimmed if the story about the earlier marriage was revealed."

"Crazy first wife in the attic. This is turning out to be totally Jane Eyre," I murmured. "And Charles-Henri went along with it?"

"Until he simply got tired of paying and canceled the wedding. We are not sure that Madame Carroll and Monsieur Dubrovski were ready to stop milking such a wealthy cow. As I said, Delphine Carroll was seen in Bordeaux the night of Monsieur Banville's death. Her alibi for the night appears to be very fragile. Very fragile indeed."

"But there's someone else who doesn't have a good alibi for that night," I observed.

Bertrand looked puzzled for a moment. "Oh, do you mean Carlos Ortega? It was perhaps not an accident that he was alone that night. The false alarm set off in the house of his friend, the professor, is quite suspicious. At any rate, when Professor Fourget returned from his holiday in Sao Paulo two weeks ago, he was able to remember the alternate restaurant that he suggested to Mr. Ortega. The waitresses in the café were quite taken with the young Spaniard, and once we had the location, we were able to trace his steps with some of the area's closed-circuit television. No, Monsieur Ortega is no longer a suspect."

"I'm glad for him."

"Are you not glad for both of you?" When I didn't answer, he continued. "Carlos Ortega is a good man, Melody. He is intelligent and quite courageous."

"He has some issues with the truth."

"Doesn't everyone?" asked Bertrand. Come to think of it, he still hadn't confirmed whether or not he had the last diary written by Charles-Henri Banville in his possession. "Secrecy," he said as he escorted me out of the precinct, "is often of great importance in police affairs."

"But not in love affairs," I told him sadly.

"Do not be so quick to judge," he said, patting my shoulder.

I was past passing judgment, at least as far as Carlos was concerned. I spent Friday afternoon helping Jenna decorate the top floor of a pizzeria with balloons and streamers for her cousin's birthday bash. The party was better than my senior prom, which had been spoiled by a pimple quartet bigger than Mount Rushmore. Acne-free in Paris, I danced almost all night with Michel, and while I didn't follow him back to his apartment after the party, I accepted his invitation to Sunday lunch with his parents in Chartres.

"It will be a little family gathering. You do like strawberry cake, don't you? It was my favorite when I was a child, and my mother bakes one every year for my birthday." We made plans to meet at the train station at eleven-thirty next Sunday. Dating someone so normal, someone with a normal family relationship, and a normal birthday cake, had its good points.

Michel kissed me goodnight, and how could I resist the birthday boy? I was surprised to find that I enjoyed it. My body didn't respond in the soul stirring way it did when Carlos touched me, but Carlos had proven over and over again that there was nothing real about our love. Carlos was just a memory, and a memory that I was determined to forget. Carlos was my past.

I was at the theater with Jenna on Saturday night when I checked my email during intermission. *Would you meet me at the Café de la Paix tomorrow at noon?*

The Café de la Paix.

My emotions were all over the place as I showed the text to Jenna.

"Don't go," she said. "Don't even think about it."

But I'd already thought about it. *"Ten o'clock but no later."*

"You shouldn't have agreed to meet him at all," Jenna reproached me. "He'll think you still care about him."

"Unfortunately," I said, "I do."

But despite caring more than I should, I felt defiantly single when I strode into the Café de la Paix on Sunday morning. Carlos was at the same corner table, but he didn't have a newspaper to hide behind this time. He didn't need one. *Le Parisien,* and all the other Paris papers, had already run their cover stories about Delphine Carroll, now accused of complicity in the blackmail of her ex-husband. There had even been a picture of her, snapped at the Banville funeral at Père

Lachaise, where my partial profile showed up in the frame behind her. My fifteen minutes of fame.

Carlos looked as handsome as ever but noticeably less sure of himself than he'd been at our first meeting. He rose when I crossed the room to his table but had difficulty meeting my eyes. "*Un café crème,* as usual?" he asked when the waiter stopped by our table.

"Mint tea," I told the waiter. "What's on your mind, Carlos?"

"I just wanted to know how things have been going for you. Here in Paris."

"Just fine," I told him. "How was jail?"

"It was…" He shut his eyes. "It was horrible, but it didn't last long. As soon as the publicity about my arrest died down, they transferred me to a safehouse, far in the countryside, to hide."

"Was there a swimming pool? A tennis court?"

"It was not a damn vacation, Melody!" He slammed the table with his fist. "For heaven's sake, I'm not a criminal. I *volunteered* to go to prison."

"Why couldn't you share that with me?"

"Melody, Melody, Melody, my dearest love, don't you understand?" He drummed his fingers on the table. "At first, the police were convinced that I'd killed my father. They thought I was a murderer. How could I subject you to that kind of pressure, my darling? Later, when it seemed like my false arrest was the only way to see justice done quickly and expediently, I didn't feel it was fair to force you to act in a charade."

"Why did it have to be done so quickly?"

"Because I needed…" He stopped and closed his eyes again. "Because I needed…"

"What did you need, Carlos? What did you need?"

"I needed the money." He whispered the last word and drew a deep breath. "I needed the money for my mother. I couldn't wait for the wheels of justice to turn slowly and surely. You see, my mother, she has…what she has…it's a difficult situation…"

"I know about her illness, Carlos, and I'm sorry for all you and she have suffered. But I only know about her illness because Bertrand told me. You didn't."

"Then you must understand that if all this has been hard for you, it's been much worse for me." He reached into his pocket and laid the sapphire bracelet on the table before me. The catch, I noticed, had been repaired. "This hurt. This hurt me a great deal. This was a token of our honesty and of our faith in each other. You lost faith in me."

"Because you weren't honest with me."

"I simply did what had to be done, Melody. But that's all in the past now, isn't it? We can find each other again, can't we?"

"I'm not sure," I said, leaving the bracelet on the table as I rose. "I'm not sure anymore."

Right now, I had a train to catch. Tomorrow, as some other girl said in another book, was another day.

A word about the author...

Recovering journalist Corinne LaBalme lives in the Right Bank (Is there a 'wrong' bank?) of Paris. Her work has appeared in Passion, La Belle France, the New York Times travel section, and France Revisited. Screenplay credits include Cuisine Culture episodes for PBS. Catch up with her on Twitter @corinnelabalme